MURI GREENWICH PALACE

Shadow Cutpurses Thrillers Book One

Adele Jordan

SAPERE
BOOKS

MURDER AT GREENWICH PALACE

Published by Sapere Books.

24 Trafalgar Road, Ilkley, LS29 8HH

saperebooks.com

ISBN: 978-0-85495-385-1

Map picture credit to Paul Schilling.

ACKNOWLEDGEMENTS

I wish to thank the whole team at Sapere Books for publishing this book, including Amy, Caoimhe, Matilda and Natalie. If it had not been for their diligent work and their devotion to the written word, I would not have had the opportunity to finally write some stories in my own name.

Lastly, I'd like to say a huge thank you to Paul Schilling for his creation of the map of Greenwich Palace. Inspired by the archaeology completed at the palace and some existing creative interpretations, this map was designed for the purpose of this story. Paul has designed a beautiful map, and I am very grateful for his hard work.

Map of Greenwich Palace

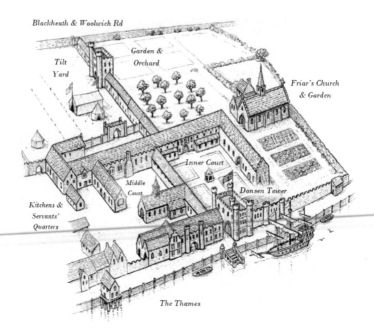

Blackheath & Woolwich Rd

Tilt
Yard

Garden &
Orchard

Friar's Church
& Garden

Inner Court

Middle
Court

Donsen Tower

Kitchens &
Servants'
Quarters

The Thames

CHAPTER 1

Greenwich, London, Thursday, 20th January 1536

"Stick to the shadows, Gwynnie."

Gwynnie Wightham tutted at her mother's words. "I know, Ma. In the shadows we are safe. You've been telling me that for as long as I can remember." Pulling the dark navy hood of her cloak over her head, she wrapped the garment around her body, masking the blue kirtle of the servant's gown she wore underneath.

"Stick to the shadows," Emlyn muttered again, striding forward down the narrow lane.

Gwynnie raised her head, her eyes fixed on her mother's back as she realised that Emlyn's words were meant for herself. Tall and grand in figure, Emlyn's dark brown hair, twisted into a tight bun, could have been mistaken for black in this darkness. Around her shoulders hung a green cloak that had been mended many times, the patchwork visible, the hem resewn so often that it was now scraggy.

Gwynnie walked across the wet cobbles between the tall buildings of Greenwich Palace. The puddles were shallower here than in some parts of the grounds, yet her boots still sank into the water. The rain had continued for so long that parts of the palace estates were flooded, with the south road cut off completely. Greenwich Palace and its grounds had become an island in the Thames.

"You know what to do." Emlyn paused at the end of the lane and glanced back at Gwynnie. The warm glow of candlelight escaping from a nearby lead-lined window in the palace fell on Emlyn's features, revealing pale skin and dark eyes, which now darted about the lane.

Gwynnie nodded, remaining in the shadows as her mother continued down the lane. Where Emlyn had walked carefully before, she now strode with confidence as she approached the door at the base of Donsen Tower. The red-brick tower, visible from the Thames, was tall and domineering against the dark rain clouds scudding across the sky. A yeoman of the guard dressed in red silk robes and carrying a pike stood in the doorway, guarding the entrance to the royal apartments.

Gwynnie pressed herself against the cold brick wall as she watched her mother approach the yeoman. Whatever she said to the man made him smile, and by the time Emlyn laid a hand on his arm, the man was captivated.

The first time Gwynnie had seen her mother charm a man, she had just been a child herself. Emlyn knew how to make a man smile. She also knew how to lift his purse from his belt.

As Emlyn encouraged the yeoman to turn his back to the lane, Gwynnie took her cue. Slowly, she stepped out from the shadows and moved toward the nearest window in the tower. Planting her back to the wall, she shifted a thin metal rod out of her sleeve, balancing the cold metal between her fingertip and thumb.

Soundlessly, she pressed the flattened edge between the window and the frame, reaching for the catch to try and lift it. The window refused to budge, its heavy iron resisting her effort.

Cursing under her breath, Gwynnie raised a hand in the air, a signal she prayed Emlyn would see in the darkness.

A sudden loud laugh permitted Gwynnie to be harsher with the window. Gwynnie allowed herself a small smile. Emlyn knew their signals all too well to mistake this one. Thrusting the rod deeper into the frame, it clunked rather noisily, though the sound was muffled by the laughter. As the catch released, Gwynnie pushed against the window, and this time the glass swung inward.

Gwynnie exhaled, her breath a white cloud in the cold night air. She glanced around, but in the darkness of the winter's night, no one but Emlyn and the guard were nearby. Bracing her hands against the frame, Gwynnie pulled herself up and through the window, being careful to close it behind her.

Inside, a corridor stretched out, a stark contrast to the cold, wet and dark world she had just left. On King Henry's orders, the Palace of Placentia had been filled with light and heat. A fireplace at the end of the corridor raged with red flames, and the walls were peppered with burning torches that emitted a warm, buttery light. Gwynnie and her mother had broken into the palace two weeks ago, disguised as maids, to scope out the layout, and she quickly recalled the map of the corridors in her mind. As Gwynnie stepped forward, the heels of her boots tapping on the flagstones, she heard voices approaching.

Gwynnie acted fast. Spotting a coffer, she shrugged off her cloak and stuffed it inside before she straightened her gown, pulling the white coif she wore down over her ears as she attempted to hide as much of her light brown hair as possible.

Three ladies appeared in the corridor, their gowns so grand that even as Gwynnie dropped into a curtsy, her eyes trailed over their fine clothes, the damask and printed skirts of their kirtles glimmering in the torchlight.

Two ladies hurried behind the first, who clutched her slightly rounded stomach as she walked, betraying the fact she was carrying a child.

"Your Highness, all will be well. You need not fear anything," one of the ladies muttered, her voice so high-pitched it bounced off the stone walls.

"Foolish girl." The lady at the front spoke with clear derision, her voice inflected with a French accent. "You think any woman in my position is safe? Look at what happened to the last one. Where is she now, I ask you?" The lady abruptly stopped walking and turned to face her ladies-in-waiting. The two skidded to a stop and dropped into deep curtsies.

"I ask you, where is she?" she cried wildly, her anger making her nostrils flare. Her long, skeletal fingers gripped her hips, then brushed the bell-shaped sleeve of her purple gown. "I'll tell you: she is dead."

"They say with a black heart," one of the ladies dared to whisper. "They cut it out of her chest. As black as ash. It is a sign of poison, is it not?"

The fine lady's dark eyes shot to the younger woman.

"I will not have such words spoken here. You would think I would be dancing, would you not? Singing, performing in a masque, anything to celebrate that I am rid of that woman at last." She turned and started pacing in a small circle as Gwynnie lifted her head a little higher.

Now, she could see the gold threading in the woman's French hood and the pearl necklace at her throat, bearing a gold initial, 'B', and adorned with three pearls that hung from the bottom curve of the lettering. Gwynnie stifled a gasp. The elegant woman was Queen Anne Boleyn.

One of the ladies dared to speak again, standing from her curtsy. "Your Majesty, Queen Catherine is dead these last two weeks. You *can* rejoice."

"Can I?" Anne halted, her hands on her hips. She no longer looked at her ladies but stared out of the nearest window. She didn't acknowledge Gwynnie's presence. As a maid, she was as important as the yellow stonework of the wall behind her. "Ghosts linger, Arianna. They walk this earth when they are not rested."

She turned abruptly from the window, her heels clicking on the flagstones. "Enough of this; I cannot walk these corridors and fear seeing *that woman* around every corner." She hastened down the corridor, calling, "Come, to my chambers."

Voices continued to murmur, yet Gwynnie could no longer hear what they uttered as she stepped away from the wall. She watched the retreating figures and the last flap of the skirt of a farthingale as it disappeared up a staircase.

"Not the queen's chambers then," she muttered with a sigh and reached for the bare space at her throat, tapping on her collarbone.

She would have to change her plan. She followed Anne's path down the corridor and toward the staircase, but at a much slower pace. The queen's chambers had always been the target, with Gwynnie and her mother hoping that Anne would be elsewhere, entertaining at this hour. The fact that Anne would now be there made Gwynnie fidget, reaching for the light-blue wool of her kirtle and screwing it up between her fingers.

The plan for the last year had been these chambers. With the jewellery that Gwynnie could take from the queen's chambers, she and her mother could turn their backs on this country at last. Emlyn would no longer have to rob and thieve, as she had done since she was a child. Gwynnie could see her mother safe, no longer looking over her shoulder in case she was being chased by a constable or a magistrate. Their lives could change.

"We were supposed to be safe," Gwynnie murmured under her breath as she reached the top of the stairs.

Further down the corridor and bathed in candlelight, she caught a glimpse of Anne again. She stood against a wall, a hand over her face. It was a moment of weakness. The rigid spine was gone, and her ladies were doing their best to usher her into a chamber.

"Who gave it to her, do you think?" Anne asked, stammering between her tears. "She carries a locket at her throat." Her fingers were splayed around the ornate gold 'B' hanging from her own necklace. "It is pure gold, and those gems…" Her breath hitched. "*He* must have given it to her. Who else would give Jane Seymour such a gift?"

"Your Highness, I beg of you, come inside." One of the ladies-in-waiting ushered her into the room, glancing back in Gwynnie's direction, clearly fearful of how much a passing maid could hear.

Gwynnie waited until the door shut firmly behind them, then she hurried forward. Moving to a long bank of lead-lined windows, she raised herself onto her toes, her short stature making it difficult to see out. Down below, she saw her mother in the courtyard, still talking to the yeoman of the guard.

Emlyn was smiling at the guard, but Gwynnie saw something in her mother's face. There was a tightness around her lips, a hint at the stiffness with which she held her body.

Soon, they would be free. She would see her mother smiling genuinely again, with a happiness that Gwynnie had not seen for fifteen years. All Gwynnie had to do was find her new target — the king's chambers.

Turning away from the window, Gwynnie recalled the rough path her mother had outlined to her earlier that day. The queen's and king's private chambers were placed on either side of the main tower, set in the frontage of the palace.

She walked calmly in the opposite direction to the queen's chambers until she found a discarded tray on a window ledge nearby, laid with pastry doucets and dates. She collected the tray and carried it on her shoulder, half covering her face as she walked down the corridor. She passed an open doorway that led to another corridor.

This corridor was darker with fewer candles, but she could hear sounds emitting from within. When a cry of pain pierced the air, Gwynnie lowered the tray and peered down the corridor. She could see nothing beyond the shadows, but someone was mumbling something. The sound was followed by the laughter of a man and a woman.

Gwynnie glanced over her shoulder, wondering if Queen Anne knew there was a woman in the king's chambers, then she walked on, heading toward the other royal apartments, reserved for special guests and members of the court whose company was highly valued by the king.

Stepping out into a wide corridor with multiple doors, Gwynnie held her tray higher, masking more of her face. There were ladies giggling in the corridor, whispering to each other. The French hoods that covered their heads flicked back and forth, the pearl trims twinkling in the light of the candles. The ladies didn't even acknowledge Gwynnie as she passed by; it was as if she was a ghost, invisible to the living.

"I heard the tale this morning," one of the ladies said to another as Gwynnie reached the end of the corridor. "They struck last night. The steward is certain of it. The lawyers and the clerks were robbed. What jewels they and their wives had with them were taken."

"It is not possible," another voice argued fervently. "How can anyone steal from a palace? Least of all this one. It is impenetrable. The king declared so himself."

"Yet it is true. I saw it with my own eyes," a third woman claimed, her high-pitched voice betraying her youth. "The chambers were turned upside down. Some say it was the Shadow Cutpurses."

A sudden heat made Gwynnie's palms clammy on the tray and as she paused at the end of the corridor, she chanced a glance back.

"Nonsense, child," another lady said. "The Shadow Cutpurses are just a legend. You mark my words. They do not exist."

Gwynnie turned away, unable to keep the smile from her face.

At the end of the corridor, there was a vast door. The carving of the wood suggested whoever occupied such a chamber had to be wealthy indeed. Even the framing around the door suggested affluence and respect from the king, for the stonework had been carved into a myriad of cherubs and angels, their faces shining amber in the candlelight.

Gwynnie knocked lightly on the door and waited. No one answered. She knocked again, louder this time, but there was still no answer. She turned the handle and, finding the door locked, she placed the tray down on the floor. Taking out the metal rod she had used to lift the latch on the window before, she thrust it into the lock and turned it back and forth. She didn't watch what she was doing, but trained her eyes on the corridor behind her, searching for shadows or any movement that could indicate someone had seen her.

She'd picked locks for many years. The first lock she had ever picked was of the shackles that were secured around her mother's wrists. Since then, no lock had defeated her. Each one had their trick.

With two turns to the left and a flick of her wrist, Gwynnie popped the lock out of place. The door swung open, and she stepped inside, her eyes darting about the room.

No candles were lit inside the chamber, but the moonlight streaming through the windows revealed it to be empty. The main privy chamber was full of furniture, with a grand oak table and high-backed chairs, and settle benches pressed against the wall. Tapestries draping the walls flanked two doors that led to more rooms.

Gwynnie hurried to close the door behind her and moved toward one of these doors. The first led to a bedchamber, the four posts draped in thick curtains with the bedding laid flat. The second door was a garderobe. Stepping inside, Gwynnie reached for the coffers first. They held fine clothes, each garment made of silk or precious satin, embroidered with gold and silver thread. As finely made as they were, they were not what she was here to seek out.

Turning her back on the coffers, she crossed to a buffet cabinet and opened a mahogany box, more akin to a small bible box than any coffer. Inside, gold chains and bright jewels glittered. Gwynnie lifted the lid higher.

"There you are," she whispered, a smile creeping across her face.

A floorboard creaked and a door opened in the outer room. Gwynnie froze, her head jerking toward the door of the garderobe. Someone had returned to the chamber.

CHAPTER 2

"We need some light," a man grunted.

Gwynnie jumped toward the door of the garderobe and pushed it so it was nearly closed, leaving a gap just wide enough for her to peer through. Her heart thudded as she saw two men enter the room, their figures indistinct in the darkness. The taller of the two moved toward a tinder box resting near the window to light some candles.

Gwynnie glanced around the garderobe. There was one window. It wasn't much of an exit, but it was the only choice she had. She moved to the window, then glanced back at the box of jewellery.

If she left it, then her mother would have to continue stealing to survive. Gwynnie could not pass up this chance now, not when there were so many jewels before her. Tiptoeing back to the mahogany box, she collected the jewels one at a time and slipped them into a leather pouch she carried at her belt, trying to avoid chinking the pieces together.

"Light," the voice from the other room said impatiently once more. "If we are to have this discussion, Your Grace, I must first see the whites of your eyes."

The choice of words made Gwynnie pause, but not for long. She lifted the jewels hurriedly, spying thickly ridged gold brooches, some inlaid with red rubies, others bordered with pearls. Three brooches designed with triskeles were peppered with blue and red jewels, while on two medallions, designed to be worn from heavy chains, white enamel had been shaped to form the initials H and F.

Gwynnie dropped them into the pouch and was about to close the box when something glinted in the roof of the lid. A much smaller brooch was pressed into the velvet lining of the box. She took the brooch, turning it over in her fingers. To see it better in the darkness, she raised it closer to her eye. In contrast to the other brooches, this one formed a Celtic knot, the gleaming silver pattern turning back on itself multiple times. There were no jewels on this brooch. It was a plainer item, one that did not belong with the rest.

"Ah, light at last," the man said with satisfaction from the adjoining room.

Fearing discovery at any second, Gwynnie dropped the Celtic brooch into the leather pouch with the others. Seizing the hem of her gown, she tucked it into her belt, knowing that if she was going to clamber out of this window, she would need to do so without being incumbered by her long skirts.

"Why did you wish for this meeting, Florian?" the other man asked. "You know any discussions with me should be conducted through my father first."

Gwynnie froze as she recognised the voice of the man who had spoken. When she and Emlyn had first crept into the palace two weeks before, to act the parts of maids in the household, she had seen this man performing at court and in masques.

"Woe betide whoever wishes for a private audience, eh?" the amused voice of the first man asked. "Mind if I sit down?" The unmistakable sound of a chair being moved revealed that this man was not waiting for permission before he took a seat.

"Your arrogance, Florian, knows no bounds. I should call Renard now to tip you out of that chair."

"We both know you do not want him here. Not yet anyway."

Gwynnie turned her back on the window. Slowly, she crept toward the door and pressed her face to the gap.

In the main privy chamber, the man named Florian sat in one of the high-backed chairs at the large oak table. From the light of the candles, she could see that he was smiling, completely at ease, his dark hair curling around his ears. He scratched languidly at the stubble on his jaw as he stared at the other man.

"I am not wrong, am I?" he asked, his voice husky. "You do not wish for another to hear this conversation, do you?"

Gwynnie's eyes darted to the other man in the room.

Henry Fitzroy, the illegitimate son of King Henry VIII, stood by the window. He was young, practically still a boy. Tall and lanky, his body was yet to fill out. The doublet he wore was made of rich magenta silk, heavily embroidered with flowers and leaves. His dark auburn hair was neatly coiffed, without a single wisp out of place.

"Speak your mind," Fitzroy said eventually, his light voice a stark contrast to the husky tones of the seated man.

"Well, Fitzroy, I thought you and I should have a little chat about a certain arrangement." Florian sat forward, his face leaning further into the candlelight. He was older than Gwynnie had first thought, perhaps even twice the age of the king's son. He drummed his fingers along the edge of the table, the confident smile never slipping from his face.

"What arrangement?" Fitzroy asked, folding his arms across his chest. He looked ill at ease, shifting his weight between his feet.

"An arrangement for silence. Some men's tongues can be bound not to speak, when offered the right price."

Gwynnie reached for the pouch at her hip. She could be discovered at any second if Fitzroy came toward her. She glanced back at the window, knowing it was time to make her escape. Yet she didn't move.

"What is it you think you know, Florian," Fitzroy asked, "which could possibly make me wish to pay you?" He attempted a nonchalant tone, even forced a laugh, but the youthful cheeks quivered, revealing a weakness.

"You do not have the strong expressions of your father. Do you know that?" Florian asked, tilting his head to the side. "Better you learn from him fast, boy."

"You will not address me as 'boy'," Fitzroy declared forcefully. He stepped forward. "I am the king's son, and I... I —"

"Command respect?" This time, Florian was the one to laugh. The sound reverberated around the room and made Fitzroy back up again. "Think what dear Pa would say if he knew your secret."

Fitzroy ran a hand through his hair, making the tendrils dance and fall out of place. "What secret?" he asked.

"The secret I suspect your young wife must know by now..." Florian tipped his head to the side, watching Fitzroy as a falcon would its prey, his dark eyes gleaming. "She is in your country house, I suppose. Not particularly welcome at court. Yet your marriage was not consummated — you and I both know that."

Fitzroy's hands quivered at his sides and his breathing grew laboured.

"How many men have you entertained in your bedchamber?" Florian asked, pointing toward the door. "Such practices may be common in the theatre and in the streets of London, but at a royal court? The son of King Henry himself?

What do you think your father would say, Your Grace?" He was enjoying himself now, leaning forward in his chair. "A man who prides himself on his masculinity and stands astride in every painting on these palace's walls with a codpiece to rival some of the towers…" He broke off, laughing deeply.

The sound made Fitzroy flinch.

"The son who would sooner bed his manservant than his wife. Your father would despair of you."

"Stop! Not another word, I beg of you." Fitzroy dropped down onto a settle bench, his face in his hands. "Y-you want paying?" he managed to stammer eventually, lowering his hands enough that Gwynnie could see his cheeks were tear-stained. "What is your price?"

"That depends on how many secrets you wish me to keep." Florian stood abruptly and walked around the table, reaching for a silver flagon of claret in the middle of the table. He poured out a glass for himself, as if he was the owner of this chamber rather than the visitor.

Fitzroy stopped trying to dry his tears, his gaze darting to Florian.

"What happened to Master Woodville, Your Grace?" Florian asked as he lifted the glass to his lips. "He has not been seen for some time, has he? I hear at one time you and he were great friends. Never seen without one another." He took another sip of his wine.

Fitzroy wiped his cheeks abruptly, standing up with such suddenness that the settle bench behind him wobbled.

"The last I saw him was at New Year."

"You see, if you could at least put on a stoney expression, then maybe I would have believed you knew nothing of his disappearance. As it is, your acting skills are as poor as those of the boys they get to play girls on the stages in Southwark."

Fitzroy turned away, pacing in a small circle. His hands went to his hair again, pulling on the dark coppery tendrils. "I have not seen Master Woodville. I do not know where he is."

"No? Your lover disappears, and yet you have no inkling as to where he could be now —"

"Do not call him that." Fitzroy turned to face him. His tears could not be stopped, and they ran down his cheeks uninhibited.

"Yet that was what he was," Florian said with a shrug. "Did you see him here, I wonder?" He pointed to the bedchamber door again. "I bet you did. Under the nose of your father, scarcely two corridors away from his chamber —"

"Enough!" Fitzroy shouted.

"You will not halt my tongue. I have told you already, there is only one way to make that happen. Pay me what I want, and these secrets shall stay with me. No other shall hear of them."

Gwynnie breathed deeply. She too had now heard these secrets.

"I cannot pay you. My father would want to know where the expense was going. It cannot be done."

"Was that an admission, Your Grace?" Florian asked, stepping free of the table and marching toward Fitzroy.

"What? No!"

"An admission that Master Woodville was your lover? Or the fact that you were responsible for his disappearance?" Florian halted beside him, the shorter of the two, yet the elder. "Did you end it, my lord? Was that why he vanished? Or perhaps he threatened to reveal the truth to your father? Maybe he wanted more…"

"Stop it, I pray you." Fitzroy stepped around Florian, putting the table between the two of them.

"You have my price, Fitzroy. You want your secrets hidden? You want it to end, then you pay me." He thrust his palm down onto the table between them, making the jug of claret dance and the glass topple over. It rolled off the table and shattered on the floorboards, the shards glittering in the candlelight. "You want me tongue-tied? That is the way to obtain it. Now, do I have your agreement?" He stared hard at Fitzroy. "Speak! Do I have your agreement?"

Fitzroy turned his back on Florian, his hands pulling at his hair once more. When Florian took his shoulder, the young man spun around, pushing the hand away, and reached for Florian's throat. He pushed Florian back until he collided with the table behind him.

Florian grappled with the hand at his neck, the shards of glass crunching under his feet as he coughed and spluttered.

Fitzroy raised his other arm and gripped Florian's throat with both hands. He may have been younger, but his greater height gave him the advantage in this fight.

"There is more than one way to tie a man's tongue," he said darkly, leaning over Florian.

Gwynnie stifled a gasp and took a step back from the door. She couldn't bear to watch anymore.

Florian tried to speak, but the words he attempted to say were just gargled noises. Thuds followed as he must have kicked out, fighting for his life. When something heavy hit the floor, Gwynnie inched toward the gap in the door, her whole body trembling.

The table had toppled over in the tussle. Florian was now on his back on the floor, with Fitzroy above him, squeezing the life out of him. With wild hands, Florian tried to pull at Fitzroy's arms, even attack his face, but Fitzroy had longer arms and could simply raise his head out of the other man's reach.

Gwynnie couldn't take her eyes off Fitzroy's face. The tears were still there, but his face was now flushed red. Sweat gleamed on his temple and at the base of his jaw. With his breathing so laboured, spittle formed at the edges of his lips.

Florian's legs twitched a few times as he tried to kick out, to dislodge Fitzroy from him. Fitzroy merely pinned him down further.

Gwynnie held herself as still as possible, her hand over her mouth to stop the cries of terror that nearly erupted from her body.

She wished to go and help Florian, to fight Fitzroy and push him away, but what good would that do? She was scarcely as tall as his shoulder, and much weaker. If she tried to fight him, she could end up dead too.

As Florian's life was drained, Gwynnie stumbled back into the corner of the garderobe, half falling onto a coffer. She didn't know which was worse, the guilt that swelled within her, her fear for her own life, or her sorrow for Florian.

CHAPTER 3

Gwynnie crept back to the door and pressed her face to the gap, watching as Fitzroy stumbled backwards away from the unmoving body on the floor. He collided with the fallen table and cried out, as if he had been wounded.

"Ah! No! No, this cannot be happening. Not again." Finding his feet, he reached for the main chamber door, but simply leaned against it for a moment. Great gasping cries wracked his body. Then, inhaling sharply, he wiped his cheeks with the sleeves of his doublet and stood straight, laying a hand on his stomach as he attempted to breathe evenly.

Abruptly, he opened the door and fled through it. The door slammed shut behind him and the key turned in the lock. Gwynnie heard his footsteps the other side of the door, running fast.

Her legs trembled as she opened the garderobe door. Her eyes immediately darted to Florian. Hastening toward him, she dropped to her knees and reached for his face.

"Come on, sir, please." She tapped his cheek, but there was no response. His eyes stared sightlessly upward. She reached for his neck, trying to find a pulse. There was no flutter beneath the skin. "You cannot be dead. Please," she whispered, somehow hoping that her desperate pleas could rouse him.

Sitting back on her haunches, she reached for the middle of his chest and pressed down upon his ribcage. She'd seen a man revived in the street once by such an action. She continued to press down repeatedly, feeling her eyes well with tears although she refused to let them fall. It didn't matter how many times she thumped his chest; Florian did not move. She inched forward to look at his face, but her eyes darted to the newly formed bruises on his neck instead. Already, they were black and purple, the finger marks plain against the pallid skin.

"I am so sorry," Gwynnie whispered, guilt threatening to overcome her.

Suddenly there was a sound in the corridor, two people shouting at one another. One of the voices was distinctly recognisable as that of Henry Fitzroy.

"Do not say it, Your Grace. Do not say it," another man was urging.

"How can I not? It has happened again —"

"I shall remedy it. I sorted it before, and I can do so again. Now, give me the key to your chamber."

Gwynnie scrambled to her feet and ran back into the garderobe, closing the door so only a gap remained.

The key clunked in the lock and the door to the main chamber swung open. Gwynnie tiptoed to the window of the garderobe, her body trembling so much that she struggled to undo the window latch.

"Shut the door," the voice Gwynnie did not recognise ordered. It struck her that the accent was distinctly French.

The door clicked shut.

"It's the same as before," the same voice said. "Fitzroy … with your bare hands."

"He would not stop, Renard," Fitzroy said in panic. "He knew! He knew everything. About me and…" He trailed off, his breath ragged.

This time Gwynnie managed to unlatch the window and it swung open. Peering out, she swallowed, realising the danger she was in.

Not only was she trapped with a murderer, but her only means of escape was a lead guttering pipe that led from the rooftop down to the ground far below. The clouds had gathered, and rain was falling again. The cobbles beneath her were wet and shiny and the rooftop that was a short climb away would no doubt be slippery.

"Listen to me," Renard instructed from the other room. "I can remedy this, but to be certain, we need to make sure no one saw Florian come to your chamber. Now, think, Your Grace. Did anyone see you together in the corridors? Anyone at all?"

"No, no. We took the back stairs. He was plain about not wishing to be seen."

"Then he signed his own death warrant."

"I did not mean to do it."

Gwynnie glared back at the door. She had seen the rage; she had witnessed the way his hands had clamped around Florian's throat. Squeezing the life out of a man was no short task, yet he had done it anyway. At any point he could have stopped, but he didn't — he was a brutal murderer.

Gwynnie stepped up onto the windowsill. The stone was even damper than she had been prepared for and her boot slipped. She grappled with the iron frame as the thud echoed loudly.

"Shh," Renard commanded Fitzroy.

Gwynnie held herself still, her body half through the window as she looked back into the garderobe. Her heart raced as she stared at the door.

Slowly, the door creaked open. With no candles in this room, she could not see their faces, and she had to pray they could not see hers either.

"Who's there?" Fitzroy demanded.

Gwynnie launched herself through the window. She jumped at the lead guttering and clamped on tight with her hands, feeling her legs swinging out in the air.

"Stop!" Renard bellowed.

Without looking back, Gwynnie scrambled down the guttering as quickly as she could. She was no great climber, and the pipe was slippery in the rain, causing her to nearly lose her grip. What hair had escaped her coif was now plastered to her cheeks in the rain.

"Step back," Renard ordered Fitzroy from far above her.

Gwynnie glanced up. It was so dark, she couldn't see Renard's face, though she saw him lift something out of the window, ready to be thrown as a missile.

Gwynnie's feet slipped on the wall as a heavy box was flung through the air. It thudded against the wall, smashing into pieces as she dropped to the floor. Landing on her back, Gwynnie grunted, feeling the pain ricochet up her spine.

"Get her!" Fitzroy cried in panic from the window above.

"Shh! Do you want the whole palace to hear?"

As they disappeared from the window, Gwynnie scrambled to her feet. The pain in her back was so strong that she could not stand easily. She took a deep breath before heading down a lane, away from the front towers of the palace.

In the conduit of the inner courtyard, where there had once been grass, the puddles now swamped her ankles, the icy water making her toes numb. If she continued this way, and Renard and Fitzroy caught up with her, then the sound of her splashing through the flood would draw them nearer.

Backing up, she looked for another way around the courtyard. In the darkness, all she could make out was the faint outline of the fountain in the middle of the square, which was now overflowing because of the rain.

"This way!" Renard's voice called behind her. Clearly, he had found his way outside already and was not far behind.

With no time left to make a decision, Gwynnie ran across the courtyard. Her heavy footfall betrayed her position and when she reached the distant corner, she glanced back to see two shadowy figures appear on the other side, heading in her direction.

Knowing she couldn't outrun them forever, Gwynnie changed her plan. She headed toward the back of the palace and the servants' quarters. Darting past discarded carts and empty crates left out by the kitchens, she found the nearest door and pushed. She was in luck. It had been left open. She stumbled in, kicked the door shut behind her, and ran down the corridor. She knew this part of the castle, from spending two weeks pretending to work here with Emlyn, and rather than avoiding the kitchens, she ran straight towards them.

The two lofted rooms were largely empty, apart from two cooks who sat on a bench close to the vast fire. One grasped a flagon of mead in one hand whilst stifling a yawn with the other, while the other counted things off on his fingers.

Even though no one was preparing food at this time of night, the scent of cooked meat and spices still hung in the air. Clouds of cinnamon and nutmeg tickled Gwynnie's nose, urging her to sneeze as she neared the cooks, one of whom she knew to be called Samuel.

"Two peacocks, three pheasants, venison, and one boar ... is that enough?"

"It will have to be. The king will make do."

"Aye, and the king is one to make do, is he?" the first cook, Samuel, asked with a deep laugh.

Gwynnie approached and dropped down on the bench beside Samuel.

"Gwynnie, you well, lass?" he asked, lifting his head to look at her. "You look as if you have seen death itself."

Gwynnie flinched at the words and forced a smile. "Oh, I'm just basking in this lovely warm weather we've been having," she said wryly, eliciting a hearty chuckle from the two men.

"Here, have this, lass. You need it more than I." Samuel shrugged off a grey woollen cloak and passed it to her.

Gwynnie eagerly pulled the cloak around her own damp shoulders and took off her coif so that her hair would dry faster.

"Now, how many was that again?" Samuel turned to the second cook, ready to count out their planned feast for the morrow once more.

Just then a short stocky figure appeared in the doorway. Gwynnie might not have been able to see Renard clearly before, but the silhouette had been enough to tell her she was looking at the same man now. The greying hair and pointed beard revealed his age, though the litheness of his figure suggested a younger man. His dark eyes darted over the three of them by the fire. When his eyes landed on Gwynnie, she ducked her head, praying he had seen so little of her that he would not recognise her now.

"Strange place for you to be, Master, at this time of night," Samuel said, standing from the bench. "Is the king in need of something?"

"No." Renard took a step forward. "I am looking for someone."

A shadow flickered behind him and Gwynnie glanced up, realising that it was Fitzroy, skulking in the shadows.

"Who?" Samuel asked.

"A woman." Renard glanced at Gwynnie then turned away, as if dismissing her as a possibility.

"If you're looking for company for the night, Master, you're in the wrong part of the palace," Samuel said with a grin. "You'll find no lasses here are willing to share your bed."

The second cook laughed, as did Gwynnie, trying to appear at ease.

Renard nodded and retreated. His hands curled around the belt at his waist, revealing short, stubby fingers. Briefly, he laid a hand on the wooden grip of a dagger, then he released it and stepped through the doorway once more. When a door closed in the distance, Gwynnie sighed in relief.

"Saw you, did he? Tried to take you to his bed?" Samuel resumed his seat and leaned toward Gwynnie, nudging her with his shoulder. "That's why you ran in here as if hounds were at your heels. Take my advice, Gwynnie, don't get caught by men like him. Bad things can happen in places like this when there's no one watching."

"I know. Thank you, Samuel," she said softly, glad that Samuel merely thought Renard was preying on her and did not know the truth. "I shall go find my mother."

"Aye, the safest place for you, I'll bet." Samuel encouraged her to keep the cloak with a wave of his hand. "Go, lass, but avoid going outside again. That man will be waiting for a lass on her own."

She tapped his shoulder comfortingly and walked calmly through the kitchens. The moment she was out of the door, she stumbled down the corridor, repeatedly glancing over her shoulder just in case Renard or Fitzroy reappeared. She did as Samuel had suggested and stayed inside the palace. She trailed through the corridors. At this time of night, most of the servants were in bed and the corridors were dark, with no candles to light the way. She navigated by trailing her hands along the stone walls toward the spiral staircase that led up into the rafters and the servants' quarters.

Her hand grasped the thin iron rail nailed into the wall as she climbed the stairs. At the top, she moved towards the only room with a glimmer of orange candlelight beneath the door. She tapped on the door using their code, two quick knocks, then three small light ones.

The door opened quietly, and Emlyn stood with a hand on her hip, a satisfied smile on her face.

"We did good, Gwynnie. That guard never suspected me."

Gwynnie stepped into the room, walking past her mother, who closed the door. The chamber was little more than a cupboard, with barely enough standing room between the two cot beds.

"So? How did we do?"

"Ma…" She managed to croak out the word, but Emlyn wasn't listening. She reached for the leather pouch at Gwynnie's waist and grinned at the weight.

"This is it, Gwynnie. It's what you always wanted, is it not?" Emlyn sat down on the edge of one of the beds, tilting her head back and revealing her full smile. The crow's feet around her dark eyes were more noticeable these days, as were the lines around her chin. "We'll be free at last."

"Ma…" Gwynnie tried again, but her mouth was dry, and no words came.

Emlyn tipped the contents of the pouch out onto the bed. She gasped in awe and ran her fingers over the gold brooches.

"These are beautiful," she whispered. "We can sell it all, Gwynnie. Start somewhere new, just as you wanted. Where do you want to go? Ireland? Scotland? Maybe even France?" Emlyn laughed suddenly. "The world is open to us now, my girl." She held her arms wide. "Never have we made such a steal before."

"Ma, I need to talk to you."

"I think maybe France." Emlyn nodded to herself, sifting through the various pieces of jewellery. "I'd like to see the Continent. Wouldn't you?"

"Ma?"

"We could leave next month."

"God's blood, Ma!" Gwynnie snatched up the leather pouch and shook it in front of Emlyn to get her attention. "I have seen something tonight that I cannot unsee." She closed her eyes as a tear slipped down her cheek. "I saw a murder."

CHAPTER 4

"Well?" Having changed into a warm woollen chemise, Gwynnie sat huddled in the bed with the blanket around her. Her light brown hair was loose around her shoulders.

"We must think," Emlyn whispered as she paced up and down the small room, her hands on her hips.

"You have been thinking for hours," Gwynnie murmured. "Clearly without success."

"Thank you for the reminder." Emlyn halted by the window. Between their two beds was a small stone windowsill with a window no bigger than a child's face, looking out over one of the courtyards by the stables. The lead-lined lattice cast shadows on Emlyn's strong features as the sun rose over the rooftops. "We could run."

"Run?" Gwynnie repeated. "Run where? How?"

"Gwynnie, think about it. Whether this Renard or Fitzroy recognised you last night in that kitchen is beside the point. You are a witness. If you can point the finger at Fitzroy, then you are too much of a risk to go free. They will hunt you down."

Gwynnie pulled the blanket over her head, wishing she could hide from the world.

"You haven't done that since you were very small," Emlyn said, reaching for the blanket and trying to tug it off Gwynnie.

"I'm still small!" Gwynnie pointed out in frustration.

"Well, you get your petiteness from your father." Emlyn succeeded in pulling the blanket off her head. "He wasn't very tall either."

It was so rare to hear Emlyn talk of her late husband that Gwynnie waited with bated breath to see if her mother would say more, but she did not.

"We cannot run," Emlyn said instead, answering her own question as she returned to the window. "The Thames has burst its banks, and the flood has cut off the road on the south side of the palace. Woolwich Road is completely under water and Blackheath is unreachable. The wherrymen aren't working because of the cold, and there are tales of the river freezing in places. No, our best way out of here would be to swim and in this cold, we're likely to die in the attempt." She looked at Gwynnie.

"I cannot keep sitting here." She knelt forward. "Ma, I have to do something."

"Do what?"

"Tell someone. Anyone! If someone knew what had happened last night, what Henry Fitzroy is capable of —"

"Shh!" Emlyn clamped a hand over Gwynnie's mouth and looked toward the door. "And who do you expect will believe you when you make such a claim, my miting?"

Gwynnie managed to pull her mother's hand off her mouth. "Do not call me that. You know I hate being called that."

"You'll always be my miting, my little one." Emlyn smiled softly and ruffled Gwynnie's hair. "Even though you have your first grey hair." She plucked a hair from Gwynnie's head.

"Ma!" she complained to little effect. She'd seen her twenty-seventh summer the year before, yet at times Emlyn still treated her as if she was a child.

"Gwynnie, listen." Emlyn's face turned serious. "No one will believe the word of a maid over the word of the king's own son. No matter what tale Fitzroy gave to his father, it is he they would believe. You breathe a word of what you saw, and…" Emlyn trailed off.

"And what?" Gwynnie asked, noting the fear in her mother's eyes.

"And they'll hang you for lies. Maybe even for treason."

"What about those?" Gwynnie jerked her chin toward the other bed where the jewels she had taken from Fitzroy's chamber still lay.

Emlyn laid a hand on the jewels. "We must hide them," she whispered. "If we have to stay in the palace for longer than we expected, then we do not want these found in our possession."

Emlyn stood and moved toward the windowsill. Reaching for the stone slabs beneath the lead-lined glass, she shifted one from side to side, loosening it. They had discovered the weakness around the stone on their first day in the chamber, and sensing the potential, they had used smaller stones to wear away the remaining mortar that held it in place. Emlyn now lifted the slab, revealing the gap beneath where they had already hidden the jewels that they had taken earlier in the week.

Gwynnie stood to peer into the gap. The other jewels were wrapped in linen and wool.

"Find me something to bind them," Emlyn whispered as she gathered the jewels from Fitzroy's chamber together.

Reaching into a leather bag, Gwynnie pulled out a strip of linen once used for stockings. Together, they put the jewels in the linen. Gwynnie paused when she found the Celtic brooch.

In daylight, she could see the silver was rather dulled, and the pin on the back was broken.

"Quickly," Emlyn urged.

Gwynnie dropped the brooch into the linen with the others, allowing Emlyn to place the jewels into their hiding place and return the slab.

"There, it is done," Emlyn said, stepping back with a satisfied smile. "So we have our plan."

"Plan?" Gwynnie shook her head. "Oh yes, a grand plan it is too. Let us just continue working here under the same roof as a murderer."

"Your sarcasm isn't helping, miting."

"No? You think not? Because it is cheering me up no end!" Her outburst merely made Emlyn raise her eyebrows. "God's blood, Ma, we cannot simply hide here and hope for the best."

"That cursing tongue of yours —"

"I got it from somewhere —"

"Not from me —"

"Then from Pa." Her pointed words made Emlyn look away.

"Neither can we flee with the water the way it is," she said with a sigh. "No, for now, we act out our parts and we stay the course. Remember what I told you?" Emlyn looked at her. "Where is the best place to hide?"

"In front of another's eyes. As if you are not hiding at all," Gwynnie muttered angrily as she stood and moved toward a small looking glass that hung from the whitewashed wall. In the glass, she half expected to see someone different.

It felt as if the last night had changed everything, that perhaps she would no longer see her own small face when she looked in the mirror, but that of someone else entirely. A woman with a black heart that would stand and do nothing when a man was fighting for his life. Was that not who she was now?

Suddenly nauseous, she stepped back from the mirror and gagged. Emlyn reached for a chamber pot and thrust it under her nose. Gwynnie bent over it as Emlyn held back her hair.

"Ah, miting." Emlyn rubbed her back. "It is what the sight of death does to us all."

Gwynnie's stomach knotted further at her mother's words. She knew Emlyn had seen death, but being reminded of it was never easy.

"Come, there now." Emlyn offered a handkerchief for Gwynnie to wipe her mouth. "If we are to keep you hidden from these men, then we must get to work. We must hide in full view."

"They've struck again. It was them. The Shadow Cutpurses. They were here again last night."

"Be quiet, boy."

The stable boy's loud shouts were quelled by a sharp flick to his ear by the stable master.

Gwynnie glanced their way as she and Emlyn exited the wood store beside the stables, each carrying a pail of firewood.

"Keep your head down," Emlyn whispered as she strode across the puddle-filled grass toward the main palace. They passed Friars' Church on their right and hastened through Friars' Garden.

Gwynnie followed behind her, watching as many of the staff gathered to hear what the stable boy had to say. Maids tittered, pulling coifs around their ears as they whispered to one another. Gwynnie strained to hear some of their conversation as she passed by.

"They're not real," one whispered to another.

"They are," a second insisted. "My Ma says they did all the fine houses on the east coast last year. No house was left untouched."

"That cannot be true. They would be as rich as the king if it were."

"Why come here? Why steal from the palace?"

"Why not?" Emlyn whispered to Gwynnie as they walked on through an archway and into the main inner court. "Because we can."

"Ma." Gwynnie elbowed her mother. "You said we came so we could be done with this life." Her stomach knotted when she noticed Emlyn avoiding her gaze, suddenly seeming busy with the pail of firewood. "That was the deal, was it not? One last theft, then we were to be done."

"Yes, it was." Yet Emlyn walked on faster and Gwynnie trailed behind her, frowning. The plan had always been that the Palace of Placentia was to be their last job, before there were any more pamphlets about the Shadow Cutpurses taking wild guesses as to their identities.

The latest pamphlet had illustrated them as two men clad in black, moving like bats across rooftops. That particular image had made Emlyn laugh for hours as Gwynnie glared at the picture, wondering where the people got their ideas from.

"Stay calm," Emlyn whispered as they walked through the courtyard. "If anyone mentions them again, do not respond."

The flooding had receded a little from the night before, but with the morning had come a greater chill. In patches across the courtyard, the puddles had frozen to thick trenches of ice. The fine ladies and gentlemen that had come out to take the air kept slipping in their court shoes and boots, squealing like suckling pigs and clinging onto one another's arms.

"It was them. Did you not hear?" one man cried from a group of professional gentlemen nearby. Some wore the black robes of the lawyers, others the red cowls of the high clergy and the bishops. "They have stolen from the Duke of Richmond, Henry Fitzroy. All of his jewels were taken in the night."

Gwynnie's pace slowed until Emlyn bumped her arm with the wooden pail.

"Ow!"

"Walk on," Emlyn whispered. "What did I say about ignoring it?"

They walked around the group of gentlemen, aiming for the doorway that led to the gallery chambers and the great hall.

"It is not to be borne," one elderly man huffed, pulling at his long fur-lined cloak and tucking the collar around his chin. In the icy wind, he blew into the collar. "The Shadow Cutpurses are not just thieves, not from what I hear. There's blood on their hands too."

Gwynnie and Emlyn exchanged a look.

"Not now," Emlyn whispered. "Now is not the time."

"I know." Gwynnie nodded and reached for the door.

A sudden cry from the other side of the courtyard made them turn.

"He's dead! He's dead!" a young woman cried, running through the archway from the middle courtyard, her light blonde hair falling from her French hood in her panic.

"They've found him," Gwynnie murmured.

"What is it, Mistress Ellenheim? What is wrong?" The elderly gentleman with the fur collar hurried forward, taking her arm.

"Master Florian Battersby is dead — murdered! Oh, the blood!"

"Blood?" Gwynnie frowned. "There was no blood. Something is wrong."

"Where is this, Mistress Ellenheim?" others called. "Tell us, what is happening?"

"See for yourself. Oh, it's madness. Death, as pale as this infernal frost. Oh!" Mistress Ellenheim swayed on her feet. A gentleman reached for her, catching her before she could fall to the ice-covered ground.

A group of gentlemen hurried toward the archway. Most of the ladies hung back, trying to attend to Mistress Ellenheim.

Gwynnie strode forward.

"Gwynnie!" Emlyn tried to pull her back, but Gwynnie did not stop.

She walked past the crowd of well-dressed ladies and darted under the archway, hastening into the middle courtyard. The gentlemen that had gathered in front of her were in uproar, some complaining loudly at the sight of the blood on the ice, others sending prayers to heaven, with the red-cowled clergy crossing themselves.

Gwynnie crept between the men, her stature so small that no one glanced her way. She reached the front of the group and saw for herself the sight that had left Mistress Ellenheim stricken with horror.

Prostrate on the red and black tiled ground of the courtyard was Florian, yet not as Gwynnie had last seen him. His throat had been cut.

CHAPTER 5

Gwynnie's eyes darted over the scene, noting how the bruising on Florian's neck had been completely masked by the ruthless cut to his throat.

"We have a killer in our midst," said a man behind her.

"It's what you were saying just now, is it not? That the Shadow Cutpurses have blood on their hands."

Gwynnie looked up at the speaker. It was the elderly gentleman with the fur collar. He crossed himself, sending a prayer to God.

"It seems they have more blood on their hands today."

"No," Gwynnie whispered, too quietly for anyone to hear her as she looked down at Florian again.

She and her mother were to take the blame for the murder.

Casting her eyes over the body, she tried to take in as much of the scene as she could. In order to cover up Fitzroy's crime, Renard had dumped the body out here in the open and cut the throat to cover up the bruising. Any hint that Fabian had been in Fitzroy's chambers was gone. Something glinted in the sunlight, and Gwynnie realised that she had been mistaken. There was one thing. On the bottom of Florian's boots were the shards of glass he had trodden on in Fitzroy's rooms.

"Out of my way." A booming voice erupted across the courtyard.

Gwynnie's arm was grabbed, and she was pulled back. She scrambled to look around and see who it was. A young man, perhaps even younger than herself, stood at her side. His dark copper hair and heavy beard did a good job of masking his features. The hand he had on her arm was covered in black ink spots. His grey eyes flitted between the corpse and the two men who were now marching toward it across the courtyard.

When Gwynnie saw the king, she immediately bowed her head along with everyone around her. She lifted her chin a little, watching King Henry as he calmly stood beside Florian.

She had only seen the king from a distance during her time in the palace, and now she could see him up close, she realised he was not quite the fine figure of a man some had described. He was broad-shouldered, and certainly masculine in build, with a heavy chin bearing ginger hair. The small beady eyes were without expression as he stared down at Florian. His clothes were yellow — shocking, considering his first wife had only recently died. He plainly wished to make a statement: he would not be mourning her.

"Well?" he barked at the small man beside him, making his rotund belly jiggle. "Who did this?"

"We do not know yet, Your Majesty." The man bowed his head, his black cap hanging over his haggard features. "May I advise the body is moved, with your permission? Such scenes as this —" he paused and cast a glance around at the gathered gentlemen — "they can cause scandal."

"Who is it?" King Henry didn't answer his man's question but stepped forward, peering at the face of Florian. His top lip curled, and he raised a lavender-scented handkerchief to his nose, warding off the stench of death.

The small man's eyes found the bearded young man standing beside Gwynnie. "Who is he, Tombstone?" he asked sharply.

"Master Florian Battersby," replied Tombstone in a West Country accent. "He was the Lord Chamberlain's man." He again bowed his head in acknowledgement of the king.

"Then he was a man of gentry." King Henry huffed and turned away, his yellow robes trailing across the ice.

"Cromwell," he said in a low tone to the small man beside him, "find out who did this. And find somewhere to put the body: dump it in the river if it will keep the crows away."

Beside Gwynnie, Tombstone bristled at the king's words.

The king walked away, leaving the crowd of gentlemen gossiping and pointing at the retreating figure. Cromwell bent down over the body, sweeping his long grey cloak behind him.

Gwynnie had heard much about Thomas Cromwell, Earl of Essex and Lord Privy Seal to the King. Though she had heard people whispering about a man of great power, she saw only a man of slight stature with a rounded belly visible against his grey robes. His dark hair peeked out beneath his black cap, trembling in the cold breeze. He said nothing, his manner quiet and careful as his eyes darted over the body.

Gwynnie crept forward, wishing for another look at Florian. Her eyes fixed on the shoes and the shards of glass pressed into the soles. As far as she could see, it was the only hint that something more was amiss. To any casual observer, Florian could have been attacked here in the courtyard and left for dead.

"Take care." A hand took Gwynnie's elbow once more. She turned to see the tall figure of Tombstone, who had not moved from her side. "The stench is enough to make a man fall."

"And you think the sight would be enough to make a woman swoon?" Gwynnie asked.

"What is your interest here?" Tombstone lowered his voice, stepping closer to her.

"A man has died. Nothing remotely interesting in that, is there?" she said wryly, yet Tombstone didn't seem to understand her irony. The coppery threads of his brows drew closer together.

"Tombstone?" Cromwell called his name again as he stood from the body. Tombstone walked around Gwynnie, moving to the other side of Florian and talking to Cromwell in hushed tones.

Gwynnie did not know how long she stood there, staring at the immovable figure of Florian. She lost track of what the gossiping crowds were saying around her. She thought only of Florian and the way she had thrust her hands into the centre of his chest the night before, trying to rouse him.

Eventually, men started to walk away, but Gwynnie continued to stand at his side, her stare only broken when someone threw a discarded cloak over the body, masking from view the blood and the pale face with the slackened jaw.

"Gwynnie?" Emlyn took hold of Gwynnie's arm. "Come away."

"This is wrong," Gwynnie whispered as Emlyn drew her aside.

"What is?"

"I mean, they have dumped his body," Gwynnie hissed. "They've disguised the bruising." She raised a hand to her throat, rubbing the spots where she had seen the bruises on Florian's neck. "They're covering it up."

"Keep your voice down." Emlyn tugged her into the corner of the courtyard.

Gwynnie breathed deeply. "Henry Fitzroy will never face punishment for what he has done," she said. "Ma, that is not right."

"And who will you tell? Hmm? Remember what I said." Emlyn thrust one of the wooden pails of firewood back into her hands. When the steward for the household proper walked past, she forced a smile and wrapped an arm around Gwynnie's shoulder. "If you breathe a word of it," she whispered, her lips close to Gwynnie's ear, "they will try to silence you."

Gwynnie felt a shiver run down her spine.

"No one can know what you saw," Emlyn continued, drawing her back toward the archway. "It is done, Gwynnie."

"Done?" Gwynnie turned to stare at her mother. "What are you talking about?"

"I mean there is nothing we can do." Once more Emlyn looked around them, clearly fearful of being overheard. "Trust me when I say that staying quiet is for the best."

"But..." Words failed Gwynnie. It was contradictory to everything she had ever been taught by Emlyn. When it came to bloodshed, someone had to serve justice.

"Is that what you did? When you saw a murder?" Gwynnie whispered.

Emlyn flushed. They both knew which murder Gwynnie was speaking of. Emlyn stepped toward her, her dark hair escaping her coif now tangled by the wind.

"I am protecting you, miting. You may not like it, but justice cannot always be served." She took Gwynnie's arm, making their wooden pails clatter together. "Now, come. We must return to our duties."

They walked through the archway toward the great hall. Feeling numb, Gwynnie tried to persuade herself that her mother was right. For the sake of her own life, she would have to stay hidden and silent.

"What if we are blamed for this?" Gwynnie asked, a new fear taking over. "I have already overhead one man say it must be the Shadow Cutpurses' doing."

"They haven't found us yet." Emlyn's strained voice faltered as a woman in a green gown ran past them.

"No! No!" the woman screeched as she sprinted through the icy puddles. "Tell me it is not him. Tell me!"

"Who is that?" Emlyn whispered, pulling Gwynnie out of the anguished woman's path.

She was barely dressed, and her black hair trailed behind her, without a hood or a bongrace to cover it. Her gown hung loose at the front as she flung herself into the courtyard, pushing past the men in her effort to reach the body.

"Let me see him — please, let me see," she pleaded desperately.

"Mistress Battersby." Tombstone emerged from the crowd and reached for her, taking her shoulders in a gentle grip. "Do not come any closer. You do not wish to see this."

"By this light, I shall see my husband. Let me through." She wrenched free of Tombstone's hands and ran around him.

Gwynnie could no longer see the lady as she reached Florian, but the strangled cry that erupted was enough to make Gwynnie flinch. Emlyn took her arm and gently pulled her away, through the inner courtyard. Gwynnie glanced back and saw Tombstone doing his best to console Mistress Battersby.

Woodenly, Gwynnie allowed her mother to steer her through the nearest door and down a corridor. They reached the great hall, the vast fireplace that stood at the edge of the chamber unlit. This room, usually full of people in this weather, was empty. Every soul was outside, trying to catch a glimpse of Florian.

Emlyn dropped to her knees and attended to the fire, throwing wood from her pail into the grate.

Gwynnie stared into space as she thought about Mistress Battersby's scream. It had sounded unearthly, her pain no doubt as great as Emlyn's on the day that she had lost her own husband.

"Gwynnie?"

"Yes?" Gwynnie looked around.

"You're shaking." Emlyn reached up and gently took the pail out of Gwynnie's hands. "Are you well, miting?"

"Oh, perfectly well. Can you not see how I am dancing for joy?" Gwynnie stepped away, her hands moving to her hips as she looked around the hall. It was cold with the fire not yet lit, the emptiness foreboding.

"Your sarcasm does not help matters."

"God's blood, Ma —"

"What did I tell you about that tongue of yours?"

"Who cares if I curse after what has just happened?" Gwynnie marched to her mother's side and dropped to her knees. "You wish me to act normal? You wish me to make up a fire?" She tossed far too much wood into the grate and fumbled for a tinderbox, her fingers dropping the iron wool multiple times in her effort to retrieve it from the small plain case.

"Gwynnie —"

She tossed the burning wool onto the wood. It caught light so suddenly that they both veered back, with Gwynnie kicking the fire screen into place to prevent the flaming wood from rolling out.

"Well, yes, you seem normal," Emlyn said, her tone equally sarcastic.

"Do not pretend this has not changed everything, Ma." Gwynnie shook her head, watching the flames as they danced. "I cannot sit here and do nothing."

"Then what is it that you intend to do?"

Gwynnie remained silent, uncertain how to answer the question.

"Anything you do endangers us both," Emlyn reminded her. "Was this not to be our last job? You wish to risk that now by pointing the finger at the king's son?"

A door opened in the distance and they both lowered their voices.

Gwynnie breathed deeply, knowing her mother was right. For so long her only goal had been to keep her mother safe, but now she didn't know what to do.

CHAPTER 6

"Wait! You there, maid!" a voice called.

Gwynnie halted with the tapers in her hands. She stood in the withdrawing chamber behind the great hall, having just lit another of the palace fires. Emlyn continued to scrub down the fireplace, as if no one was shouting to them at all.

On the other side of the room, beneath an archway flanked by green and red tapestries revealing the hunt of a white hart, stood two men. Gwynnie's stomach had lurched when she first saw the figures, thinking briefly that it was Renard and Fitzroy come for her again. She breathed a sigh of relief when she recognised Tombstone.

The tall young man wore a black robe over his rich doublet, his collar stiff and high around his neck. At his side was a second man, far older, with a shining bald head, a slightly hunched back and bushy white eyebrows.

"Is this who you spoke of?" the older man asked Tombstone, pointing at Gwynnie as they entered the chamber.

"Yes, Master," Tombstone replied, before turning to Gwynnie. "What is your name?"

"I am Gwynnie Wightham." Gwynnie stood tall, looking between the two men. "I saw you this morning. With the … body." She almost said Florian's name but realised that as a maid she would not be expected to know who he was.

The elderly gentleman gestured dismissively toward Gwynnie. "She is little more than a child, a mere girl," he said, as if she was not present.

Gwynnie frowned. "And you, sir, are an old man. For what reason are we pointing out one another's state?"

The gentleman's bushy eyebrows shot up. Before he could reply, Emlyn approached, offering one of those sweet smiles that usually had gentlemen bending to her will.

"Gwynnie, dear, that is no way to greet a gentleman," she said, dropping into a deep curtsy. "Good day to you, Master. I apologise for my daughter's manners. She can sometimes be uncouth, and the dramatic events of this morning have left her a little lacking."

"That is quite understandable." The elderly gentleman smiled back at Emlyn.

Gwynnie had to stop herself from sighing in exasperation.

"May we have the honour of an introduction, Master?" Emlyn asked as she raised herself from the curtsy.

"Well, quite the manners of a fine lady. What a surprise." The elderly man's smile grew all the more.

Gwynnie would have happily pointed out that if he knew her mother at all, he'd realise she was no fine lady. Born in one of London's slum districts, any manners Emlyn had learned she had copied from the fine ladies she had watched as a girl, before stealing their purses.

"This is Master Neville Pascal, Magistrate for the City of London and the Palaces," Tombstone said, indicating the senior man. "I am his lawyer and clerk, Elric Tombstone."

Gwynnie noticed the ink stains on his fingers once again. He wore an elegant doublet beneath his cloak, embroidered with gold. For a lawyer, he dressed quite finely.

"We have been asked by Lord Cromwell to look into the recent robberies here at the palace and, of course, Master Florian Battersby's death." Elric Tombstone's eyes turned to Gwynnie. "I noticed that you, Mistress Gwynnie, were particularly interested in the body this morning. I thought it strange and wished to ask what drew you to look at it?"

"Is it so strange?" she asked, anxiously fidgeting with the tapers in her hand.

"It was the way you looked at the body." Tombstone stared at her. "Most looked away, but not you."

"My child is not afraid of the realities of the world, Master." Emlyn spoke with a sad sigh. "Having grown up as serving women, we see much darkness and despair on these streets."

Pascal and Tombstone exchanged a look. Pascal fidgeted so much that his black court shoes squeaked on the tile flooring. In contrast, Tombstone stood perfectly still. His grey eyes now flitted from Gwynnie to Emlyn.

"We have spoken with the yeoman of the guard who stood by Donsen Tower last night. I am sure it will come as no surprise to you, Mistress Wightham, to learn that he remembers you from last night. You stood and talked with him outside the tower for some time."

Gwynnie's hands tightened around the tapers. Emlyn merely smiled broadly.

"Indeed I did. Master Cuthbert is a kind man indeed. His conversation quite enamoured me, so much so that I stayed from my bed when I should have been in it." She giggled and laid a hand on Gwynnie's shoulder. "You were quite in despair by the time I returned to our chamber, were you not? Wondering where I had been at such an odd hour."

She gave Gwynnie the alibi, and she was forced to agree with it, slowly nodding.

"Is that how it happened, Mistress Gwynnie?" Tombstone shifted his focus back to her. "Were you in your chamber as your mother —" he paused, clearly choosing his words carefully — "conversed with the yeoman of the guard?"

"That I was, sir." Gwynnie nodded again.

"May I ask what these questions are in relation to, sir?" Emlyn addressed Pascal, clearly judging him to be the more amenable of the two men. Tombstone, in contrast, seemed unmoved by her sweet smiles. Gwynnie judged he may be too young to be impressed by her mother's more mature beauty, but it was rather as if Tombstone hadn't noticed her at all.

"Last night, Donsen Tower was robbed," Pascal said in a low whisper, as if it was a great secret, despite the fact half the guests at the palace that morning had been talking of it. "We believe that the thieves are also responsible for Master Battersby's death."

"Oh!" Emlyn covered her mouth, looking dutifully shocked. "That is too awful. To think that someone in this world would hurt another for the sake of taking something that glitters. Oh, my heart." She flung a hand to her chest dramatically.

"There now, good lady, calm yourself," Pascal said, as he escorted Emlyn to the nearest chair and urged her to sit down.

"Thank you, sir, you are most kind." Emlyn fluttered a hand in front of her face. "It is just the thought of the depravity; the depths that humanity can sink to. It makes my poor heart ache."

"There is no need to concern yourself." Pascal patted her hand. "Whilst Elric and I are investigating this matter, all will be well. I judge that you and your daughter will be quite safe."

Tombstone cleared his throat, clearly unaffected by Emlyn's histrionics. "I should still like to know where you went, Mistress Wightham, after your conversation with the yeoman." Suspicion made the lines of his face firm.

"I told you — to our chamber," Emlyn said distractedly, waving a hand at Gwynnie. "You were worried for me, weren't you, Gwynnie? You stayed up to wait for me."

"Yes, that's right."

"There's just something I do not quite —"

"Enough, Elric." Pascal turned to his lawyer. "I cannot allow this questioning to continue when the poor lady is obviously quite overcome by this morning's events."

"So I see," Tombstone responded drily. Gwynnie moved to her mother's side. She placed a protective hand on Emlyn's shoulder and offered a handkerchief, allowing Emlyn to dab at her cheeks.

"Besides, no lady could be a jewellery thief. Could she?" Pascal's sudden question made Emlyn drop the handkerchief in her lap.

"You thought that we were thieves, sir? Oh! My heart! Oh, Gwynnie, it cannot take much more of this." She turned in the chair and latched her hands onto Gwynnie's arms.

"Calm your blood, Ma," Gwynnie soothed, picking up the handkerchief and urging her mother to take it again.

"We must investigate all eventualities." Tombstone calmly crossed his arms over his chest. "No one else was seen in the vicinity of Donsen Tower last night."

"Then I suggest we find more witnesses." Pascal bristled, standing tall with his hunched shoulders pulling back a few inches.

Tombstone remained silent, his eyes locked on Gwynnie's.

"You have my sincerest apologies, good lady," Pascal said ingratiatingly, taking Emlyn's hand and bending over it. "Do rest yourself before you return to work. I would not want to think we are the cause of any further distress today."

"You are most kind, sir. I thank you." Emlyn adopted a tearful smile and waved at him with her handkerchief.

As Pascal turned to his clerk, his smile vanished. The two of them left swiftly, with Tombstone casting one more glance back in their direction.

The moment they disappeared from view, Emlyn dropped the handkerchief into her lap, all signs of tears gone. "Well, that was a little too close for comfort."

"A little too close?" Gwynnie repeated, rounding on her mother. "You may have old Pascal eating out of your hand, but that lawyer is no fool. He is suspicious of us, Ma."

"And what can a lawyer do when the Justice of the Peace is helping me to a chair?" Emlyn smiled victoriously and stood from her seat.

"Ma, be serious for a minute," Gwynnie said. "You heard what they said, did you not? They believe the jewellery thief and the killer are one and the same. If they were to —"

"Hush now." Emlyn took Gwynnie's hand. "Do not think on it, miting. Do not think on it at all." She winked. "We shall be quite safe here."

"Of course we shall. Just as the sun is shining beautifully outside today." She waved a hand at the window, beyond which the rain came down hard, lashing at the glass.

"I thought I warned you about that sarcastic tone of yours."

"God's blood, Ma —"

"Gwynnie!"

"Shh!" Gwynnie spun towards the open archway at the sound of a tile being scuffed beneath a boot. Moments before, Pascal and Tombstone had stridden out of the room. Now, there was a shadow cast across the doorway, intimating that someone was there.

If someone was eavesdropping or intending to sneak up on them, Gwynnie was not inclined to find out why. There had been enough unsettling events for one day.

"Gwynnie," Emlyn said again.

"I said shh." Gwynnie grasped the hearth brush and spare tapers from the fireplace, throwing them into the wooden pail.

Taking her mother's arm, she pulled her toward the edge of the room.

The withdrawing chamber was vast, with a dividing screen down the middle that they now darted behind. As they reached the corner of the room, where one of the tapestries overhung a small door in the wall, someone stepped into the room through the main archway. They crept forward on their toes, clearly not wishing to be seen or heard.

"Who is —" Before Emlyn could say any more, Gwynnie pushed her mother through the door. She stumbled into the corridor beyond as Gwynnie shoved the wooden pail in after her. She quickly turned back, hiding behind the tapestry as she strained to get a glimpse of the newcomer. A man moved toward the fireplace they had just left, the toe of his boot brushing the stone as if inspecting it for dust. He huffed under his breath and looked around, his eyes narrowed.

He was well dressed, in a rich black doublet that wasn't overly embroidered. His breeches were tucked tightly around the tops of his legs, and his long boots showed signs of water from the puddles outside.

Gwynnie suppressed a gasp. It was Renard.

When another set of footsteps crossed the tiles, Gwynnie lowered the tapestry and ducked back through the doorway, her ears straining to hear their conversation.

"Well?" an all-too-familiar voice asked. "Have you found her yet?"

"I do not know." Renard's voice was quiet in comparison to the shrill tones of Henry Fitzroy.

"You said you could find her. Renard, if we do not find her—"

"Patience, Your Grace. If Pascal and Tombstone have come to question those two maids, then there has to be a reason for it."

"You think a maid is a jewellery thief? Pah! Like they would have the wherewithal for such a thing."

Gwynnie glanced back at her mother in the shadowy corridor. Emlyn raised a single eyebrow, clearly irked at the criticism.

"You and I saw the same thing," Renard said. "The person that climbed out of your window last night was a woman. You know it, as do I."

"But a maid?"

"Anyone is capable of anything, Your Grace. I would have thought you of all people would have known that."

Renard's words made Gwynnie step back. Indeed, who would have thought the son of the king would be a murderer? He was so young, so fair of face and innocent in his appearance. She still remembered the heavy tears and despairing expression before he had wrapped his long fingers around Florian's throat.

Anyone was capable of anything, when given the right push.

Gwynnie took her mother's arm and urged her down the corridor.

"Was that them?" Emlyn whispered, when they were far enough away not to be heard.

"No. It was pups barking adorably."

"By this light, Gwynnie, you never say anything serious."

"Well, how about this, Ma." Gwynnie's hand tightened on her mother's arm. "If Renard is hoping to discover who witnessed Florian's murder last night by watching Tombstone and Pascal's movements, then we need to make sure they do not realise that I was the one in Fitzroy's chambers."

CHAPTER 7

"You're injured. You need to rest," said Emlyn.

"I do not have time to rest, Ma." Gwynnie lifted the trug of sheets, her nose wrinkling at the stench as she crossed the orchard toward the outer walls of the palace, ready to do the laundry. "Were you not the one who said we have to continue our act as maids? I'm beginning to realise why we ended up as cutpurses in the first place." She dropped the trug and reached for her back, which still ached from her fall, trying to stretch it out. "Any other task would be preferable to this."

As she bent down to retrieve the trug, pain radiated up her spine and she yelped.

"That's quite enough. You need to rest." Emlyn took Gwynnie's arm and steered her toward the servants' quarters and their own chamber. Gwynnie didn't argue.

Inside, the corridor was busy with servants going about their tasks. As they passed by, Gwynnie caught snatches of whispered conversation.

"What thief would kill too?" one maid whispered to another as they carried baskets of vegetables down the corridor, heading to the kitchens. There were onions and cabbages piled high, along with bunches of parsley and rosemary that had been tied with string. "They must have been desperate."

"I hear they were a killer already," the other maid said. "Murderer. When judgement day comes, they'll burn in the fires of hell. That's what my mother says."

Gwynnie's head spun toward her mother. Emlyn avoided her gaze as they climbed the spiral staircase.

"What she said —"

"Not now, Gwynnie."

"But … do you think it's true?"

"It depends whether you're asking a Catholic or a Reformer. They all have their beliefs, and one should run for the hills if you have the wrong beliefs these days." Emlyn laughed, as if the idea of any religion at all was baffling to her. When she reached the top of the staircase, Gwynnie pulled on her arm.

"But do you think there's any truth in it? About the burning?" Gwynnie felt sick as she stared at her mother.

Emlyn stared back, a sudden tightness around her lips. "No, I do not."

"You mean you pray it is not true? After what you did…"

Emlyn took Gwynnie's shoulder and steered her toward their chamber. "Today I am just worried about keeping you and me out of the Tower of London. I can worry about the flames of hell another day." She pushed open the door to their room.

Inside, the chamber was in chaos. Their cot beds were turned over, the straw pillows pulled out of their coverings so loose straw was scattered across the room. Even the rush matting that had once covered the floor was rolled up, cut in places, as if sliced through with a blade. The latticed window had been pushed open and rain entered through the gap, soaking the windowsill and the matting beneath it.

"Ma…"

"I know. I see it." Emlyn stepped over the mess, avoiding crushing the matting or their gowns that had been tossed onto the floor, leaving a small coffer empty. "They were thorough."

Gwynnie moved to the coffer to see her mother was right. Whoever had searched their chamber had practically turned the coffer upside down. Running her hand over the lid, she found the wood fractured, the lock broken. In danger of getting splinters, she pulled her hand back suddenly. "They were looking for a hiding place."

Emlyn closed the window. Gwynnie moved to her side and scrambled to press her fingers into the grooves around the stone in the windowsill.

"Together," Emlyn urged. "One, two … now." They lifted the stone and rested it on the sill. Peering inside, Gwynnie reached for the various linen cloths in which they had hidden the jewels. Each one was sodden, for the rain had seeped through the gaps between the slabs, but as she unfurled the first cloth, she found the jewels safely inside.

"They didn't find them," Gwynnie murmured. "It was what they were looking for, though."

"It must have been." Emlyn nodded. "Whoever came looking was searching for our guilt. The question is, who? Was it Renard?"

"Or your new friend, Pascal?" Gwynnie muttered, then she shook her head. "No. Pascal didn't believe we were capable of being thieves, and you had him dancing to your tune. He would not have agreed to a search of our chamber in this manner."

"Then it is the other? Renard?"

Gwynnie couldn't answer. She righted the beds and slumped down onto hers with a wince as Emlyn dropped the linen cloth back into the gap in the windowsill, before hurrying around the space and tidying the mess. Gwynnie sat up, grimacing as she used what she could find of the straw to cushion her back. Her eyes repeatedly flitted to the closed door, fearing that if Renard had broken in once, he could do so again.

As if reading her mind, Emlyn turned her attention to the door. She lifted the latch, opening it an inch and bending down to examine the lock.

"He must have picked it," she whispered. "Almost as good a job as you can do, Gwynnie. There are only a few scratches in the wood."

"He wanted to find the jewels," Gwynnie murmured, more to herself than her mother. "If he could find the jewels, it would prove that one of us was in Fitzroy's rooms last night. That one of us witnessed Florian's murder."

Gwynnie closed her eyes. The whole reason she had come here in the first place was to protect her mother, to give Emlyn the chance to escape from a life of hardship and poverty. Instead, Gwynnie had placed her mother in even more danger than before.

"We need to get out of here," she whispered.

"What?" Emlyn's head shot up.

"Ma, we need to get you out of here."

"Me? What about you, miting?" Emlyn moved to stand. "Last time I looked, I was the mother here. I was the protector."

"Ma," Gwynnie said, wincing. "If the justices catch you, they will charge you with more than just larceny. You and I both know that."

"If they believe either of us are responsible for Master Battersby's death, then the past hardly matters today." Emlyn walked toward the windowsill and laid her hands protectively on the stone. "If Renard finds these, he will use them to reveal our guilt for the theft and hope he can pin the murder on us too."

Gwynnie stiffened, her back contorting with pain. "You mean..." She paused, breathing deeply. "Rather do anything to us himself, he'll hope to see us convicted of the murder, to protect his master?"

"It is the way the world works." Emlyn's expression grew dark as she looked out of the window at the rain. "Hornets fly away before they can be blamed for their sting."

The light was already fading as Gwynnie wandered through the courtyard. Having rested for a short while at the insistence of her mother, she was back out with the trug of laundry, intent on doing her job and hoping to disappear amongst the other staff that attended Greenwich Palace. Darkness crept in over the tiled roof, enveloping the courtyards. People scurried to and fro with lanterns clutched in pale fingers, each person hurrying to their task.

Gwynnie didn't bother with a lantern. Both of her hands were taken up carrying the basket as she moved toward the outer walls. In the middle court, four large shadows appeared, making her pause.

The men carried a slat of wood, upon which something was laid, a clean white sheet hanging over it. The toe of a boot hung out from one end of the sheet, revealing what was underneath it. Florian Battersby's body.

Behind the party walked Florian's wife, Goodwife Esme Battersby. Her head was lowered, and her black hair was now tied at the nape of her neck, no longer loose and wild as it had been the last time Gwynnie had seen her.

Gwynnie crossed the courtyard and headed toward the group. Not a single person looked her way or gave any sign of acknowledging her presence. As she moved closer, she could hear Goodwife Battersby muttering to herself.

"Someone must pay. They will pay. God's righteousness will be served upon this earth, by someone's hand, if not by my own. Lord, I pray it is my own. I pray you, God, show me the way. Show me who did this. I shall see your justice is served."

The need for vengeance was not new to Gwynnie. In her mind's eye, she was a child again, little more than thirteen. She stood in the corner of the attic rooms she and her mother shared after her father had gone, trying to light a candle. Repeatedly, she struck the iron wool from a tinderbox against a piece of flint. Sparks flew in the darkness until at last the flame took.

She had watched that wax burn down for hours, the flame a small orb in the corner of the room. Gwynnie brushed away the spiders that threatened to land on her shoulders from overhanging cobwebs as the door at last opened.

Emlyn stumbled in, dressed in hose and a jerkin, with a heavy cloak across her shoulders. She could have been mistaken for a man at a casual glance. She didn't see Gwynnie at first and leaned heavily against the nearest wall, a moan escaping her lips.

"*Ma?*" Gwynnie had whispered the word, capturing her mother's attention.

Emlyn didn't have the strength to step off the wall, but as she half turned toward Gwynnie, she revealed her palms. They were stained with blood.

"*Vengeance has been served tonight, miting.*"

Gwynnie blinked and stared after Goodwife Battersby as she left the courtyard, following the four men that carried her husband away. Try as she might, Gwynnie could not move. She was fixed to the spot, with the laundry in her trug dampening by the second and the loose hairs escaping her coif sticking to her cheeks.

"Curious, is it not?" a voice called to her, inflected with a French accent.

Gwynnie's body grew cold as she turned around. Standing in the shadow of a tall archway was a figure. By now, Gwynnie could recognise the silhouette, for she had looked for it with fear throughout the day. The lithe body was clothed in that same black doublet, his long boots covering his knees. Calmly, he took a step forward, out of the shadow of the archway. Candlelight from a nearby window fell on his features. The greying hair and angular beard glistened in the light.

"Forgive me, I have frightened you." He nodded politely, a casual smile on his lips. "We met briefly last night, in the kitchens."

"We did." Gwynnie kept her voice level, feeling her throat grow tight. She bobbed a curtsy, remembering just how many times her mother had told her over the years that to survive, one merely had to pretend that they were not the prey an animal wished to hunt. She had to make Renard believe she was not afraid of him, if she had any chance of persuading him that she was not the jewellery thief he had nearly caught the night before. "You described something as curious, sir?"

"I did." His eyes flitted past her, toward where Goodwife Battersby had retreated with her husband's body. "I have seen you twice now, lingering near Master Battersby's body."

"I was one of the unfortunate souls in this courtyard this morning, sir." She hung her head, having no need to feign a sad tone for it came naturally. "I saw Master Battersby's body along with many others."

Renard stepped closer. His face briefly disappeared from the light until he stopped in front of her, and the candlelight fell across his eyes, revealing their dark depths.

"You ought to be careful, Mistress…?"

"Gwynnie Wightham, sir. I'm a maid here at the palace."

"So I hear. Even more curious, for I do not remember seeing you here before this last month."

"I am new, sir."

"Ah, that must be it." He tipped his head back, looking down his long nose at her.

As the silence stretched out, Gwynnie's adjusted her grasp on the trug. She felt the urge to flee, but to do so would be announcing that she was afraid of him.

"Is there anything you need, sir? I should return to the laundry." She held up the trug for him to see.

"By all means, return to your duties." He waved a hand, urging her to carry on, but he did not step out of her way. Slowly, Gwynnie walked around him. She kept her distance as much as she could, glancing back only when she was at the far end of the courtyard.

Renard had started to follow her, his silhouette barely discernible in the darkness.

Turning forward again, Gwynnie kept her pace even as she turned down a narrow lane between two of the palace buildings. Only when she was certain she was out of sight did she run. Sprinting on the toes of her boots, she tried to avoid making any sound at all. She glanced back but didn't see another figure enter the lane.

When she reached the far end, rather than heading to the outer walls and the laundry room, she stepped up onto a stone platform erected outside the gate that led to the wider estate of the palace. A great statue adorned the plinth, depicting the king's father, his heavy robes hanging down as if billowing in the wind. Hiding behind the statue, she waited, her palms clammy despite the chill of the evening air. When footsteps sounded close by, she held her breath.

Glancing at the nearest window, Gwynnie caught a glimpse of a figure in the reflection. It was Renard, turning in a circle as he searched for her.

"Renard?" a voice called.

Gwynnie closed her eyes, hearing the unmistakable shrill notes of Henry Fitzroy.

"Renard?"

"Quiet, Your Grace." Gwynnie opened her eyes and saw Renard's reflection disappear back down the lane, toward Fitzroy.

"Well? Is it her?" Fitzroy hissed.

"I do not know. Yet have no fear, Your Grace. I shall find out."

As their voices and footsteps faded, Gwynnie breathed a sigh of relief. A memory shot across her mind. It was of her mother the night she had appeared with those blood-stained palms.

"*Do you know what they do to people with blood on their hands, Gwynnie?*" Emlyn had plunged her hands into a bowl of water, scrubbing madly to try and remove the dried blood. "*They hang them from the gallows.*"

Gwynnie dropped to the ground and ran.

CHAPTER 8

"I'm not doing it." Emlyn flapped the clean sheet in the air of the laundry room. Gwynnie snatched it from her mother's hands, raising her brows in silent challenge. The morning sunlight streamed through the glass, making the dust particles dance in the air between them. "I pray you, do not look at me like that. You're a sorry sight this morning. There are shadows under your eyes and you're walking at a strange angle."

Gwynnie flopped down onto the nearest stool, to give her back a rest. She was not going to admit to her mother that she'd had another dreadful night's sleep, with her back aching so much that she'd practically crawled out of bed when the sun rose. The running she had done the night before to avoid Renard hadn't helped matters, and she feared that if she didn't recover soon and she had to run from him again, he would be able to catch her all too easily.

"Ma, think about it," Gwynnie urged. "If you and I continue to do nothing, then Renard will keep watching me. What if he finds the *jewels*?" She whispered the last word despite their being alone, yet her mother still looked around sharply as she continued to fold the next clean sheet. "You know as well as I that he will use them against us. I promised long ago I would not see you at the gallows," she hissed. "I will not see it happen now."

As Gwynnie watched her mother, a pain radiated through her body that had little to do with the injury in her back. It was the thought of losing Emlyn that caused that ache.

"If we wish to live, then we need a way to help the truth come out." Gwynnie stood and took one end of the sheet, to assist with the folding.

"How are you going to do that then?" Emlyn asked tartly. "Do you plan to just walk up to that nice Pascal and his difficult lawyer, and announce that you saw the whole thing? Think it through, Gwynnie. They'll hang you."

"I know that."

"Do you?" Emlyn huffed, taking the folded sheet from Gwynnie's hands. "At this moment, I think a newly weaned pup has more sense than you."

"I have sense, Ma."

"That is debatable."

"And you wonder where I get my sarcasm from." Gwynnie crossed the room to the barrel of water and lye. Emlyn followed, helping as Gwynnie plunged more soiled sheets and chemises into the barrel. "There must be a way to reveal what Fitzroy did."

"How?"

"Perhaps we could find out more about why Florian was blackmailing Fitzroy in the first place."

"What do you mean?" Emlyn plunged the sheets into the water as Gwynnie chewed her lip, trying to recall what she had overheard in Fitzroy's garderobe.

"Florian said that Fitzroy had a lover. A man named Master Woodville."

"Woodville?" Emlyn paused in her task.

"You know the name?"

"I do. About a week before you and I arrived, I heard through the other servants that Master Jerome Woodville went missing. It was New Year's Eve." Emlyn's brow wrinkled. "Do you not remember me telling you? Most thought he had left in the middle of the night, abandoned his duties to the palace."

"Well, Florian plainly thought there was more to the matter." Gwynnie frowned as she recalled Florian's exact words. "He asked, 'Was that an admission?'"

"An admission of what?"

"Either an admission that Master Woodville was his lover, or that he was responsible for Woodville's disappearance."

Emlyn dropped the sheet back into the barrel and stared hard at Gwynnie.

"Florian thought that Fitzroy had killed Woodville."

"Exactly," Gwynnie murmured. "And when Renard arrived, he said something about it being the same as before; how Fitzroy had done it before with…" Slowly, she lifted her eyes to stare at Emlyn. "With his bare hands."

"By this light!" Emlyn gasped.

"We need to ask about Master Woodville. If we can find out what happened to him, then perhaps we can point Tombstone and Master Pascal toward the truth. It is worth a try, is it not, Ma?"

Emlyn turned away. She busied herself pulling out more dirty chemises, which she plunged into another barrel of lye and water.

"Ma?" Gwynnie followed her, stopping on the other side of the barrel. "What was it you once said to me about vengeance? How someone has to take it into their own hands?"

"This is different."

"How is this different?"

"We did not know Florian. Nor did we know Master Woodville. Let another take their vengeance and let us save our own necks." She flapped one of the chemises in the air, nearly catching Gwynnie with it.

"And what would you have thought if someone had the chance to catch my father's killer, and they did nothing about it?"

There was a sudden silence between them. Emlyn stared down into the water; her lips pursed. Gwynnie held her breath, fearing she had taken it too far.

"No more," Emlyn whispered, her words barely audible. "No more, Gwynnie, I beg you."

"We need to do something, Ma."

Before they could discuss the matter anymore, the door opened, and another maid bustled into the room carrying a trug of laundry. She was much older, her face as wrinkled as the creased sheets being washed.

"I hope you two aren't shirking," she said with a thick northern accent. Then she grinned. "Been impressed with you two since you arrived. Won't have that changing, I hope."

"No, Sarah." Gwynnie forced a smile.

"I always make sure my daughter works hard," Emlyn said with a wink.

"Ah, you take good care of her." Sarah dropped her trug. This one was full of men's shirts, and she wrinkled her nose as she pulled them out, one at a time. "I bet you take good care of your mother too, don't you, Gwynnie? Can't say I blame you with all these strange tidings."

Gwynnie moved to help her with the shirts.

"Ma was telling me that the thefts and poor Master Battersby's death are not the first ill things to happen as of late." She lifted a jug of water and stared pouring it out into a third barrel, into which Sarah dropped some of the shirts. "I hear a gentleman also went missing."

"Master Woodville? Oh aye, you're right about that. Bad business, if you ask me." Sarah shuddered.

"How do you mean?" Gwynnie asked.

"I mean that Master Woodville was one of the lower gentries of the palace, well liked, and because of it, he seemed to have access everywhere. Aye, nice lad. Always had a kind word to say to us servants. Not like some of the high and mighty you get in these corridors." Sarah wrinkled her nose, but it was no longer because of the foul scent. "He was younger than you, lass. Scarcely more than a boy." She sighed heavily. "He was last seen at New Year."

"I heard he left the palace and ran away to make his own life," Emlyn said calmly from across the room as she started to wring out some of the sodden sheets.

"You can think that, if you like." Sarah dumped the last of the shirts into the barrel.

"What do *you* think happened?" Gwynnie asked, adding a lye mixture from a small brown jug into the water.

"I think that Master Woodville was happy here," Sarah said softly. "He never had a desire to go anywhere, so why would he leave? And then there's the fact he didn't take anything with him." She halted her movements and looked straight at Gwynnie. "A man who runs away takes a coffer and a few things. Nothing was taken from Master Woodville's chamber. Not even a spare shirt." She thrust her hand into the barrel and worked the shirts together with the lye. "If you ask me, something happened that night. He wouldn't be the first lad to drink himself into a stupor or to end up in a fight from all that liquor. Poor boy probably ended up in a ditch or tripped into the Thames, too drunk to pull himself out."

Gwynnie gulped, watching the pain on Sarah's face.

"Poor boy," she murmured again. "Nothing good comes from these wet winters. One man disappeared, another dead, and now all these robberies? Nah, the rain is an omen if you ask me."

"What sort of omen?"

"Of bad tidings." Sarah nodded. "I'm not the only one who thinks it. Ravens have been seen over the river. And, on Yuletide Day, two great fish the size of carts washed up on the shore of the Thames. Bad times are to come. Last time such omens came to the palace, we lost a queen." She looked at Gwynnie. "Queen Catherine was sent from this palace. Now, poor Queen Catherine is dead. The king wears yellow to celebrate and there are tales that when Queen Catherine's heart was cut from her chest, it was found to be as black as night. You want my thoughts? I think Queen Anne should be watching where she treads."

Gwynnie said nothing but glanced across at her mother. Emlyn was strangely quiet, staring into a barrel of water and chemises. Gwynnie crossed the room to her mother, so Sarah could not hear her.

"We have to do something," Gwynnie whispered. "For Master Woodville's sake."

"Then do something." Emlyn nodded. "But be careful what path you choose, miting."

"What do you think?" Gwynnie held up the letter. Her handwriting was shaky, the words barely legible.

"You know I can't read," Emlyn said. "You'll have to read it out to me. Your father was the one who could read a little."

Gwynnie remembered all too well. Her father was a learned man, who had taught Gwynnie to read and write. Now, it was a skill that might prove useful, if the intended reader could believe what was in her letter.

71

Gwynnie cleared her throat and flattened the letter upon the stone windowsill. "*To the Master Neville Pascal,*" she began. "*You and your clerk are searching in the wrong place for your killer. If you wish to know who killed Master Florian Battersby, then forget the jewellery thieves. We know what happened that night, and it had nothing to do with jewels, and everything to do with a secret. If you wish to search for the truth, then look to where Master Battersby went that night. Yours etcetera, the Shadow Cutpurses.*"

Gwynnie dropped the letter onto the windowsill and sat down on her bed, her sore back making her wince.

"You could tell the truth of what you saw that night, I suppose." Emlyn chewed her lip, then shook her head. "No. That is a poor idea. If you accused Fitzroy, they would never believe you."

"Precisely. It is better they find out the truth for themselves. They are more likely to believe it that way."

Emlyn picked up the letter and folded it, passing it to Gwynnie. "You know what to do," she whispered. "Though I pray you are right about this." Her brow furrowed. "I will not stand by and watch you go to the gallows."

Gwynnie stood, taking the letter from her mother's hands. "It's what I've been trying to protect you from all these years too."

"I know." Emlyn's words were barely audible. "Now, go. Before anyone wonders why you are not at your duties."

Gwynnie slipped the letter inside the sleeve of her gown and left the room. She headed toward the kitchens. It was not long now until the feast would be ready, and the usual clamour and uproar sounded in the kitchens. Cooks shouted at one another, Samuel's voice booming above the others. Maids hovered by the hatches, some carrying trays of spiced wine in flagons, others great trenchers of pig cooked until the skin caramelised, and pheasants that had been tucked back into the skin.

Gwynnie stepped to the side of the maids. They were talking so loudly that not one paid attention to her.

"Do you think the thieves will strike again?" one maid whispered to another. "I do not want to die."

"You have nothing to steal, remember?" the other maid laughed. "I'd say you are quite safe."

Gwynnie's stomach knotted at the idea that anyone could think she was a killer. She picked up a tray full of doucet pastries and sweetmeats, and followed the other maids toward the great hall, where the feast was being held. Shortly before they reached the great double doors, she hung back and turned down another narrow corridor. She passed through many corridors, moving around the middle court to the south wing of the palace. Passing through a gate and the tiltyard, she moved toward the curtain wall.

Master Neville Pascal and his lawyer were set up in the southern wing of the palace, not far from Cromwell's own chambers and the other rooms in which the clerks, lawyers and privy councillors worked. Gwynnie passed down a corridor with dark tapestries on one side and mahogany panelling on the other. On this side of the palace there were no grand paintings or portraits, no royal figures adorning the walls.

Myriad doors were before her, some closed, others ajar. She crept toward the nearest open door and poked her head inside. The sun streaming through the window revealed it was empty. She stepped in, peering down at the paperwork on the nearest desk. The name referred to one of Cromwell's officials, but not to Pascal.

Stepping back out of the room, Gwynnie chose another open door. On the desk were many letters, each one bearing the name of Neville Pascal. Lowering the tray of doucets to the desk, she pushed these letters aside, creating a bare space on which she laid her own letter. Smiling, certain that it would be seen, she picked up the tray and turned to leave.

Footsteps sounded in the corridor.

"There are no other witnesses." It was the voice of the lawyer, Elric Tombstone. "I have combed through every testimonial of those staying in the tower that night, all except for the king and queen themselves."

"You know we cannot talk to them."

"Then accept my word, Pascal. No one saw anything."

There was no way Gwynnie could escape the room without being seen. Her eyes darted around for a place to hide. There were no tapestries to tuck herself behind, no other doors to slip through. To hide under the desk would be obvious and she'd be discovered in a few seconds.

The only other space in the room was the fireplace. The grate was empty, without a burning ember inside it.

"I must be mad," Gwynnie whispered to herself as she moved toward the fireplace.

CHAPTER 9

"Elric, give me a minute to think, I pray you." Pascal's words rang out as he entered the room.

Gwynnie held her body completely still, trying not to cough from all the soot in the confined space. Her feet were jammed against the stones in the wall of the chimney, her hands on either side of her, braced against the wall. The pastry tray she had been carrying now rested precariously on a ledge beside her. She watched as it teetered on the edge.

A heavy thud sounded from inside the room, suggesting that one of the men had sat down on a settle bench, making the wood creak.

"So, there are no witnesses," Pascal sighed heavily. "No one saw anything. This is madness. How can a man be attacked in the middle of a courtyard, his throat slit, and yet there was no ruckus? No shouts of fear or anger, nothing to awaken anyone to even peer out of their window?" He paused. "Perhaps if someone did see something, they are nervous of coming forward?"

"Perhaps," said Tombstone. "Or maybe there was no fight at all."

"See sense, boy. The man had his throat slit. I struggle to believe he would not have put up a fight."

"I agree. But do you not think it odd that there was glass under his boots? Where did it come from?" Tombstone's perceptive question made Gwynnie smile. At least someone had noticed the glass.

"Why is that important?"

"There was no glass in the courtyard — I checked. Then there is the fact that most men react impulsively to damage at their throat. Their hands go to their own neck, trying to hold the wound closed. Do you not see, Pascal? His hands were free of blood."

"Hmm. I had not thought of that."

Gwynnie shuddered, trying not to think about the blood on Florian's neck.

"Shall we light a fire?" Tombstone's question made her freeze, looking down at the grate beneath her. If they lit a fire now, she'd either be smoked out of her hiding place, or she'd drop down into the flames and end up with badly burnt feet.

"Wait ... what's this? Elric, look."

Footsteps moved away from the fireplace, and Gwynnie allowed herself a small sigh of relief.

"That is some shaky handwriting," Tombstone murmured.

"Do you recognise it?"

"No."

They must have opened the letter as both men fell quiet.

"The Shadow Cutpurses, eh?" said Pascal eventually. "I still remember the first time I heard that ridiculous name. Given to them by some foolish pamphlet writer in London. They'd robbed a ship as it stood in the Thames, stealing all the jewels on board that belonged to the wife of the captain. They disappeared into the night…"

"Like shadows," Tombstone finished for him. "I've heard the tale before."

"You have?"

"You've told it before."

"Oh."

There was something about the dynamic of their conversation. Where Gwynnie had judged before they were merely employer and lawyer, she now wondered just how well they knew each other.

"If you ask me, the thieves wrote this in an effort to save their own skin," Pascal went on. "They want us to look elsewhere, so that they can escape with the jewels. The lower classes are all the same: thieves, killers — any skullduggery and they'll turn their hand to it."

Gwynnie's heart thudded hard as she listened to Pascal. He had no idea how hard servants worked just to be able to put food on the table.

Tombstone grew grave. "I am not sure what this letter means, but I am not convinced I believe it either. They claim to know what truly happened. But if that is the case, and someone else is responsible, then why do they not just say who it is?"

"They are responsible," Pascal said with feeling. "Trust me, boy. This is the knaves' attempt to push the blame elsewhere. That is all."

Tombstone did not reply.

"Find out who has been seen near this room in the last hour. See if anyone witnessed who placed this letter here."

"Very well." Tombstone's footsteps moved toward the door.

Gwynnie shifted her hand on the wall, relieved that they no longer had any intention of lighting a fire. She brushed the doucet tray, and it wobbled even more than before, in danger of falling. She clasped it, the other hand slipping on the wall.

"What was that?" Tombstone asked. He must have heard her move.

"Crows in the chimney again. They never do anything about it. Elric, there's something else."

"Yes?"

Gwynnie froze, not daring to move in case she gave away her location.

"The rain has stopped. The flood has already retreated a little since yesterday."

"You believe Woolwich Road could soon be open if the flood retreats far enough?"

"Exactly, boy, exactly," Pascal said eagerly. "If the Shadow Cutpurses are waiting for the flood to retreat before they make their escape, then we do not have long. If the weather continues dry, we could only have a few more days before they are gone and beyond our reach."

"We will find them, Pascal." Tombstone's voice grew firm. "No killer has escaped me yet, has he?"

"Your arrogance will be your downfall someday." Despite his words, Pascal's tone was soft. "Now, go. Find what you can about who delivered this letter. I shall report to Cromwell."

Gwynnie waited until she heard the door close and the key turn in the lock, clunking loudly, before she snatched up the sweetmeats tray and climbed down the chimney. She slipped and landed on her knees in the soot.

"God's blood, this will be the death of me," she muttered, clambering to her feet. Finding the pastries were now covered in ash, she hastened out of the fireplace and moved to the window.

Beyond the glass there should have been a grassy bank that led up to a copse of trees, but in its place was the flood Pascal had spoken of. Gwynnie reached for the glass and pushed open the window, peering down at the water. She could risk picking the lock and leaving through the door, but if anyone was wandering around, she risked being seen.

Climbing up onto the windowsill, she looked at the dirtied doucets. They could hardly be eaten now, and they no longer served as an excuse for why she was wandering these corridors. She tossed the tray and pastries into the flood. They splashed in the water, disappearing into the muddy depths.

Gwynnie craned her neck, checking that no one had heard the sound and poked their head out of a nearby window. When all remained quiet, she lowered herself out of the window and dropped into the flood.

The ice-cold water enveloped her, snatching the breath from her chest. She gasped until she could breathe again, before swimming through the flood. Judging by how deep the water was, there was no chance she and Emlyn could escape the palace any time soon. Out of fear that it would get deeper, she stayed close to the palace walls.

When she reached a small footpath above the level of the water, she clambered onto it, her body shaking as she fell onto her hands and knees. Her back ached and for a minute, she didn't think she would move again.

A sudden shout from above urged her on as a window was flung open.

"Tombstone! Down there! There's someone there."

Getting to her feet, Gwynnie found energy she didn't know she had left. She darted back toward the palace buildings and chose a small door that led into the laundry rooms, hiding herself inside. She fell against the door, breathing deeply.

"Gwynnie? Is that you?" Emlyn called from the main room of the laundry.

Her legs shaking beneath her, Gwynnie moved toward her mother's voice. She stepped through a small antechamber, where there were laundry mangles and shelves full of bars of lye beside small brown-and-white-chequered bottles, full of mixtures of soap and lavender. Entering the main chamber, Gwynnie stalled in the doorway.

Emlyn dropped the sheet she was washing and covered her mouth when her eyes settled on Gwynnie.

"Deliver a letter, you said. Easy, you said," Gwynnie murmured in a wry tone. "God's blood, my bones have become ice."

"Language, Gwynnie." Emlyn snatched up a linen towel and hurried across the room, throwing it around Gwynnie's shoulders. She took off the coif and ruffled Gwynnie's hair with the linen.

"You wish to preach to me about my language now?"

"They don't believe us?" Emlyn asked as she continued to wash the sheets.

Gwynnie sat beside the fire in the laundry room, trying to get warm. Her hands still shook as she held them out toward the flames and her hair was loose around her shoulders, drying in the heat.

"Well, Pascal does not." Gwynnie chewed her lip as she watched the flames dance.

"When the flood retreats, we'll have to run."

"What?" Gwynnie turned toward her mother. "You said yourself that if we run, they'll know it was us. They'll think us guilty of the murder too, and we'll be hunted down like dogs."

"Think on it, Gwynnie," Emlyn said. "Would you rather be cornered in this building when they come to take us? Or out there —" she waved a hand at the window — "running on our terms? I know where I'd rather be."

"It's not so simple." Gwynnie shook her head. "We still have to wait for the flood to retreat. It's too dangerous as it is."

Emlyn said nothing more and returned to her task, her movements sharper than before.

Watching Emlyn perform such a mundane activity, when so much else was going on, made Gwynnie think of the way that Florian had calmly drunk his wine, shortly before Fitzroy had latched his hands around the man's throat. The everyday and the monstrous. Gwynnie shuddered.

"We must make them believe us," she whispered. "We must make them see the truth."

"And how do you expect to do that? Eh?" Emlyn laughed, but without any real humour. "You want to walk up to them and tell them with your own lips?"

"There must be something we can do." Gwynnie thought back to that night in Donsen Tower when Florian had attempted to blackmail Fitzroy. The missing man, Master Woodville, was at the centre of it all.

"What if we were to do Pascal and Tombstone's job for them?" Gwynnie whispered, watching the red and yellow flames dance in the grate.

"In case it has passed you by, we have enough of our own work to do here," Emlyn called as she wrung out one of the sheets.

"I mean, what if we were to find out what happened to Jerome Woodville?"

Emlyn's hands stilled on the sheet and water dripped off it, running into a puddle on the flagstones.

"Ma?" Gwynnie said. "Think on it. What if we were to find Jerome? We could point them toward where he is. It would lead them to Fitzroy, as he was seen in Master Woodville's company the night he disappeared —"

"A body."

"I'm sorry?"

"You are not asking us to find a *man*," Emlyn said, her eyes flashing in anger. "You are asking us to find a *body*."

"I… Yes, I am." Gwynnie swallowed around a sudden lump in her throat.

"You saw your first dead man only a couple of days ago. Let me warn you of something now." Emlyn crossed the room toward her. "It stays with you. Once you have seen death, you cannot unsee it."

"I thought you never liked to talk of what you have seen before —"

"Gwynnie!" Emlyn snapped. "Looking for a dead man is the most foolish idea you've ever had." She sat down beside Gwynnie, leaning toward the fire.

"What other choice do we have, Ma?" Gwynnie whispered. "If we find him, it could lead Pascal and Tombstone to Fitzroy."

"It's still a foolish idea." Emlyn looked at Gwynnie. "But maybe it's the only choice we have."

Gwynnie nodded, a breath escaping her lips.

"Then here's the next question. How do we find him?"

"We find out what happened at New Year, the eighth night of Yuletide."

CHAPTER 10

"You're getting worse."

"I'll be fine." Gwynnie rubbed her sore back. Following the fall from Donsen Tower and her subsequent jump from Pascal's office, her back was now smattered with bruises and when she walked, a throbbing pain radiated up her spine. Yet she couldn't afford to sit down and rest. She had to push on.

She nodded to her mother as they reached the door to the kitchens. Emlyn walked away, heading toward the bathing room where the maids took their baths, and Gwynnie stepped into the kitchen. The bells from Friar Church rang out across the palace grounds, calling the courtiers to Sunday morning service.

It was the early hours of the morning, and the sunlight was just filtering through the lead-lined glass windows of the kitchens. At such an early hour, only a few cooks had risen. Bread was being baked in the fiery ovens, the flour spread on nearby wooden blocks, as the scent of dough lingered. Samuel was in his usual merry state as he kneaded dough on a slab of marble, humming a happy tune as he repeatedly pelted the dough with flour across the palms of his hands. Beside him were Seville oranges, imported from the Continent, and pomegranates, ready to make the bread sweet.

Gwynnie stepped up in front of the cook, offering an easy smile.

"Gwynnie! How are you, lass?" he asked as he broke off from his tune. "Not here to steal more pastries, are you?"

"What?" Gwynnie stiffened, fearing he had seen her take the doucet tray the day before.

"Pastries have gone missing." He shook his head and sighed. "Between you and me…" He paused and leaned across the marble. "I suspect old Rudyard over there." He jerked his head toward the oldest cook in the room.

A man in his seventies with a crooked back, he was currently trying to take a spit of cooked meat off the fire, but his hands shook, and the spike wavered precariously in the air.

"He's grown forgetful these days. I reckon he ate them and forgot all about it."

"Probably," said Gwynnie, feeling a little guilty. "Samuel, can I ask you something?"

"What is it, lass?" Samuel returned to pounding the dough.

"What have you heard about Master Woodville?"

"Not much." Samuel sighed and loosened his hands from the dough, rubbing them together to get rid of some of the excess flour. The scent of the cinnamon spices that had been added to the dough leapt into the air. "You know he went missing on eighth night?"

"Yes, I had heard," Gwynnie whispered, chewing her lip. "It all seems so strange. One man missing, another killed. It's awful."

"That it is."

"Sarah thinks the poor man must have tripped and fallen into the river when he was drunk."

"Could be."

"What do you think?"

Samuel watched her with slightly narrowed eyes as he rubbed the flour off his hands.

"Why all the questions, lass?"

"I suppose I'm worried, that's all." She shrugged. "I thought coming to work here in the palace with Ma would be safe. Now I'm not so sure."

Samuel beckoned her to walk around the bench, so they could talk quietly.

"If you ask me, there's nothing to worry about when it comes to Master Woodville. I saw him that night myself."

"You did?"

"He was with the king's son. When we went to the great hall to serve the food, I went too; none of the maids are strong enough to carry the boar's head." He chuckled, shaking his head. "Fitzroy and Woodville were sat close together, drinking so much wine that as much of it went on their clothes as in their mouths. I think Sarah's probably right. Poor boy drank himself into a stupor and fell into the Thames. No need to worry, lass." He tapped her shoulder comfortingly and turned away, returning to the dough.

"Why would he be walking alongside the Thames, though?" Gwynnie whispered. "I thought the lower gentry's rooms were in the south wing."

"They are." Samuel didn't look up from his task. "Old Rudyard saw Woodville walking on the docks with Fitzroy that night during the celebrations. Said they were hooting like owls at the moon." He laughed softly and shook his head. "Here, take that." Samuel reached across to a tray of pastries and passed a small one to her.

"I thought you said a whole tray had gone missing?"

"Then no one will miss another, will they?" He laughed and winked. "Take it quickly and don't you worry. You and your ma are safe here."

Gwynnie forced a smile and turned away, thinking how little he truly knew.

She wrapped her woollen cloak around her shoulders as she stepped out into the cold. It wasn't raining this morning, but the air was chilly and as she walked across the cobbles between the palace buildings, she slipped more than once, the puddles having turned to ice.

She headed through the main gate at the front of the palace, beneath Donsen Tower, and out to the docks that looked over the Thames. The water had risen so high that half the docks were underwater, making it impossible for the wherrymen to get close to the building.

Stepping out gingerly onto what remained of the docks, Gwynnie peered over the edge and into the water. If, as she suspected, Fitzroy had killed Woodville at New Year, then it was perfectly possible that he had disposed of the body in the water. If that was the case, then Woodville's body could have been washed miles away, perhaps even out to sea. It would be impossible to find.

"This is a fool's errand," Gwynnie muttered to herself as she wrapped her cloak tighter around her shoulders, trying to ward off the cold.

"What makes you say that?"

Gwynnie whipped her head around, recognising the French accent of Renard. He stood before her where the riverbank met the dock, his arms folded across his black doublet.

"I'm sorry?" she said. She suddenly didn't feel cold anymore, but clammy.

"What is a fool's errand?" he asked, his piercing gaze unwavering.

"Trying to get across the river." She offered a small smile. "I was thinking the poor wherrymen must be having a harsh winter."

Renard slowly nodded.

"Well, if you will excuse me, I should return to my work." She walked back along the dock toward him. She expected him to step aside, but he didn't move. Instead he blocked her path, forcing her to come to a halt. "Sir…" She gestured for him to step back.

"I'm curious." He tilted his head to the side, watching her closely.

"About what, sir?"

"I seem to keep finding you in unexpected places, Mistress Gwynnie. The kitchens, very late at night, looking at the body of the dead man too. Now here…" Renard's eyes flitted down to the water.

"Have you not met maids before, sir?" Gwynnie said wryly. "We're supposed to go about our business unseen. We do not always accomplish it." She laughed and moved to step past him, but he inched to the side and blocked her path. "Sir, I need to return to my work."

"I cannot help feeling that I have seen you somewhere else, too."

"Have you? I have been working here for some weeks, sir. It is likely you have seen me around."

"I mean, somewhere that you should not have been."

"Where?" Her voice was quiet.

He stepped forward, and Gwynnie instinctively moved back, toward the flooded dock. When her heels splashed in the water, she halted.

"Careful, Mistress Gwynnie. You wouldn't want to end up in the water, would you?" His words were quiet, holding a threat within.

"Excuse me, sir." She tried to walk around him, more forcefully this time, but he caught her elbow, jerking her toward the water. Gwynnie teetered on the very edge of the dock, her back jarring so that she squealed with pain.

She stared down into the watery depths. In places, the water was frozen, especially where the shallows met the frost-covered riverbank, and in other places it was so deep, she could not hope to see the bottom. A few minutes in that water and it would be far worse than when she swam through the flood the day before. She would struggle to pull herself back out of those icy depths.

"You have an injury," Renard hissed in her ear. "How did you come by that?"

"I fell," Gwynnie muttered. She tried to pull her elbow out of his hold, but his grip was too strong. Looking around at the riverbank, she searched desperately for another face, some witness she could call to, but the area was empty.

"Where are the jewels?"

Something silver darted in the corner of her eye. Gwynnie flicked her head back toward Renard. He held a blade to the tip of her chin.

"Where are the jewels?" he asked again. He leaned so close she could see the red veins in his eyes.

"I do not know what you are talking about." Gwynnie barely moved her lips at all, in case her skin was cut by the blade. "Sir, you have me confused with someone else."

"Do I?" He thrust the blade up a little. The action was minute, but enough to score her skin.

She grunted at the pain and acted fast.

Driving her knee into his groin, she connected hard, and he grunted loudly, releasing her. She hurried past him, and as he reached for her again, she pushed out with both hands, knocking him off the dock, straight into the icy water.

A great splash erupted around him as he flailed about, struggling to catch his breath from the sudden shock of the cold.

Gwynnie scurried back along the dock, spotting the blade he'd dropped. She could see it clearly now, a dagger no longer than the span of her hand, the blade sharpened so much that it was wearing away on one side. The handle was wooden and notched.

"Good day to you, sir!" she called loudly to Renard, putting as much distance between herself and the dagger as she could. "You should be careful with your footing out here. It's quite dangerous."

He latched a hand over the dock to drag himself up, just as she reached the riverbank and sprinted for the main gate.

Darting through the archway of Donsen Tower, she headed toward the inner court. A group of fine ladies wandered out of the main building, laughing, oblivious to what had just happened out on the dock. They filled the archway, forcing Gwynnie to creep alongside the wall.

As she emerged past the ladies, into the inner courtyard, she looked back, but she was too short to see over the ladies' French hoods. Hastening to the fountain in the middle of the cobbled square, Gwynnie glanced around to ensure no one was looking her way before climbing up onto the stone rim of the fountain, using the extra height to see if Renard was following her.

His face emerged, scowling, his black doublet now sodden.

"God have mercy." Gwynnie dropped down from the fountain and ran. She ignored the few flustered ladies who squawked like startled geese as she ran past them, down the nearest narrow lane and out into the middle court. She was dimly aware of something warm trickling down her chin, but she didn't pay it any attention.

When she reached the edge of the courtyard, she could go no further. The kitchen doors had been flung open, and the servants hurried out with their trays of food, carrying them toward the great hall, ready for breakfast. There were trays of eels coated in saffron and yellow spices, trenchers of pike and perch, and a trout whose flesh had already been flaked with a knife. The stench of fish wafted in the air, not quite masked by the heavy spices and sweet scents of sugar.

Amongst the many familiar faces, Gwynnie saw Sarah. The elder woman was heaving under the weight of two jugs of claret.

"Sarah? Here, let me help you with that." Gwynnie hurried to her side and took one of the jugs. It was so heavy that she nearly dropped it. "What is this made of? Lead?"

"Aye, it feels like it." Sarah chuckled. "Thank you. Come on, the king will be wanting his claret."

Gwynnie lifted the jug onto her shoulder. Renard appeared in the courtyard, skidding to a stop. Gwynnie shifted the jug a little, using the large vessel to hide her face as she walked past him with the other maids.

Only as they stepped through the doorway into the east wing of the palace buildings did she glance back. Renard had halted in the middle of the courtyard, turning back and forth as he searched the faces of the maids who passed him.

Gwynnie allowed herself a small smile as she followed Sarah into the building, though it didn't last long. As she walked, she recalled the conversation with Renard on the dock. Rather than seeking to confirm his suspicion that she had witnessed Florian's murder, he had instead asked her where the jewels were.

"Interesting," she whispered aloud.

CHAPTER 11

"You stealing a sip?" Sarah pointed at Gwynnie's chin as they placed the jugs down in the great hall.

Distractedly, Gwynnie lifted a hand to her chin. Her palm glistened red, and her chin was sore to the touch.

"No, I suppose I must have spilt some," Gwynnie whispered.

"Go get yourself cleaned up." Sarah waved a hand dismissively.

Gwynnie turned to leave the great hall, her eyes darting around the vast chamber as she searched for Renard. Rather than finding his face, she found another pair of eyes staring back at her.

At the top table, erected on a platform, sat Fitzroy. He seemed uninterested in eating, instead clutching a goblet of claret rather tightly. At his side, his father talked to him incessantly, morsels of pheasant falling from his lips and into his auburn beard as he laughed.

Gwynnie tore her gaze away from Fitzroy, eager to leave the room. She hesitated for a moment in the doorway of the hall, looking back to the table. Fitzroy no longer stared at her but talked to his father. On the king's other side was his wife, Queen Anne.

The expression on her face brought Gwynnie to a halt.

Queen Anne was staring down at the food before her, unmoving. Even the sugared cherries at the side of her plate were left untouched. Her dark hair was coiffed perfectly, with not a strand out of place beneath her French hood. She wore a rich green gown, the bodice rising and falling rather fast. As

Gwynnie watched, Anne raised a hand and reached toward her husband, trying to ensnare him in conversation, but the king did not look at her. He waved a pheasant leg and managed to knock over a jug of claret, tipping the liquid into her lap. He offered no words of apology and continued to talk to his son.

As Gwynnie turned once more to leave the hall, she heard a commotion.

On the other side of the chamber stood a sodden figure, water dripping from his clothes. Nearby, people pointed at him.

"You been for a swim, Renard?" one courtier shouted with a rumbling laugh.

"You old fool. You'll catch your death in that," another agreed.

Gwynnie stepped away, but not before she heard more voices.

"Where are you going, Renard?"

"You dragging the Thames in here with you?"

Gwynnie started to run. If Renard had seen her in the great hall, then he might be chasing her. Two maids yelped in surprise as she pushed past them. She threw an apology over her shoulder before running down a flight of stairs, grabbing at the carved wooden banister.

At the bottom, she darted through an archway and into another much narrower hallway that led back toward the kitchens. Gwynnie looked at the walls, draped in rich sage green and gold tapestries, searching for a place to hide or a door through which to escape. She found no door, but at the end of the corridor sat a guard. Perched on a low-lying settle bench, he was fast asleep. Beside him, a pike more for decoration than defence rested against the wall. His great red and blue yeoman's cloak hung beside him on the back of the settle bench.

Gwynnie didn't think for too long. She cast a glance around the hallway, but finding she and the sleeping guard were alone, she snatched up the cloak and threaded it around her shoulders, pulling the hood over her head, then reached for the pike. It was heavy, unwieldy, and almost double her own height. She felt rather like a mouse gripping a tall candlestick.

Heaving the pike ahead of her and gritting her teeth, Gwynnie marched as she had so often seen guards do around the palace. She moved toward the nearest door that led outside and stood on the other side. The wind picked up, threatening to blow the hood down. She gripped at it with one hand, so in danger of dropping the pike that she had to lean the heavy iron blade against the wall beside her.

Footsteps echoed in the corridor she had just left. Gwynnie held herself still, her knuckles straining to keep hold of both the hood and the pike. Someone was running down the hallway, heading her way.

In seconds, a figure appeared beside her.

Gwynnie bowed her head, needing only to glimpse a pair of drenched leather boots to know it was Renard. He said nothing, not bothering to look past the yeoman's colours. Then the boots retreated, the heavy footfalls sounding across the courtyard. As they disappeared, Gwynnie looked up, daring to peek around the edge of the hood.

Renard slipped through another door, back into the palace, his increasingly quick steps revealing his frustration.

Gwynnie smiled, until the blood dripped off her chin and landed on the edge of the cloak.

"Damn thing," she muttered. Leaving the pike where it was, she stripped off the cloak, dropping it to the ground before heading back in the direction of the kitchens. Hurrying under an archway, she turned right when another stepped into her path. Gwynnie didn't see them in time and ran straight into them.

"God's breath!" She stumbled back.

"Good day to you too, Mistress Gwynnie," the smooth voice of Elric Tombstone answered her.

Gwynnie shifted to face him, noting he looked almost as harassed as she was. His copper hair was tangled beneath a black felt cap, and his clothes were not as neat as they usually were. He looked past her, then his eyes flitted to her chin.

"What happened?"

"What do you mean?" Gwynnie pressed a hand at her chin, trying to stem the blood, but it was no good. The pool in her palm only grew worse.

"Your chin — it is bleeding."

Gwynnie looked over her shoulder, nervous of Renard or even Fitzroy making another appearance. By the time she turned back to face Tombstone, he was looking over her shoulder too.

"Well?"

"I'm sorry, what did you say?" she asked.

Tombstone looked to the archway through which she had just passed, then back at her again.

"Are you hiding from someone, Mistress Gwynnie? Did someone do *that* to you?"

"Of course not. I was clumsy with the cutlery in the great hall, that's all. Nicked myself with a knife. My ma will laugh at me." She forced a laugh, one that was clearly so unconvincing that Tombstone was already shaking his head.

"Come with me." He marched past her, along the palace wall. When Gwynnie didn't follow, he halted and turned back, the thick black cloak that hung from his shoulders swirling around his legs as he moved. "I do not like giving orders. Do not make me give them again."

"If you do not like them, do not give them in the first place."

"You have a rather sharp tongue for a maid," he said with raised eyebrows.

"I mean … of course, sir." She bobbed a curtsy and moved to follow him, recalling something her mother had told her.

"To disappear in plain sight, one must act as another expects us. If you're a maid, you're obedient. If you work in the market, you catcall and jeer like the best of them. If you're pretending to be a draggle-tail, you wear your skirt too high."

Gwynnie kept her head bowed as she followed Tombstone out of the courtyard, leaving behind the scent of venison pie and roasted pheasant. They crossed the tiltyard to the lawyer's rooms. She followed him down the corridor where she had been the day before, toward Pascal's office.

Instead of stopping by Pascal's door, they halted by the one beside it. Tombstone unlocked the door, stuffing his keys deep into a pocket hidden within his cloak, before leading the way in.

"Sit." He pointed at a chair in front of the desk.

Gwynnie looked around the room. It was much smaller than Pascal's office next door, clad in red brick on one side and wooden panelling on the other. The desk was covered in papers, all neatly lined up in rows, and behind Gwynnie there was a tiny fireplace, stacked high with wood that was already burning, emitting a strong scent of ash.

Tombstone shrugged off his cloak and looked pointedly at her. Gwynnie quickly sat down in the chair, the wood creaking beneath her weight.

Tombstone reached for a small buffet cabinet in the corner of the room. Opening a tiny door that Gwynnie hadn't noticed at first in the cabinet, he pulled out a box, the wood carved with a pattern of Tudor roses and heavy vine leaves. Placing the box down on the desk, he opened it and took out pads of linen and bound cotton. Gwynnie stared as he walked around the desk and knelt before her, reaching toward her so fast with the bound cotton that she lurched back and nearly fell off the chair.

"You have one injury already today. Do you want another from falling off that chair?"

"What are you doing?"

"What does it look like?" He tried to reach for her again.

"Hmm, I wonder why I asked the question? Perhaps because I do not know." Her sarcasm was so thick that she could have sworn the corner of Tombstone's lips turned up beneath the coppery moustache.

"You're bleeding down your gown. Halt!" He was quicker this time and managed to press the bound cotton to her chin. "See? I mean you no harm."

He continued to dab the wound before standing and returning to the wooden box. He uncorked a vial so small that it was thinner than his thumb. Tipping the viscous contents onto another cotton ball, he returned to her. This time, when she veered away, he offered it to her. "Smell it," he urged.

Warily, she leaned forward and inhaled. "Honey?"

"Amongst other things," he said, adding a little more from the vial before passing it to her. "Hold it to your chin. It should help to seal the wound."

She did as he said, her fingers fumbling with the cotton.

"It's a strange thing to keep in your cabinet." She nodded at the box as Tombstone walked around his desk and sat in the vast chair on the other side. He looked strangely ill at ease in the chair, only managing to perch on the very edge. "You know medicine, sir?"

"A little of it." His eyes flitted toward the box. "My mother was a healer. Perhaps old habits linger, like cracks in wood, eh?"

"Your mother?" Intrigued, she adjusted her grasp on the cotton. "I'm holding some strange medicine to my chin then?"

"Nothing strange about it. Honey, egg whites, and turpentine. It will help. Trust me."

Gwynnie sat back, making the chair creak once more as she wondered what he would think if he knew that she had been hiding inside the chimney in Pascal's office the day before.

Tombstone's gaze never shifted from her, and she fidgeted in the chair, struggling to know where to look.

"Are we to sit here in silence?" she asked eventually.

"Very well, let's speak. But let us talk of things that matter. We shall start with this: who were you hiding from?"

"Who said I was hiding?"

"Credit me with some intelligence. I know what I saw. I saw a maid running so fast that she ran straight into me, as if she was not in control of her own feet."

"Who says I was not just attempting to escape a rather eager footman with too many hands?" she said leadingly.

Tombstone shook his head. "If that were the case, you would have told me so by now. You strike me as the kind of woman who would call any footman out with that sharp tongue of yours." He inclined his head. "Am I right?"

She matched his movement. This time, Tombstone's lip lifted enough to reveal the smallest of smiles.

"Let us begin again. Who were you hiding from? I take it they are the cause of this injury to your chin?"

"I told you. I was clumsy with the cutlery in the great hall for the king's feast. That is all." She fumbled with the cotton pad, lowering it enough to see that her chin had finally stopped bleeding.

"Someone hurt you, Gwynnie." He didn't bother with the formal address of 'Mistress'. "I've investigated enough crimes, seen enough injured men and women, to know when someone has been attacked."

"You are a connoisseur of assault then?" Her attempt at humour fell flat.

"Who hurt you?" he asked once more, his words coming slow and deep.

"Why would you care?" The words fell from Gwynnie's lips before she could stop them. "Why should it matter to you?"

"I am investigating one death in this palace. I do not need another." He leaned toward her so abruptly that she flinched.

"Just because I am clumsy enough to injure myself does not mean I am about to end up dead."

"Then why do you jump as if you are a frightened rabbit with a crossbow pointed at you?"

"I am doing no such thing." This time, Gwynnie managed to keep herself completely still in the chair. "Enough of these questions. Please, may I go?"

"No."

"I thought you said you didn't like giving orders?"

"Maybe I'm getting used to it now." He leaned forward, resting his elbows on the desk and clasping his hands together. "Gwynnie, *someone* was following you. *Someone* did that to you." His eyes flitted to her chin. "Tell me who it was."

Gwynnie's hand stilled on the cotton ball. Telling Tombstone the truth would be utter madness. It would lead to all sorts of questions, such as why Renard was following her. The frightened rabbit he had claimed her to be, would be down the rabbit hole, with the fox in quick pursuit when he realised that she was not only a thief, but one of the Shadow Cutpurses they all talked about in the palace.

"Even if I told you, you would not believe me." She remembered the discussion she had overhead between Tombstone and Pascal the previous day. "And anyway, who would believe a maid's word? Who would believe someone without a shilling to their name?"

"I will hear you out," Tombstone said forcefully. "I would not judge you for being a maid. I would believe what you told me."

"No one at the palace would," Gwynnie said.

"Then you have given me my first clue." He cocked his head to the side. "The man following you, the man who caused that cut, was a wealthy man, was he not? He had to be, for you to fear your word would not be believed against his."

Gwynnie lowered the cotton ball from her chin, letting it rest between her fingers. Tombstone was too perceptive. Even when she was trying to distract him, to evade his questions, he noticed every detail.

"Gwynnie, who did this?"

"It does not matter."

"How can you say that when you are bleeding?"

"It's my blood, not yours. Leave it to me."

"Damn that curt tongue of yours."

"You sound like my mother."

"I beg your pardon?" His words were sharp, and she looked up. "What did you say?"

"Nothing, I —"

A sudden knock at the door made them both jump in their seats.

"Master Tombstone? I must speak to you. I must speak to you at once."

CHAPTER 12

Tombstone held up a finger. It was a silent order to Gwynnie not to say a word.

"Can I —"

He raised his finger higher, and she capitulated, deciding she would say something sharp as soon as his visitor was gone.

"Tombstone!" The voice was louder as knuckles rapped on the door.

Tombstone moved to his feet and walked to the door, opening it so quickly that the woman on the other side practically fell into the chamber. Gwynnie stared, open-mouthed, as she saw the lady's face.

It was Goodwife Esme Battersby, Florian's wife. Flustered, her face red and her cheeks tearstained, she waved a handkerchief in the air as she stepped toward Tombstone.

"Have you discovered who did it yet?" the new widow asked without preamble.

"Please —" Tombstone began, but he didn't get to finish.

"Oh!" she wailed. "I know what that means. You need say no more. You have not found him. You do not know who the murderer is."

"These things take time," Tombstone offered, his voice soft.

"Someone has murdered my husband." Goodwife Battersby raised her hands to her face. Her fingers distractedly scratched her cheek, though Gwynnie wasn't sure if this was an attempt to stop the tears or some habitual movement. "Yet you sit here in your chamber, and ... and..." Her eyes darted to Gwynnie and the blood-stained cotton. "You must know something by now," the lady said with desperation, looking back at Tombstone. "Anything?"

"When I do know something, I shall tell you." Tombstone stepped forward and took Goodwife Battersby's hand before she could dart away. Gwynnie was reminded of a bee, dancing from place to place, unable to settle. "Believe me in this. I shall not stop searching for your husband's killer. I vow to you; I will discover the truth of what has happened."

"You vow it?" Goodwife Battersby's eyes glittered with unshed tears. "To God? You vow it?" Then her expression darkened. "To a Catholic God or to the new religion?"

A strange silence descended on the room.

"This is not the time for religious debate." Tombstone let go of her hand.

Around Goodwife Battersby's neck, Gwynnie spied the beads of a rosary. She was clearly of the old religion and sat on the Catholic side of the debate that currently raged through Greenwich Palace. Where Queen Anne's influence had once seemed strong, with one Protestant reform following hotly on the heels of another, things were changing again. This year, King Henry had insisted on hearing Mass at Christmas. It had brewed debates long thought to have been silenced.

"I will keep my vow," Tombstone said, his voice firm. "Now, go and rest. I shall report to you when I know more."

She nodded. "Th-thank you," she stammered, and then she was gone, her gown whipping around the edge of the doorframe as she disappeared down the corridor. Her heels clicked on the stone floor, echoing as she walked away.

Tombstone slowly closed the door behind the widow and leaned on the wood. He sighed deeply and then returned to his chair behind the desk.

"You have a strong sense of justice," Gwynnie whispered as she looked at him.

"Deaths will be answered, murder will be avenged," he muttered darkly. "I will not have it any other way. All that has happened in this palace — it makes no sense." He drew forward a sheaf of parchment from the desk. "The murder, the disappearance..."

"The disappearance? Of Master Jerome Woodville?" Gwynnie sat forward. "You are investigating that as well?"

"Of course." He frowned at her. "Did you think no one was paying attention?"

"The staff ... the whispers..."

"Ah, you are listening to gossip?"

"Well, what other way is there to learn of news? People say that he fell drunk into the river," she said hurriedly, "after he was seen drinking with the king's son on New Year's Eve."

"Wait, what did you say?" Tombstone jerked forward. He slid parchments together, pulling up another sheaf in which some notes had been written in such hasty scribble, they were barely legible at all. "Master Woodville spent New Year's Eve in the great hall in his own company, barely talking to another. He returned to his chamber alone at the end of the night."

"Well, whoever told you that was wrong." Gwynnie shook her head. "Samuel, one of the cooks, saw him in the great hall, drinking with Fitzroy. Old Rudyard saw the pair of them hooting at the moon like owls on the docks over the Thames after the feast had finished."

Tombstone blinked a few times before taking a quill from his drawer, along with blotting paper and ink. He added to his notes, his eyes repeatedly darting up to look at her.

"You keep your ears open? You hear things?"

"I try to," she murmured. "It's amazing what you can hear below stairs, if you only have the willingness to listen. I imagine men in your position do not have cause to go down to the kitchens very much. Why would you? You get served in great halls and fancy chambers instead."

His quill stilled over the parchment as he glanced at her, before he returned to his notes.

"You hear things of note? Things it would be worth me hearing?"

"Occasionally," she said softly, sensing an opportunity.

"Would you like to listen — for a price?" His quill stilled again.

"What do you mean?"

"I mean, would you be willing to keep your ears open and report to me on what you hear?"

"You mean if it relates to Master Florian Battersby?"

"To Battersby, or to Woodville." As Tombstone said Woodville's name, he looked down and busied himself scribbling notes again. "Anything that could be useful."

"Did you know Woodville?"

"We were both at the palace from time to time. I knew him a little, though not much." Tombstone avoided looking her in the eye, and Gwynnie couldn't help thinking there was more to it, an answer that Tombstone was not willing to give. "Here is what I will pay you each week to listen out for me." He reached into his desk drawer and pulled out a leather drawstring pouch. Untying the string, he took out two coins and dropped them onto the table.

Gwynnie reached for the coins, but before her fingers could close over them, Tombstone covered them with his own hand and slid them back toward himself.

"Well?" he asked. "Do we have an agreement?"

The coins weren't much, but they were enough that she and her mother would be comfortable. It was certainly more than they would ever get paid working as maids, though far less than the value of the jewels that were currently hidden in their chamber.

Suddenly another possibility opened itself up to Gwynnie. By agreeing to be Tombstone's mole in the staff, she could not only pass information on to him, but also steer him in the direction of Fitzroy.

"Very well." Gwynnie moved to her feet as Tombstone laid down his quill. "We have an agreement."

"You agreed to do what?" Emlyn shut the door of their chamber fiercely. The flame from one lonely tallow candle on the windowsill flickered with the sudden movement, making the shadows dance across the wall.

"I agreed to listen out for things. To report back if I heard anything that could be of use to his investigation." Gwynnie sat down on the bed and stretched out her sore back.

"What a clever decision that was!" Emlyn cried. "You think this wise? You think you can help Master Battersby now?" She moved to stand over Gwynnie. "No one can help him. He's dead. Soon enough, he'll be buried. What good can you do him?"

"Is that what you'd say to his wife?" Gwynnie asked softly. "Strange, I do not remember you saying such things about my father after he was —"

"Enough!" Emlyn interrupted. She couldn't bear to hear the word 'murdered'. "Gwynnie?" Emlyn sat on the side of the bed. "You have not helped yourself. If Renard or Fitzroy realise that someone is informing Tombstone that they are involved, what do you think they will do next?"

"I have to do something," Gwynnie said firmly, rolling over on the bed to face away from her mother.

Emlyn took her shoulder and pulled her back around. "What happened to your face?" She took Gwynnie's cheek, tilting her face to look at her chin. "Gwynnie? Who did this to you?"

Gwynnie pushed her mother off and scrambled to stand from the bed. "Who do you think did it?" she asked tartly. "Some angel?"

"Gwynnie!"

"Renard followed me today." Gwynnie told her mother about how Renard had cornered her on the docks and demanded to know where the jewels were, before pulling out the knife.

By the time she had finished her story and explained how she had ended up in Tombstone's chamber, Emlyn was sitting very still on her own bed, her face half hidden in shadow.

"You could end up dead, Gwynnie." The words were softly spoken. "Renard is getting increasingly dangerous. What manner of weapon do you think he will pull next?" She slowly stood from the bed and walked toward Gwynnie. She reached out. Gwynnie tried to avoid her mother's grasp, but Emlyn was too quick and took her cheek once more, tilting it up so she could examine the wound. "Not yet, though," she murmured. "You'll not die yet."

"Ma? You're talking in riddles."

"He asked you where the jewels were. He didn't ask what you had seen. Do you not see what this means, Gwynnie?"

Gwynnie tore her face away from her mother and moved to the candle on the windowsill. As she watched the flame quiver, dancing back and forth in the wind that crept in through the frame, something shifted into focus in her mind.

"He wants the jewels," Gwynnie muttered. She slowly turned to face her mother. "Everyone thinks the Shadow Cutpurses killed Florian as well as stealing the jewels." Emlyn nodded, urging her on. "So, he hopes to confirm all the rumours are correct, does he not? He hopes to find the jewels and use them to frame us — *me* — for the murder."

"Precisely, Gwynnie," Emlyn said. "Once he has the jewels, he will plant them in such a place — on your person or in this chamber — that they can be found all too easily. Then he will stand back and watch the law take its course. He doesn't need to silence you with his own hands, Gwynnie, or he would have done so today with that blade as you stood before the Thames. How easy would it have been for him to slit your throat and push you into the river?"

"Ma!"

"It is true. It would have been easy for him, yet you are more valuable to him alive than dead. You are the scapegoat for his master. If they can blame you for the murder, then all of Fitzroy's fears will fade to nothing." Emlyn sank down onto her bed. "If he gets those jewels, he'll have you in Newgate by the end of the week, and on the gallows by next Saturday."

CHAPTER 13

"Will you stop grinding your teeth so?" Gwynnie muttered as she reached for the stones beneath the window and pulled hard, trying to dislodge them from their hiding place. "It is a good plan, and you know it. You just do not like to admit it."

Emlyn said nothing, but she stepped forward and helped Gwynnie to move the slabs, revealing the gap below. Pulling out the bound jewels, they laid them out on the bed, both kneeling before them.

"You know this could work. What other choice do we have?" Gwynnie asked. She had barely slept, her plan keeping her awake into the early hours of the morning. In her excitement, she'd knocked over the one tallow candle, the flame extinguishing and the noise making Emlyn jump so much that she nearly broke the cot bed. "It's the one chance we have of pointing Tombstone and Pascal toward the guilty man. It's the one chance poor Esme Battersby has to get justice."

"Not everyone gets justice in this world. It's like some twisted demon. It transforms before you when you reach for it."

"What does that mean?" Gwynnie asked, her hands stilling over the jewels. Her mother gave no sign of hearing her now. She pushed back the dark hair that was still loose around her ears and continued to unwrap the jewels.

"We need to keep some," Emlyn said slowly, "so that when we leave, we have something to pay our way. We'll go to France, as we said before. We will start again."

Gwynnie smiled faintly. If there was the smallest chance that she could still find the future she longed for, the future where Emlyn would no longer have to keep looking over her shoulder, then she would fight for it.

They unwrapped the linen they had bound Fitzroy's jewels in.

"They are beautiful," Emlyn whispered, holding up a golden medallion attached to a chain. Each link in the chain was twisted into an ornate figure of eight shape, the links bound together tightly. The centre of the medallion was ruby red, divided into four distinct stones and bordered with more filigree gold. A single pearl hung from the heavy pendant. "Think what this is worth."

"Much," Gwynnie said in agreement. Amongst the jewels that glittered on the bed, one stood out. It was the one she had noticed the night she had been in Fitzroy's rooms, the one that had been hidden in the lid of the jewellery box.

Reaching for the Celtic brooch, she lifted it into the air. When compared to the other jewels, the metal looked dull, the silver in desperate need of a polish.

"Where did you get that?" Emlyn asked, nodding at the brooch.

"It was Fitzroy's." Gwynnie added the brooch to the others they were keeping.

"You could return it then, today," Emlyn said hurriedly.

"He will not miss that one. It is not so elaborate, and it has no jewels." Gwynnie gathered together the other items.

"You will not have long for this foolish plan of yours."

"Your confidence in me, Ma, is my greatest source of comfort!"

"No sarcasm today, miting."

"When did I agree to that? Ow!" Gwynnie winced as her mother tapped her around the arm in reprimand.

They bound some of Fitzroy's jewels together in linen, then Gwynnie stood and tucked the linen into the opening of her gown. Seizing a cloak, she pinned it to her shoulders and wrapped it around her body, hiding any sign of the package.

"At the jousting tournament, no one will be looking at you," Emlyn continued as she walked around Gwynnie, adjusting the cloak to make sure it lay flat. "The king will be in his element. The steward says he has been so looking forward to this tournament, that he has barely slept these last few nights. All attention will be on him. Just do your best to disappear into the crowd."

"Ma, this is hardly my first time sneaking through a crowd, is it?" Gwynnie huffed. "I picked my first pocket when I was thirteen."

"This time you are *adding* to someone's pocket," Emlyn reminded her, folding her arms. "Take care, Gwynnie. Please. If you are caught..." She trailed off, not needing to say the words.

Gwynnie's breath hitched as she moved toward the small looking glass on the wall. She adjusted her hair and pulled on the white coif, tucking the brown strands beneath and pulling the coif so far down, part of her face was covered. It would help her to hide in plain sight.

"I will be safe," she said aloud, trying to convince her own reflection as much as her mother. "Trust me, Ma. I can do this. I shall keep us both safe."

The tiltyard was alive with colour and activity. As Gwynnie entered the area, lawned on one side and cleared to a pebbled path on the other, she winced at the cacophony of sound. It seemed that everyone in the palace had gathered, tired of being indoors after all the rain. On this sunny morning, the sky blue with wispy white clouds over the heath in the distance, they were determined to make the most of it.

Gwynnie slipped between the crowds as people cheered and welcomed those competing in the joust. Ladies dressed in crimson and celadon gowns waved handkerchiefs in the air, choosing their favourites. Young men jeered at the jousters, insisting that they could do better if they were just given a horse and lance with which to compete. Toward the back of the tiltyard, away from the wooden barrier that separated the people from the competitors, old men sat on benches with their faces buried in great thick cloaks of black and white fur, their wrinkled hands clutching walking sticks and gloves.

In the centre of the seating was a box, erected entirely on its own. Draped in red and gold cloth, embroidered with the emblems of a falcon, the box stood out as the royal seat.

Gwynnie halted when she saw just one robed chair in the middle of the box. Queen Anne sat alone. Her thin lips were pressed together, her hands thrust into a binding of ermine cloth. Two ladies stood behind her chair; the same two ladies Gwynnie had seen with Anne on the night of the robbery. All three ladies seemed just as anxious today, with not a single smile gracing their lips.

Gwynnie stepped closer to the box, for some reason curious to hear something of the queen's conversation. She soon realised such a task was impossible. Anne lowered her voice too much and with the catcalls from the crowd, such delicate whispers were lost on the winter breeze.

To the left of the box was an important bench full of wealthy courtiers. Amongst the embroidered doublets, the fur-lined cloaks, and the heavy leather boots, was a figure Gwynnie recognised.

Fitzroy sat beside the other men; his head bent low as he conversed with another. He was in his element today, as if he was holding court, much as his father would. Many men listened to him, urging him on to tell some great tale. When he finished, all the men around him burst into laughter.

Gwynnie flinched at the laughter. If she ever did end up in Newgate Gaol, as her mother feared, then she would stand no chance against a man as influential as Fitzroy. He clicked his fingers, and two other men turned around to listen to him.

The clamour of the crowd grew louder and Gwynnie looked toward the jousting, to see what had caused such noise. Two competitors strode out from striped tents. Both were dressed ornately in the medieval style, with armour-plated chests and legs so bound in metal that they clanked as they walked toward the crowd. The first, bearing a sapphire and purple flag, lifted his arms into the air and the people cheered for him, though a few booed too, clearly taking sides. The second then thrust his arms into the air and received far more boos than the first. The crowd had their favourite.

As the two knights moved to their horses on either side of the tiltyard, the herald for the competition stood in front of the crowd, shouting the rules to be heard above the cheers. No one listened to him. They all knew the rules by now and busied themselves, making bets with one another. From what Gwynnie could overhear, the amounts ranged from a shilling to two whole pounds.

Gwynnie had to do it now. When the first joust began, every head would be turned in a particular direction. No one would be taking note of what she was doing.

"Where is he?" she whispered to herself as moved alongside the benches, looking for Renard. He was not with the other courtiers on the benches. As she reached the far side of the yard, she looked back, squinting into the crowd and against the bright sunshine, trying to catch a glimpse of him.

The knights atop their horses raised their lances, the blunted ends pointed into the air. Each lance bore a flag or some handkerchief, as a favour from a lady, to show who was their favourite to win.

The herald standing atop a crate before the crowd raised his hand into the air. A hush fell as everyone waited for the joust to begin.

"There you are," Gwynnie whispered as she caught sight of Renard.

He stood at the front of the crowd, his elbows resting on the wooden barrier that bordered the arena. His eyes were on the jousters, and he did not speak to those around him.

To approach him now, in her maid's uniform, would be too much of a risk, after all that had passed between them. She needed to find another way to get close without drawing his attention.

On this side of the tiltyard were some of the staff who had come to watch the joust. Some made their own bets, though for far smaller sums than the courtiers. Gwynnie saw Samuel and old Rudyard talking together, exchanging copper-coloured coins.

"Samuel?" Gwynnie hurried toward him.

"Have you come to see the joust, Gwynnie?"

"I need a favour." She tugged at the cloak around his shoulders, and it fell away.

"Your own not enough?"

"Not right now. I shall return it in a moment."

He was distracted as Rudyard accused him of not paying enough money for his stake in the joust.

Gwynnie turned away and wrapped Samuel's cloak around her shoulders. It was vast, with leather scraps covering the pock-marked cloth. It was so large, it swamped her entirely. Pulling the hood over her head, she crept through the crowd.

"Are we ready?" the herald bellowed, the words echoing across the yard.

Gwynnie just had time to wonder where the king was before the herald brought his arm down.

The knights charged. Each one lowered their lance as they gripped the reins of their horses and bent forward.

Gwynnie hurried forward, darting through the smallest gaps in the crowd.

"He's going to win!" someone shouted.

"No, he's not!" another cried out. "You'll lose your money."

Gwynnie ignored all the jeers, focusing on her target. She reached Renard and stood beside him, her heart thundering in her chest as the horses' hooves struck the ground so firmly that she could feel the vibrations through the earth beneath her.

Renard took no notice of her. His eyes were trained on the jousters, his gaze flitting between the two of them. The favourite of the pair thrust forward first, driving his lance into the other's shoulder as the horses charged past one another.

The crash of wood on metal echoed. The crowd gasped at the sudden splintering of wood from the lance. Renard and the others all clambered back from the wooden barrier, and Gwynnie moved with them. They jostled together, colliding, for there was so little room in the enclosure. Gwynnie reached beneath the two cloaks and into her gown, pulling out the binding that held the jewels. Without hesitating, she reached for the loose pocket within Renard's cloak, slipping the binding in.

"Get off me!" The bellow made her jerk, but it didn't come from Renard. It came from another man nearby, someone who clearly disliked the cramped conditions. The crowd spread out again, including Renard, who moved back to his position by the railing.

Gwynnie retreated, her smile growing a little wider. She had done it. If Renard had hoped to frame her with the jewels, he wouldn't be able to accuse her now. Instead, he would have to explain why *he* of all people had the jewels on him. She was playing him at his own game.

The herald yelled the result of the first joust from atop his platform. Some complained, others cheered, and money changed hands. Once more, Gwynnie slipped between all the shouting people. Not one looked her way; they were too busy thinking of money. Even as she returned the heavy cloak to Samuel, he took it without really noticing her, far too busy insisting that Rudyard pay up properly for the bet he had made.

Gwynnie reached the benches. There was someone there she had spied earlier, someone she now had to talk to if she was going to make this plan of hers work.

Further down the benches, not so high as Fitzroy and the courtiers, sat Tombstone. She could have sworn Pascal was beside him earlier, but now, Tombstone was alone.

In contrast to those around him, Tombstone didn't smile or cheer with the others. He was strangely calm, his face impassive, like it had been carved from stone. It took Gwynnie a minute to realise that he wasn't watching the joust; he was watching the crowd instead.

Gwynnie hurried forward, intent on talking to him, when she saw something that made her hesitate.

A young man walked past Tombstone, talking loudly with a friend beside him. He was handsome, with blond hair coiffed behind his head and a manicured beard across his chin. Gwynnie was not the only one to notice the handsome man.

Tombstone's eyes flicked from the crowd to the man too, and he watched him walk past. In fact, Tombstone's eyes seemed to linger even longer than Gwynnie's did.

"We have our next competitors," the herald boomed across the crowd. "The first is a man you all know well, the Duke of Northumberland." There was a general cheer of approval, until the herald turned and raised his hand. He pointed to what had to be the largest tent in the tiltyard, the great swathes of crimson material parting to reveal the rather large figure that waddled out, his armour struggling to fit across his person. "And our second competitor, unbeaten in this discipline, King Henry!"

There was such a roar that Gwynnie whipped her head around. Rather than looking at the king, as so many did, she looked at the queen.

Queen Anne raised her hands and clapped eagerly with the others, before dropping them to her swollen stomach.

"The king is jousting!" Murmurs erupted through the crowd as King Henry approached his horse.

CHAPTER 14

"Tombstone?" Gwynnie crossed toward him. "I must speak to you."

"Another time," he said dismissively. "I'm busy."

"Well, you look busy."

His brows quirked together at her sarcasm. He looked past her toward the yard where King Henry was now being helped onto his horse.

Gwynnie followed his gaze and winced. She'd heard many great things about King Henry's ability to joust, his great pageantry and skill. Yet the man she saw before her needed help getting onto his horse. The chest plate of his armour was pulled so tightly across his vast girth that he appeared to struggle to breathe in it, as he sat atop the saddle.

His face was distinctly purple this morning, contrasting with his red hair. A young man passed him a helmet, though Henry seemed to consider refusing to take it.

"Have you placed money on the joust?" Gwynnie asked.

"No. I do not gamble my money."

"That suggests you gamble something else."

He looked quickly at her, then turned away.

"I must speak to you," she insisted in a low tone. He gave no sign of having heard her. He was busy looking at the crowd. "What are you doing?"

"Watching."

"Watching for what?" She moved to sit beside him.

"Do you need ask?" he hissed. "Someone in this crowd is a killer. Who is to say they will not kill another? Such crowds as these at this time are dangerous."

"Surely you do not think they would kill again now? Not in front of so many people?" Gwynnie whispered, trying not to look obvious as she glanced in Fitzroy's direction.

He was pointing toward his father atop his horse, telling some grand tale and mimicking a joust as he thrust his hand into the air.

Even Fitzroy could surely not lose his temper in a crowd like this.

"A killer's mind does not always have to make sense," Tombstone said. He sat forward, resting his elbows on his knees as he scanned the crowd. "Some kill without reason, as if it gives them a thrill. Those are the killers I fear the most."

"You speak as if you have known many murderers."

"I am a lawyer. That means I come across killers as much as I come across litigation and land disputes." Tombstone leaned toward her as the cheers of the crowd grew louder.

King Henry was nearly ready to joust, but one of his arm plates was loose. The young man beside him adjusted it as the knight on the other side of the yard grew impatient and waved a hand in the air, urging the herald to begin the match.

"It is why I wish to speak to you," Gwynnie whispered. "You asked me to keep my ears open, to listen for anything that could be of use to you."

"I did."

"What if I had *seen* something that could be of use to you?"

"What do you mean?"

The king beckoned to someone in the crowd.

Distracted, Gwynnie looked toward Queen Anne. She stood, her hand resting on her rounded stomach. Yet she was not the lady the king had beckoned forward.

A woman approached the jousting barrier, her golden hair tucked into a gable hood. She was excessively pretty, with dark eyes and a narrow nose. Her thin lips stretched into a smile as she approached the barrier and offered up her handkerchief as a token of her favour.

To Queen Anne's credit, her face remained impassive as she stared at her husband accepting the favour of another woman.

"Poor Queen Anne." The words left Gwynnie's lips before she could stop them.

"It is not your business, Mistress Gwynnie," Tombstone cautioned. "Leave the king to his own affairs."

"Do you imagine the staff do not talk of him? They talk. As much as the courtiers do, I do not doubt."

"What was it you came to talk to me about?"

"Something I have seen." Gwynnie watched as the pretty lady retreated into the crowd and the king pulled back his lance, preparing for the joust.

"What is that?"

"Tombstone! Tombstone!" a voice bellowed.

"Get up," Tombstone said to Gwynnie. "Before he sees you."

"What?"

"I do not care if you sit here, but some men take umbrage at such things. They think maids have their place, and it is not in the courtiers' seats. Go. Now!" Tombstone took her elbow and steered her to her feet.

Gwynnie stumbled back, moving only a short distance away to the edge of the crowd. She pretended interest in King Henry and the joust, though her attention was on Tombstone and the man now approaching him.

It was the small man she had seen with the king on the morning that Florian's body had been discovered. His black hair, covered by an even deeper black cap, was distinctly recognisable.

"Tombstone," Cromwell snarled as he approached him. "Why are you here? I thought you were investigating Florian."

"Nearly everyone who is at the palace is in this yard at this moment, sir," Tombstone explained in a calm tone. "If the killer was to hurt another, in this crowd —"

"God's death!" Cromwell spat sharply. "Do you truly think such a thing could happen?"

"I do not know what to think at this time. All I know is that if the jewellery thieves and the killer are one and the same person, as Pascal seems to think, then they know how to hide all too well. They are like shadows — that's what people say, is it not?"

"You are supposed to be looking into fact, not rumour."

At that moment the crowd cheered and Gwynnie could no longer overhear what was being said. She flicked her head around to see the herald had brought his hand down. King Henry and the knight charged toward one another.

Despite the fact he was younger, and taller, the knight didn't lean as far forward over the head of his horse. Gwynnie suspected he was holding himself back. After all, who wished to be the man who would defeat the king in front of all of his courtiers at Greenwich Palace?

"See to it!" Cromwell barked, the words so loud that Gwynnie heard them this time. He marched away, leaving Tombstone staring after him. Gwynnie walked back toward Tombstone, moving so quietly that when he noticed she was there, he jumped.

"You creep around like a mouse."

"There's something you need to know," she began. She couldn't waste any more time. She had to tell him before Renard noticed that the jewels had been planted on his person.

"What is it?" Tombstone asked.

"It is him." She pointed through the crowd, pretending not to know his name. "The man with the French accent."

"Renard?"

She shrugged, as if she could not be certain of the name. "I saw him this morning as he walked here. He was looking at some jewels in his hand, then he stuffed them into some linen and put them in a pocket in his cloak."

Tombstone stared at her.

The roar of the crowd grew louder, suggesting that King Henry and his opponent were about to clash.

"They could be his own jewels," Tombstone said.

"Is he a wealthy man?" Gwynnie asked, wrinkling her nose with suspicion. "I thought he was lower gentry in Fitzroy's service. Those jewels … they were expensive indeed."

Tombstone didn't need telling again. He marched away from her, pushing his way through the crowd in order to reach Renard.

Gwynnie stood on the bench, the extra height allowing her to see what was going on.

"Get down, girl!" someone behind her shouted.

"This is no place for a maid!"

She ignored their cries, watching as Tombstone closed in on Renard's position.

King Henry and the knight clashed. Yet at the last minute the knight lifted his lance, allowing Henry's lance to strike his shoulder, knocking him cleanly off his horse. He rolled across the ground as the crowd cheered so loudly that Gwynnie covered her ears.

As King Henry thrust his lance into the air in celebration, the horse beneath him suddenly bucked.

The clamour of the crowd faded as the horse bucked again. The king dropped his lance as the horse grew wild, rearing furiously.

Tombstone had nearly reached Renard. As everyone watched the king and his horse, Tombstone's hand nearly had hold of Renard's shoulder.

With an almighty clatter of metal, Henry fell to the ground, dirt and dust clouding the air. The horse raised itself up on its back hooves, kicking the air and whinnying loudly before tipping backwards and falling upon the prone king.

The crowd gasped. Then a woman's scream pierced the air. Queen Anne clutched the edge of the royal box, her two ladies trying to pull her back as shouts rang out.

"Get to the king!"

"He's not conscious. We need a physician. Now!"

Gwynnie glimpsed blood on the ground as the horse rolled over King Henry and tried to scramble to its hooves.

In the chaos, she had lost sight of Tombstone. She searched the crowd for him, spotting him just in time to see his hand about to clasp Renard's shoulder, before the throng pushed forward, trying to get a proper look at what was going on. Tombstone and Renard were separated, Renard none the wiser.

"No," Gwynnie whispered, as people jumped onto the bench where she stood, trying to see over others' heads.

In the crush Gwynnie was pushed off the bench and fell to the ground.

"The queen!" someone cried.

Gwynnie moved to her knees and saw that the queen was no longer on her feet. She was lying on the ground with her ladies standing over her.

CHAPTER 15

"You're needed." An elderly maid thrust a pile of heavy sheets into Gwynnie's hands, a bundle so high that Gwynnie had to poke her nose over the bergamot-scented sheets to see over it. "Go to Queen Anne's chamber."

"The queen's chambers?" Gwynnie repeated in surprise.

She was a maid, yes, but her work had principally been washing sheets in the laundry, sweeping out the ashes from the fireplaces and laying the wood for later, and running errands. She was not one of the finer maids that worked in the ladies' chambers, and she certainly was not Queen Anne's maid.

"Now!" the elder woman ordered, clicking her fingers at Gwynnie. "We have no time for questions."

Gwynnie kept her head down as she walked out of the laundry room and across the courtyard, tempted to talk back, though it would do her little good.

Gentlemen and ladies were still gathered in the courtyard, talking earnestly of what they had seen at the joust. Some ladies had wrapped their fur cloaks around their mouths as they tried to hide their whispers.

"Did you see?" one lady whispered as Gwynnie walked past. "It was Jane Seymour. The king took her favour before the joust."

"I am surprised Queen Anne did not collapse at that very moment," another lady said, tilting her chin high and looking down her long nose. "The audaciousness, to offer up her favour in that manner."

"Did she offer it, though?" another lady asked. "Or did he rather demand it?"

Gwynnie had quite forgotten the incident with the young fair-haired woman, and the queen's stiff response as she watched on. Since then, much had happened, and it surprised her that the ladies spoke of this rather than the king's accident or of Queen Anne's collapse.

"Mark my words," the lady with the long nose said. "We shall have a new queen by Michaelmas."

There was a collective gasp from the others as Gwynnie walked on. She tarried by the gentlemen, many of whom were shaking their heads. One lady stood amongst them, clutching the arm of a man whom Gwynnie presumed was her husband.

"What happens now?" she asked her husband in earnest.

"A physician will see to the king."

"You fool, do you not see what I see?" she asked him in a hoarse whisper. "If the king does not wake, who does the crown go to?"

The men in the group looked at one another, none of them having an answer.

Gwynnie walked through the courtyard and toward Donsen Tower. She slowed by the door, reflecting on how different things would be had she had the opportunity to steal Queen Anne's jewels from her chambers, and had she never stepped into Fitzroy's chambers.

Stepping in through the open doorway, she found the entrance hall wet with puddles from the rain. Apparently, no one was bothered about closing the door, not when there were other things to worry the household. Gwynnie tried to kick the door shut, struggling under the weight of the heavy sheets, before hastening toward the staircase.

She climbed the steps, trying not to trip on the hem of her gown. As she reached the top of the tower, she came upon two of Queen Anne's ladies-in-waiting sitting on the stairs. One was crying with great sobbing breaths, while the other stared into the distance, as white as the sheets Gwynnie carried.

Gwynnie tiptoed past them, noting that they didn't once look her way.

As she reached the door that led to the queen's chambers, she found a priest in the doorway. He was placing the sign of the cross over the door, with rosary beads clutched in his long bony hand.

"Away." Another lady-in-waiting, perhaps twice as old as the queen herself, stood in front of the priest, blocking his entrance.

"But madam," he said in thick French accent. "The traditions must be observed."

"Traditions?" the elder lady sneered. "The queen holds onto a Protestant God, the true God. She will not take comfort in you preaching now."

The priest was outraged, his lips parting. He looked ready to argue, but Gwynnie stepped by him, holding up the sheets.

"Come through." The lady-in-waiting waved her hand hurriedly to Gwynnie.

Gwynnie stepped into the chamber, shocked by the sudden darkness. Curtains had been draped across the windows, even pushed into the gaps of the window frame, in an effort to block out every scrap of light. Just one candle stood at the far end of the antechamber, lighting a path for Gwynnie.

A table was piled high with glass bottles and vials. One had been tipped over, and the distinct scent of turpentine filled the air, making Gwynnie's nose wrinkle.

She was bustled into the second chamber by the lady-in-waiting, where she found a very different scene to the first room. Where the first had been empty, this room could not have had more people crammed into it.

There were physicians, healers, and even an astronomer who read aloud from a book, straining to see the words by the light of a candle that he clutched in his hand.

"Mars is in orbit. Oh, I fear for the health of this child."

"Do you think such things are helping?" the lady-in-waiting snapped and took the book out of the astronomer's hand. "Away. At once."

He stepped back and Gwynnie was given a better view of the room.

At the foot of the bed were three maids. One of them was mopping up blood, her face pale, tears streaming down her cheeks. The other two maids offered up towels and anything else they could get their hands on.

A physician snatched one of the sheets from Gwynnie's pile and threw it over the bed.

"Bind her," he ordered the other physicians.

The linen strip was bound around the waist of the prostrate woman on the bed.

It was Queen Anne. Her French hood had been tossed to the floor, and Gwynnie saw that one of the pearls on the headdress had broken off and rolled away across the floor.

Anne's dark hair streaked across the pillow beneath her head. She was awake, but her eyes kept fluttering closed. She was moaning, trying to clutch her stomach, but the physician batted her hands away.

A cold chill washed over Gwynnie as she stood at the edge of the room, unnoticed. It was easy to judge what was happening.

The queen was losing her unborn child.

"Take this." A young physician appeared beside her and pressed a vial into Gwynnie's hands.

One of the other maids scuttled back from the bed and clutched her hand to her mouth. The next minute, she ran into the other chamber. She must have found a chamber pot or something to be sick in, for the sounds of retching soon followed.

"Are you of a sickly constitution?" the physician asked Gwynnie.

She shook her head, uncertain what good it would do if she said she was.

"Good. Then come here." He beckoned her forward. He gently tipped Anne's chin back. "For the pain, Your Highness. It will help." He took the vial out of Gwynnie's hand and tipped the liquid into her mouth.

The queen nearly retched herself, but the physician closed her mouth in such a way that she was forced to swallow it.

"Hold this." The physician passed an empty chamber pot to Gwynnie. "You will need it, for her."

Gwynnie nodded.

As Anne tried to pass the unborn child, Gwynnie pressed the chamber pot forward when it was needed, trying her best not to look at anything that spilled into it.

She wasn't sure how long she was there. Seconds turned to minutes, and perhaps the minutes even turned to hours, but Gwynnie stayed throughout and kneeled beside the bed, holding up the chamber pot when she could.

"It is done." One of the physicians stepped back some time later, wiping the sweat from his forehead with his sleeve. "Your Highness, I am sorry, but —"

Queen Anne raised a sharp hand in the air. That movement was enough to halt his words. She didn't want to hear it. They had all seen what had passed; they had seen she had lost the child.

Anne turned her face to the pillow, masking her pain from the world.

Numb, Gwynnie stepped back.

"Get rid of that," the physician instructed one of the ladies-in-waiting, and she took the chamber pot out of Gwynnie's hands. "The king must be told," he said to the elder lady-in-waiting, who had spent most of the time mopping Queen Anne's brow with a damp cloth. "He must know."

Gwynnie collected some of the bloodied sheets together and moved to stand beside them, under the pretence of tidying up.

"Has he woken?" the lady-in-waiting asked the physician. "From what I hear, he has still not opened his eyes. Not since that stallion rolled over him."

The physician stilled, his hands falling to his sides.

"Are you telling me the king shall not wake again?" she asked.

He looked away abruptly. "Take those for cleaning."

The lady turned to Gwynnie and dismissed her with a wave of her hand.

Gwynnie dropped the bloodied sheets into a large barrel in the laundry room. It was now dark beyond the windows, with the only light to keep her company coming from a tallow candle she had lit and placed over the fire. Try as she might, she couldn't start a fire. Too much rain had come down the chimney and the damp wood in the fireplace prevented any chance of it lighting.

With shaking hands, Gwynnie returned to the barrel and added lye to the water, knowing the sheets would have to soak after what had passed.

The door opened and Emlyn entered the room. To Gwynnie's dismay, she too was carrying bloodied sheets, but these had not come from Queen Anne's room.

"Has the king woken?" Gwynnie asked her mother.

"No." Emlyn shook her head. "They've had me changing his sheets, preparing a bath that would not make him wake, and cutting linen into strips to bind his wounds." She sat down wearily on a chair, the sheets still in her grasp. "His eyes are closed, and if you believe the physician who watches over him, his mind is elsewhere."

Gwynnie took the sheets from her mother, added them to the barrel and began to stir everything together with the lye. "They're whispering about who will be next king already."

Emlyn looked at Gwynnie, her eyes wide. "Or queen," she whispered. "There's Princess Mary, his daughter by Queen Catherine."

"I thought she had…"

"I know." Emlyn waved a hand in the air.

Catherine had been removed from the line of succession, they all knew that, but who else was there? Princess Mary hadn't been spoken of in the palace since the news of Queen Catherine's death had broken.

Gwynnie stopped stirring the barrel as a sudden thought struck her. "Surely not…" She couldn't bring herself to say the words.

"Fitzroy cannot be king. He is illegitimate, Gwynnie. The king's advisors would not allow the son of a dancing courtier, Bessie Blount, to take the throne. Any claim he made would undoubtedly be challenged."

Gwynnie was not as certain as her mother. She recalled how many men had gathered around Fitzroy in the tiltyard. They had hung on Fitzroy's every word at the joust. And he had men like Renard dancing to his tune, happy to jump like puppets at the flick of a string.

And an illegitimate claim to the throne had triumphed before. Was not William the Conqueror once known as William the Bastard?

"I am not sure," Gwynnie whispered. "Somehow, it would not surprise me if Fitzroy made a claim to the throne."

Emlyn sat forward in her chair, the movement making the wood creak beneath her. "We shall have to wait and see what happens next."

CHAPTER 16

"Is he awake?" Tombstone asked.

Gwynnie overheard the familiar voice and scurried back. She'd been walking down a narrow lane in the palace grounds, carrying a tray of doucets she'd been asked to take to the queen's rooms. She held the tray of pastries against her chest and flattened herself to the wall, straining to hear the words.

"He is," Pascal replied.

Gwynnie sighed, startled at the relief she felt filling her chest. She hardly cared for the King of England, but she'd rather he was on the throne than his murdering son.

"It took two hours to revive him, I'm told." Pascal sighed heavily.

Gwynnie craned her neck, peering around the corner of the lane to look at the two men speaking together in low tones.

Tombstone and Pascal stood facing each other, with the early morning shadows cast over their faces. Pascal was restless and exhausted, judging by the way he continuously yawned.

"King Henry is awake, but depending on who you ask, his health varies."

"Has he been told about the queen?"

"Not yet." Pascal shook his head. "His health is delicate enough as it is. So many children … so many sons have been lost over the years." He shook himself, making his jowls tremble. "I think the court wishes to delay the news for as long as possible. At least one good thing has come from this flood. It will be days before London hears of the queen's condition. I would not wish to be the man to tell the king of this grave news."

"Most men would run for the hills," Tombstone muttered quietly.

Pascal nodded. "No man wishes to hear such tidings, do they?" His voice softened, and he took Tombstone's shoulder, clasping it tightly.

There was something affectionate in the touch. Gwynnie again wondered at their relationship, if there was more to it than simply that of an employer and employee.

Tombstone nodded at the older man. "We must continue as before," he said.

"Yes, yes, we must." Pascal inhaled and stood tall. "There is no other way. What was it you were saying about the joust yesterday? Something about that man who works for Fitzroy?"

"Renard? One of the maids mentioned seeing him with some jewels. I intended to ask him about it, but before I could reach him, the king fell from his horse and pandemonium broke out." Tombstone sighed and ran a hand over his face.

As Gwynnie watched, Tombstone suddenly looked in her direction. He stilled so abruptly that she whipped her head back around the corner. Had he seen her? Had he caught her watching the pair of them?

"I see," said Pascal. "Well, I must go to Cromwell, though I daresay he will not be pleased with us."

"He'll have other things on his mind rather than who killed Florian Battersby now." Tombstone's manner sounded stiff. "He'll be plotting who will sit next on the throne should the king have further complications."

"You should not speak so. What have I told you?" Pascal admonished him. "Do you want to find yourself in Newgate, Elric?"

"We can discuss this another time."

132

"That is what you always say, foolish boy." Pascal sighed. "I must go. Report to me later."

As his footsteps retreated down the lane, Gwynnie leant back against the wall with a sigh of relief. She had not been discovered eavesdropping. But then another set of footsteps sounded, and they were moving toward her. Tombstone appeared, angling his head around the corner, his eyes narrowed.

"Is this how you learn so much about people? You listen around corners?"

"Sometimes." She stood straight and adjusted the tray in her grasp. "Who is Pascal to you?" Her question came so suddenly that his eyebrows shot up.

"My employer."

"He does not speak to you as if you are merely a lawyer under his care. You must have known him for some years."

"I do not remember agreeing to pay you to look into my life. I asked you to listen to other people."

"That you did."

"And have you discovered anything more? Or do you listen in on my private conversations for your own pleasure?" Clearly, he didn't expect her to answer. His eyes darted down to the doucet tray. "Who is this for?"

"The queen. She still has no appetite, so I have been asked to carry this to her chambers."

Tombstone nodded and stepped back, waving her on her way.

"Wait, a minute more." Gwynnie shifted her weight between her feet, her hands fidgeting with the tray. "You said you had not managed to speak to Renard."

"You truly did hear much of our conversation." Tombstone adjusted his cloak, pulling it tightly across his body.

"Will you speak to him?" She tried not to sound too desperate.

A whole day had passed since she had informed on Renard; plenty of time for him to have discovered the jewels in his pocket and hidden them elsewhere. Yet she had to try, for there was still a chance it could point Tombstone in the right direction.

"I am going to see him now." Tombstone frowned as he turned away. "You seem most eager."

"I wish to help." She followed him down the lane. "And I remember what you said yesterday, about how the killer may strike again…" She swallowed around a lump in her throat. An image flashed into her mind of a body laid out in the courtyard, its throat cut. However, it wasn't Florian Battersby this time, but herself.

"You never know with these things," Tombstone said. "Hasten to your tasks, Gwynnie, and leave me to mine." He walked back down the lane and turned out of sight.

Gwynnie hesitated, tempted to follow him until he found Renard, but what good would that do? It would only make both Tombstone and Renard more suspicious of her.

Instead, she carried the tray to the Donsen Tower. Climbing the steps, it was immediately clear that the queen's quarters were a little calmer today. The two ladies she had seen commiserating together on the stairs the day before now stood in front of the window, bemoaning the rain.

"It is an omen," the lady that had been crying said to the other. "All this rain. Was it not predicted by the astronomer at Yuletide? He said dark times were ahead."

"Dark times are always ahead," Gwynnie muttered to herself as she walked past, rather glad the two ladies didn't hear her. She had seen such tricksters all the time in the streets of

London. They'd vow to read a man's palm or the stars in exchange for money, then reveal what was in their future. Invariably, dark times were coming. It was a mysterious enough phrase that it could be interpreted in any number of ways, so when the punter lost a dear friend or merely tripped into a ditch the next day, they believed the star-reader and came back to pay again.

"They said a dead whale washed up on the shores of the Thames," the lady continued. "Oh! What an omen it is."

Gwynnie reached the door to Queen Anne's chambers and knocked lightly.

The elder lady-in-waiting who had taken charge the day before opened the door and looked down at the doucets in Gwynnie's hands.

"To tempt the queen," Gwynnie explained, hopefully.

"Very well." She smiled, rather sadly. "Though I fear nothing will tempt her." She took the tray and stepped back. As she did so, Gwynnie caught a glimpse through the antechamber to the private bedchamber beyond.

Queen Anne sat at the foot of the bed, draped in lace and fine cloth. She looked pale and gaunt, her dark eyes hooded. She said nothing, even as the ladies around her attempted to draw her into conversation.

Then the lady-in-waiting closed the door and Gwynnie could see the queen no more.

She turned to leave, passing the two gossiping ladies who were still talking of ill omens. Every time a hare had crossed their path, or a dog had howled at the moon, they had seen it as an omen of death, of the child's passing. When Gwynnie reached the main door at the bottom of the stairs, she heard voices beyond, outside in the main courtyard. She hesitated before peering around the wood.

"It is a simple question, Renard." It was Tombstone. "I wish to see inside your pockets."

"How dare you?" Renard raged, his French accent even stronger than before. "I am in the employment of the Duke of Richmond, the son of king, and yet you speak to me as if I am a common urchin, a street pickpocket."

"I do not remember calling you anything of the kind." Tombstone remained calm.

The pair stood in the middle of the inner courtyard, before the vast fountain that was beginning to freeze over.

"I simply asked to see inside your pockets. Your reluctance makes me believe you have something to hide."

This was too much for Renard. He dropped his cloak from his shoulders and tossed it to the floor. It landed in an icy puddle, scattering droplets over Tombstone's boots.

"Search it yourself," Renard ordered and then reached for his overgown, showing it had no pockets, just as his doublet did not.

Tombstone took the cloak and searched it, feeling for a pocket.

Gwynnie watched, holding her breath, desperate for the jewels to be found.

"Please, please," she whispered. The wind whistled through the courtyard, and time seemed to slow down as she waited for something to happen.

Tombstone reached a hand into a pocket and turned it inside out. There was nothing but empty cloth, no jewels, no scrap of linen, nothing.

"God have mercy," Gwynnie muttered, leaning against the door.

"Now that is done, may I have my cloak back? I will need to send it to be cleaned." Renard snatched the cloak from

Tombstone's grasp and glowered, as if he was the one to blame for it being dropped in a dirty puddle. "I see I will have to tell my master what a dismal job the lawyers here do, searching men such as myself."

"Every man is under suspicion," Tombstone replied through gritted teeth. "Surely you can appreciate that, Renard."

"I'd suggest you're looking for a madman, not a courtier or gentleman." Renard stepped toward Tombstone and spat the words.

"Who says they are not one and the same thing?" Tombstone's question made Gwynnie smile.

"You shall be made to apologise for this, you knave." Renard turned and marched away, his boots splashing in the puddles.

The insult hung in the air. Tombstone was stony-faced, his hands clenched into fists at his sides. For a second, Gwynnie thought he was going to strike out at Renard, but he made no move to follow.

Slowly, Gwynnie stepped out from her hiding place by the door. Tombstone turned to her and crooked a finger, silently ordering her to follow him. They walked across the courtyard to another lane, where she stood with her hands folded in front of her.

"You made me appear a fool."

"A fool?" Gwynnie repeated. "I simply told you what I saw. It is hardly a wonder if he has moved the jewels when a night has passed since I told you."

Tombstone grunted and thrust his hands into his hair. "Are you certain of what you saw?" His voice was sharp.

"Why are you so angry with me, when you hold your temper for everyone else?"

"Perhaps I am beginning to realise how troublesome it can be to pay a maid to listen from the shadows," he muttered darkly. "If Renard reports me to Fitzroy, then what I have done today will be in the ear of the king by tonight. By tomorrow, my coffers could be packed, and I'll be turned out of the palace."

"They cannot send you anywhere with this flood, remember?" Gwynnie said tartly. "It is why you are so certain the killer is still here, in the palace."

"I do not remember telling you that."

Gwynnie could have kicked herself for revealing what she had overheard in Pascal's office.

Tombstone's eyes narrowed and he cocked his head. Gwynnie was reminded of the buzzards she used to watch hunting mice in the street of her first home. Tombstone had the same copperish tinge to his hair, and the same fixed glare. "How much do you listen in on things you should not hear?"

"Not much."

"Yet you have plainly heard enough of *my* conversations, hmm?" He sighed. "If you are not useful to me, I cannot rely on you, Gwynnie. I will not pay you for giving me nothing."

"I gave you something." She stood taller, refusing to back down. "It is your fault if you did not act on my information quickly enough for it to be useful. As for what I hear, I hear plenty. I hear the queen mumbling about Jane Seymour, and her fears over losing her throne. I hear men guessing who the next king will be if King Henry cannot rise from his bed again. And I hear Fitzroy ordering his man to search for these thieves himself."

"What did you say?" Tombstone whipped around on the spot. "Why would Fitzroy ask Renard to investigate himself?"

"Is that not for you to discover?" In her anger, she had given far too much away, and Tombstone was giving her that same buzzard-like stare. She quickly curtsied, remembering she was a maid and he was a lawyer, and retreated down the lane.

"Gwynnie!" he called after her, but she had no desire to continue their conversation. If he disliked her so much for simply making him search Renard, then perhaps he never would believe the killer was Fitzroy.

Gwynnie kept walking, lost in her thoughts, until she reached the corridor outside her own chamber. She tapped on the door — two quick knocks, followed by three light ones — and the door opened immediately. Gwynnie stepped over the threshold.

"Oh..." She gasped in horror as she peered around her mother into their room. "That conniving bastard!"

CHAPTER 17

"Gwynnie, curb your tongue."

"Ma!" Gwynnie stepped into the room to look around the small space. On every surface, something glittered. The jewels she had planted on Renard were now back in their chamber. There was a gold pendant on Gwynnie's pillow, with a rich blue stone in the middle of an ornate cross, and pearls at either end of the struts. A hat pin had been stuck directly into the pillow, the ruby gleaming in the sunlight that shone through the window. The gold filigree around the ruby was shaped into a fleur-de-lis. Other jewels were laid out on the windowsill, where the tallow candle stood. "Would you look at what he has done?"

"I have eyes." Emlyn went to close the door, but Gwynnie grabbed it and bent down to examine the lock.

Whoever had picked the lock to get into the room — presumably Renard himself or another man in Fitzroy's employ — had not done as good a job as Gwynnie would have done. There were scratch marks around the lock in the wood, where they had repeatedly slipped with their choice of tool.

"What is his aim?" Emlyn strode across the room and reached for the stone sill, beneath which the other jewels were hidden. She tapped the stones, which were fortunately still in place.

"We know his aim!" Gwynnie snapped, closing the door and firmly jamming it in the frame. "He intends to make us look guilty. You were right, Ma. I am more valuable to him alive, so he can frame me —"

"Quiet!"

"I will not be quiet!"

"Look out of the window!" Emlyn grabbed Gwynnie's shoulders and turned her around to face the window. Through the glass, Gwynnie could see two figures walking across the courtyard.

One was Pascal, speaking hurriedly and waving his hands. The other was Tombstone, shaking his head.

"They are coming this way," Gwynnie murmured. "Well, just as Renard managed to make the jewels disappear, so can we."

They each reached for the various jewels, gathering them together as quickly as they could. Emlyn reached for the stone slab, her hands fumbling, shifting it to the side. Gwynnie didn't bother to bind the jewels neatly in linen this time. She just dropped them into the gap as quickly as she could. Collecting the jewels from the pillow, she turned to drop them in too, but suddenly found the ruby-studded hat pin missing from her grasp.

"What is it?" Emlyn asked as Gwynnie turned on the spot.

"I think I dropped one."

Footsteps outside their chamber revealed they had no more time. Quietly, they replaced the stone in the windowsill. Gwynnie threw herself back on the bed, instantly regretting it for her bruised back complained at the sudden movement. Emlyn moved to their looking glass, adjusting what curls of her hair hung down from her coif, framing her face.

A sharp knock at the door made them both halt. They exchanged a look and Gwynnie nodded curtly. It would hardly be the first time they were searched with suspicion hanging over their heads.

Gwynnie had witnessed a search the day after her mother had returned with blood on her hands. A constable came, claiming someone had been seen coming to their rooms with blood on them. Yet he believed he had been looking for a man. Finding no man hiding in their attic, he'd left again soon after. Gwynnie had stood in the corner the whole time, trying to hide her trembling hands behind her back.

"Who is it?" Emlyn asked, her tone perfectly calm.

"It is I, Mistress Wightham, Master Pascal." Pascal answered lightly.

Emlyn reached for the door and opened it wide, revealing Pascal standing in the doorway, his hunched form bent forward, with the tall Tombstone towering behind him.

Gwynnie moved to the edge of the bed. Out of the corner of her eye, she saw something glitter. She glanced down, seeing she had indeed dropped the hat pin. She stood up and placed her boot over the jewel, where it was pressed into the rush matting.

"My apologies for the intrusion," Pascal said, bending his head to Emlyn solicitously, "but we have received some information. It is nonsense, I am sure, but we are obliged to act upon it."

"Poor Pascal." Emlyn stepped toward the magistrate and took one of his hands in both of hers. "You seem in such distress. It worries me to see it."

Gwynnie chewed her lip to prevent herself from laughing at how easily Emlyn could charm any man. Well, nearly any man. Tombstone sighed with exasperation and walked into the tiny room, striding past Pascal. She began to wonder if there was a reason Tombstone seemed unaffected by Emlyn's charms. Was it possible that he had no eye for any woman at all?

"Oh, dear." Emlyn gasped. "I am sure you have a task to do, sir, but is there a reason to barge into our chamber so? My daughter was resting after her hard day."

"So I see." Tombstone's eyes raked over Gwynnie and the position she occupied by the window. She had no choice — she could not move, or she would reveal the hat pin beneath her boot.

"I should explain," Pascal said. "You have my greatest apologies for this imposition, Mistress Wightham, but we have been informed that some of the stolen jewels have been seen in this room."

"I beg your pardon?" Emlyn affected perfect surprise. She tightened her hold on Pascal's hand, her lips parting.

Gwynnie shifted on the spot, frowning deeply, well aware that Tombstone was watching her intently, clearly waiting to judge her reaction.

"It seems to me you are being toyed with, sir," Gwynnie whispered to Tombstone. "Shall I guess who accused us of such a thing?"

Tombstone looked away and reached for Emlyn's bed.

"What is this?" Emlyn stepped away from Pascal. "You are searching our chamber now?"

"Again, my deepest apologies," Pascal said placatingly. "I of course know that two ladies such as yourselves could have nothing to do with any of this, yet we have to act on our information. We must search the chamber, then we shall be done and on our way."

"But —"

"Let them search, Ma," Gwynnie said, being careful to keep her tone calm.

"Miting?" Emlyn looked at her. Most people would not have seen a change in Emlyn's expression, but Gwynnie knew her mother's face so well, she caught the brief twitch around her eye. It was a hint to the fear she felt, that if they allowed Tombstone to search, he would indeed find the jewels.

"If we refuse, they will believe we have something to hide, will they not?" Gwynnie's question seemed to settle the matter. Emlyn nodded and moved to sit on the edge of Gwynnie's bed.

"This is all so very distressing," she muttered. "Are all the maids' chambers being searched?"

"No. It is just yours," Tombstone answered tartly.

He turned Emlyn's bed upside down. Gwynnie expected him to leave the bedding on the floor, but she was wrong. He replaced the bed and then turned to Gwynnie, gesturing for her to move aside so he could search her bed. Gwynnie nodded and took a step back. Fortunately, the room was so small she could not go far. It meant she could drag the rush matting and the hat pin under her boot with her.

Emlyn was forced to stand, and Pascal took her hand, taking it upon himself to calm her. Emlyn acted up her shock even more, making him sympathise with her.

"Oh, how awful. To think I brought my daughter here, thinking we'd be safe working in a place such as this. And yet suspicion is cast over us. Oh, it is too much. My heart…"

"Please, calm yourself." Pascal helped her to sit down on the edge of her own bed. He took out a handkerchief and offered it to her. She dabbed her neck with it, as if it was helping to cool her, but it simply drew Pascal's gaze to her skin.

Tombstone finished searching Gwynnie's bed and stood straight, shaking his head.

"See, Tombstone? What did I tell you?" Pascal barked with laughter. "Renard's implications this morning were laughable indeed."

"Implications?" Gwynnie repeated the word, looking straight at Tombstone. "What does that mean?"

"Renard came to see us this morning and made a complaint. He claims to have seen jewels in this room. Curious, do you not think?" Tombstone asked her, his words slow and deliberate. "You accuse him and now he accuses you. You might as well be children in the street."

"I do not know what is going on." Pascal shook his head gravely and knelt down before Emlyn, who was still gasping and dabbing herself with the handkerchief. "But rest assured, I know the truth. I know how mad it is to accuse any woman of being one of the Shadow Cutpurses."

Emlyn began to wail and conveniently, tears reached her eyes.

Gwynnie glanced down and saw her mother was discreetly pinching herself hard through her skirt, not that either of the men noticed. It was a quick tactic indeed to produce tears when needed.

"You believe that we could be those thieves? Oh, it is too much."

"I would have thought you more concerned to be accused of murder." Tombstone stepped past Gwynnie and moved to the windowsill, peering out at the courtyard below.

"What do you mean?" Emlyn sniffed through her tears. "You believe that these thieves, these cutpurses, are also responsible for Master Battersby's death?"

"Of that we are certain," Pascal said, perfectly calmly. "Which is why I urge you not to distress yourself. I know, despite the claims of Renard, that you and your daughter have nothing to do with this appalling business."

"Thank you. What a good heart you have, sir." Emlyn gave him a winning smile.

"To think a woman would do any of it. Pah! The whole idea is monstrous. Ladies are too delicate for such a thing." At

Pascal's words, Gwynnie folded her arms, uncertain whether to be relieved or angry. She supposed at least his belief that women were as fragile as spun sugar meant that she was safe from his suspicion.

"And what do you believe?" Gwynnie asked Tombstone, who had remained silent.

Pascal was no longer paying attention to their conversation. He was asking if Emlyn needed anything for her present relief. As he wittered on, Gwynnie waited for Tombstone to answer. He was taking his time, thinking through his answer carefully.

"I do not believe that just because you are a woman you are innocent."

Gwynnie's stomach knotted tight.

"But there are things that do not make sense to me." Tombstone shook his head and turned away, looking out of the window. Gwynnie turned with him, careful to keep the hat pin firmly pressed beneath her boot. "I saw the body of Master Battersby, and I am certain of one thing — his body was moved."

"Moved? What makes you say that? The glass on his boot?"

Tombstone jerked his head toward her.

"I saw you looking at his boots," Gwynnie rushed to explain.

"Well, the glass is one concern." Tombstone shifted, leaning his weight against the stone windowsill. Gwynnie held her breath, fearing the stone would slip. If it did, it would give away the hiding place for their jewels. "The lack of blood is another."

"I heard you speaking of that. You said a man who had had his throat slit should have more blood."

"I did say that." He frowned. "How many conversations have you listened in on that you were not a part of? Do you hide whilst listening?"

"I am a maid." Gwynnie forced a smile. "We maids do not need to hide. People simply do not look at us — they see through us."

Tombstone shifted position. "Well, either Master Battersby was moved from where he was killed — and there would be more blood where he died — or he died of something else, and his throat was slit later. If his body was moved, then a woman would struggle to do that alone." Tombstone eyed her carefully. "Two women might just be able to do it."

Gwynnie's brows lifted. Was he accusing her?

"You believe Renard's tale?" She shook her head. "Of course you do. When he is a gentleman, what would my word stand for?"

"Gwynnie —"

"Am I allowed to take something to Newgate? Or will you take me as I am? I do not suppose people live long there, even if they are innocent."

"Gwynnie, I did not say I believed him."

Gwynnie turned back to face him, hearing the hat pin scratch the matting beneath her boot. Tombstone either didn't hear the sound or did not realise what it was, for he didn't react.

"You have just intimated that you did."

"No, I said two women together could have done it. I have my reservations, the first being chiefly this." He nodded at the window. "Renard claimed to have seen the jewels in this chamber. Now, as I do not believe either your mother or you would invite that man in here, how is it possible he saw what was in your chamber at all?"

Gwynnie followed his gaze to the window. As they were in the rafters of the building, and the window was small, it was impossible for Renard to see into the room from the courtyard. They always kept the door locked too.

"He would have to force his way in here to see anything, and why would he do that?" Tombstone said calmly. "No, I'm beginning to believe that Renard's claim was one of revenge. If he believed that you were the one to point the finger at him, then that would explain it."

"Then … you believe me?" Gwynnie asked with hope.

"Perhaps."

"You do not look pleased about the idea."

"I am not." His fingers drummed on the stone sill. Gwynnie watched his hand, fearing that at any second the stone would slip. "I do not trust people on their word alone."

"Ah, was that a suggestion you are inclined to trust my word? Oh, what a nightmare!" She held her hands to her chest, mimicking the rather dramatic tone of her mother. Tombstone smiled a little.

"I think we have intruded on these ladies' privacy quite enough for one day, Tombstone," Pascal said, standing. "Mistress Wightham, you have recovered?"

"Quite recovered. I thank you for your kindness." She offered the handkerchief back to Pascal, but he insisted she keep it with a wave of his hand.

"Come, Tombstone." Pascal left the chamber quickly as Tombstone nodded at Gwynnie. His voice dropped to a whisper as he passed her.

"Stay away from Renard. It does not do to make enemies in such high places, especially when…" He trailed off. She nodded, showing she understood.

"Especially when I am not high born myself."

Tombstone gave a small nod, closing the door behind him.

Emlyn and Gwynnie waited until the sound of footsteps had retreated down the corridor before they moved. Gwynnie reached down and snatched the hat pin up from beneath her boot as Emlyn stood up from the bed, all signs of her tears now vanished.

"He believes you," Emlyn whispered, shaking her head in disbelief. "You have not attempted to charm him in any way, and yet he is inclined to trust you. Why is that?"

"I believe Tombstone is immune to any woman's charms, Ma." Gwynnie raised the stone in the sill and dropped the hat pin inside, watching as it landed amongst the others, the hidden treasure glittering. "He is simply inclined to trust my word on reason alone."

"What do you mean by that? About him being immune to any woman's charms?"

Gwynnie didn't answer as she replaced the stone.

CHAPTER 18

"We are being followed."

Gwynnie halted at her mother's words. They stood together in a corridor in the lower part of the great tower of the palace. Emlyn carried clean gowns as Gwynnie struggled with the fresh farthingales she was taking to the courtiers' chambers. Either side of them, candles flanked the walls, their flames dancing back and forth.

"You are dropping them. Here, let me help you." With the pretence of assisting Emlyn with all the freshly laundered gowns she carried, Gwynnie helped adjust the bundle, looking past Emlyn's shoulder.

It was difficult to see, but further down the hallway there was a shadow in the corner. The unmistakable outline of Renard stood there, his arms folded, his head turned toward them.

"What does he want?" Emlyn whispered.

"He is looking for an opportunity," Gwynnie surmised, as she finished adjusting the gowns. "He will know by now that Tombstone and Pascal did not believe his claim. He will be looking for another way to point the finger at me."

Emlyn nodded, her expression grave. "Do not let him get too close, Gwynnie. We must be on our guard. If he has a chance to plant something on us, we may not be prepared enough next time to cover ourselves."

Gwynnie knew her mother was right. They had been close to discovery that morning. A few minutes sooner and Pascal and Tombstone might have seen the jewels planted in their room.

"Then let us lose him in this rabbit warren of corridors." Gwynnie hitched the farthingales over her shoulder and led the way, heading toward a vast staircase. She moved slowly at first, so that Renard would not think they had detected his presence. They reached the top of the stairs and turned toward the courtiers' chambers.

When they reached the first chamber where they were to leave one gown and farthingale, Gwynnie used the opportunity to glance back the way they had come. Once more, she caught sight of Renard hiding in the shadows. From how well masked his body was in the darkness, she judged this was not the first time he had been sent to watch someone by his master.

"How many, do you think?" Emlyn asked.

"What?" Gwynnie looked at her mother as they walked on.

"How many times has Renard covered up his master's crimes?"

"That is anyone's guess." Gwynnie's hands tightened around the farthingales. "We know of one for certain — possibly two."

Her whole body shuddered as she remembered the conversation she had overheard in Fitzroy's chambers; how Fitzroy had trembled with fear then attacked Florian, as if his body had been possessed by some demon.

As they reached a second chamber and deposited the laundry, Gwynnie glanced back again. Renard was rather slower to mask himself in the shadows this time, and Gwynnie saw something glitter in his hand from the nearby candlelight.

It was a blade. It had to be the same dagger he had pressed to Gwynnie's neck the day they had tussled on the docks over the Thames.

Gwynnie did not intend to dawdle any longer. Either Renard planned to confront them, to force some confession, or he intended to act without words. It struck Gwynnie that if he hurt either of them, then it would simply draw even more attention their way from Tombstone and Pascal. No matter what Pascal thought of the feebleness of women, he would have to take notice then. "We need to lose him."

Gwynnie walked down the corridor and then changed course. Rather than following their intended path to the other ladies' rooms, she cut around a corner and headed in the direction of Queen Anne's chambers. Emlyn followed, not questioning what she was doing. With the sharp turn in the corridor, they were masked from Renard for a few minutes.

Gwynnie headed to another staircase and ran up lightly, trying not to make a sound. Emlyn hurried to follow, though because she was taller, she could not avoid making the stairs creak beneath her. On the floor of the queen's chambers, Gwynnie darted through a narrow hall.

"This way." Gwynnie pulled on her mother's arm.

"When did we switch places, miting? When did you become the one giving orders?"

Gwynnie didn't answer. Emlyn had always been the one in control, but since the day Emlyn had come back to their attic rooms with blood on her hands, Gwynnie felt as if she had been looking out for her mother, dragging her out of trouble, like a parent rescuing a child who had swum out of their depth.

She directed their steps toward the end of the corridor. To their right was a small door, behind which was a tightly spiralled set of stairs Gwynnie had seen used by the staff, so they could slip unseen between the floors.

Pushing her mother through the door, which was so short that even Gwynnie had to duck, they stumbled against the stairs, the yellow stones appearing practically black. With no candle, it was difficult to see what they were doing. Gwynnie tossed the farthingales onto the floor and gestured for Emlyn to put on one of the gowns in her arms.

"What? No!"

"What of it? It would hardly be the first time you had dressed up as some courtier. Now hurry. Before Renard catches us up."

Gwynnie tore the other gowns from her mother's grasp and ushered her into one of them. She yanked it over her mother's head and hurried up one of the steps in order to tie the laces at her mother's back, fastening them so tightly that Emlyn gasped in surprise. There was little more they could do in the time they had left, so Gwynnie settled herself with tearing the coif off her mother's head and brushing the loose tendrils back behind her ear.

"Just look important and imperious."

"That is my bread and butter, miting."

"I had noticed. Just look important enough to scare him away. He may be happy to threaten two maids, but if he thinks a fine lady is walking these corridors, someone of higher class, he will not risk being seen." Gwynnie thrust her mother back out of the door and hid on the staircase, leaving the door ajar so she could peer through.

Emlyn stood calm and still, her hands locked formally together in front of her as she raised her head and admired a tapestry on the wall nearby.

Renard's footsteps could be heard approaching. He must have halted, for the sound abruptly stopped. Gwynnie pressed her face to the gap between the door and the frame, straining to see him.

His figure appeared at the other end of the corridor. Renard would know that he should not be in this part of the tower, near the ladies' chambers, for it would be considered scandalous. He backed up slowly, anxious about being seen by Emlyn, who he had clearly mistaken for a courtier. He continued to creep backward until he disappeared entirely. His distant footsteps on another set of stairs echoed as he ran away.

"He is gone," Emlyn called to Gwynnie as she opened the door. She placed her hands on her hips, looking quite the part of a fine lady. "You think fast," she said admiringly. "That is good. I have taught you well."

Gwynnie said nothing as she tiptoed into the corridor, closing the door behind her. Her mother had taught her much, yes, but a lot she had learned herself over the years, desperately thinking of ways to keep her mother safe.

"What's that?" She strained to listen, her head cocked to the side. More footsteps were coming their way, but they did not belong to Renard. This tread was much lighter than his.

"Quick! Back to the stairs." Emlyn pointed at the door to the spiral staircase.

They pushed through the door again, leaving it open just a crack.

A lady appeared in the corridor with two younger ladies behind her. One carried a tall wax candle, while the other struggled to lift a carved wooden box. The lady who led the way, her golden hair shining in the flickering candlelight, carried gowns and a leather bag on her shoulder. The golden embroidery of her gable headdress had slipped a little, as if she had pulled it on in a hurry.

"Are you certain of this, my lady?" one of the younger ladies asked. "It is so close to the queen. Your chamber will be practically beside her own."

"Yet it is not for me to judge the commands of the king, is it? He is God's word on earth. If he wishes me to move chambers, then I must obey." She paused by the small door.

154

"He has said my brother will accompany me. Naturally, he wishes to avoid any suggestion of a scandal."

Gwynnie held her breath and felt her mother's hand curl around her arm. If the lady turned to their staircase, they would surely be discovered.

They could see the lady's face clearly now. There was a sadness in her eyes, a sadness Gwynnie had not seen when she had witnessed this same lady at the joust handing her favour to the king.

"It's Jane Seymour," Emlyn whispered unnecessarily in Gwynnie's ear.

"My lady?" One of the women halted by Jane's side and placed a hand on her arm. "Is all well?"

"But of course." Jane raised her head, a smile on her face. But Gwynnie had seen enough forced smiles in her time. She'd seen them on Emlyn's face, noted the tight lines around her lips and the way her eyes didn't brighten with true joy. "Let us be quick now. If we are to do as the king asks, then I must be in my new chambers before the morn."

She hurried away, the ladies following closely behind her. As they retreated, taking their bright candle with them, Gwynnie stood straight, moving back from the door.

"What is he doing?"

"Who?" Emlyn asked, shrugging off the fine gown that she had pulled on over her maid's dress.

"King Henry," Gwynnie said. "He is inviting another lady into his tower, when his own wife…" She trailed off, recalling the woman's voice she had heard coming from the king's rooms on the night she had first broken into the tower.

"Not all are faithful in marriage," Emlyn said, hurrying to fold the gown up with the others. "Some take their vows as lightly as they take their laundry." She pushed the clean gowns into Gwynnie's hands.

"How romantic."

"Just so." Emlyn picked up the farthingales and they stepped out into the corridor together, both glancing in the direction that Renard had retreated. The corridor was empty.

"You took your vows seriously," Gwynnie whispered. "You took them so seriously that after my father died, you…"

"We do not need to speak of what I did." Emlyn walked away. Gwynnie hastened to catch up, nearly tripping on the hem of her gown in her haste.

"You said it was self-defence," Gwynnie said, hurrying after her mother. "You had no choice."

"I know what I said." Emlyn abruptly stopped walking and turned to face Gwynnie, her expression grave. "It does not do to dwell on the past. We must look to the future."

"That is what I hope for. I look for a future in France or Ireland, somewhere far from the thieving, far from our own pasts," Gwynnie said in a rush. "Yet I cannot help but wonder sometimes if you have no wish to leave this life at all."

"I vowed to you I would, did I not?" Emlyn smiled.

Gwynnie felt as if she had been kicked in the gut, for it was another one of those false smiles.

"Come, we must be quick. Before that man finds us again." Emlyn turned on her heel and walked away, urging Gwynnie to follow.

Gwynnie did not speak again as they hurried to their tasks in the laundry, watching out for Renard, for she was too caught up in her own thoughts. She began to wonder why they had come to the palace, and if it was possible that her own mother had lied to her. Perhaps Emlyn had never intended to leave England and turn her back on being a cutpurse after all.

CHAPTER 19

"I cannot sleep." Emlyn's voice sounded in the darkness.

"Well, I am enjoying an incredibly peaceful sleep myself. Such dreams of serenity, it is practically a blissful heaven fallen to this earth." This time, Gwynnie's sarcasm didn't even earn her mother's reprimand.

Emlyn sat up, swinging her legs off the bed. Her nightgown slipped from her shoulders and she pulled it up again, reaching for a woollen shawl that she wrapped tightly around her body.

Gwynnie rolled over on the bed, lying on her side as she looked at her mother. Her back twinged with the movement, but she said nothing.

In the moonlight that shone through the window, her mother's face looked gaunt. The shadows were noticeable beneath her eyes, as if someone had smudged black ink there.

"You need to sleep," Gwynnie whispered.

"I said such things to you when you had nightmares as a child." Emlyn frowned. "After I came back that day, with…" She waved her hands in the air, not needing to say the words 'with blood on my hands'. "You had nightmares again. You said it was always the same. There was blood everywhere, all over our chambers."

Gwynnie remembered the dreams all too well. She sometimes saw her father's face in those dreams. He was always smiling, always teasing, looking for a reason to be happy. At the time, Emlyn had smiled too. So often had Gwynnie seen the pair of them together, incapable of halting their laughter at some jest. She had a particular memory of the two of them dancing, celebrating something, though she was not sure what. They had danced and drank all night in their chambers, with small Gwynnie watching on, hopping in her chair.

After her father had died, Emlyn had never smiled in quite the same way again.

"Those nightmares were a long time ago," Gwynnie said.

"Were they?" Emlyn shuddered. "For some reason, they do not feel so long ago tonight. I keep seeing things again, keep seeing it all…"

Gwynnie swallowed, knowing that they were no longer talking about her nightmares.

"Will you tell me what happened that night?" Gwynnie held herself still, not daring to move on the bed in case it creaked.

"I have told you."

"Not completely. You've told me snippets … of how you had to defend yourself, of how it was necessary." Gwynnie spoke quietly. "That I understand, but what did you do to him, Ma? How did you end up with blood … on your hands?"

Emlyn looked away hurriedly, her gaze landing on the window.

"I'll tell you everything someday."

"That is what you always say. I am no child, Ma. I have not been for a long time now."

"I know." Emlyn nodded. "I thought that you would have left me behind by now, left being a cutpurse too. Perhaps even got married yourself."

Gwynnie wrinkled her nose at the idea. She had only ever cared for one man in her life, but that was many years ago now. She had been young and naive, which explained why she had let her heart be so ensnared by a man who had no intention of caring for her too.

158

"Whatever happened to that young man of yours? What was his name — Horace?"

"Harold." Gwynnie turned her face away. "Let us not speak of him. You are changing the subject, Ma."

She could remember Harold as if what had passed between them had taken place just the week before. He had asked her to marry him, but too afraid to abandon her mother, Gwynnie had turned him down, asking for more time to see her mother settled first. Less than two weeks later, he had married another.

"It would have brought me some comfort, I think." Emlyn leaned forward. "To have seen you settled. You would be safer than you are now. In this dreadful place..." Emlyn stood and moved to the window, flapping the shawl around her shoulders as if it was a pair of wings and she was some restless bird, eager to take flight. "The cold, the flood, the ice, all of it. It is like a frozen hell."

"You speak as if we have been given a death sentence, Ma."

"I thought I knew what they were planning." Emlyn turned on the spot. "I thought that by planting the jewels here, Fitzroy and Renard intended to see you charged with the crime, but then why follow us tonight? Why bring a blade? If that is indeed what you saw."

"It is. He was carrying a dagger." Gwynnie had told her mother about the blade once they had returned to their chamber.

"I need to think." Emlyn pulled her cloak off a hook. "I am going for a walk."

"A walk?" Gwynnie sat up. "Are you mad? When we are already being followed? Ma, that is a poor idea indeed."

"Ah, miting." Emlyn stepped toward her and patted her cheek, as if she was still a child. "You forget that I lived this life long before you were born. I have escaped people following me for many years now. Trust me. A short walk will help me clear my head and I shall be perfectly safe."

"I shall come with you." Gwynnie pushed back her blanket, but as she moved to stand, her back twinged and she was forced to sit down again.

"You need to rest." Emlyn pushed her gently back down. "Trust me, Gwynnie." She winked. "I do not always need a protector at my side."

"No?" Gwynnie asked, her eyes wide.

Emlyn offered a small smile. "I shall return soon. Sleep. You need it." She turned the key in the lock and stepped out, taking the key with her. Gwynnie heard her lock the door from the other side before her footsteps faded.

Gwynnie lay down heavily, making the bed groan beneath her. Something didn't feel right. Emlyn was in a strange humour, to be going for a walk at this time of night. She had taken many such walks over the years on sleepless nights, but never in a flooded palace where men suspected them of being jewellery thieves.

"What are you up to, Ma?" Gwynnie glanced at the door. Deciding it was best to discover the truth, rather than just lie there and drive herself mad with speculation, Gwynnie stood from the bed and dressed, pulling on her maid's pale blue gown and white apron over the top. She wrapped a thick fur pelisse around her shoulders to protect herself from the cold night air, though she didn't bother with her coif at this time of night.

Gwynnie turned to the door, her hand hovering over the handle when she remembered Emlyn had taken one of the keys. She returned across the room and sought out another key that hung on a hook when a sound at the door drew her attention.

Someone was on the other side.

Something was slowly pressed into the lock of the door, the clicking of something hard sliding against the metal catch. Gwynnie stepped back, flattening herself against the wall behind the door as she watched the handle. Someone was attempting to pick the lock, though they were making a poor job of it. Their efforts to stay quiet soon became fruitless, and they practically shoved their implement further into the lock, in danger of fracturing it completely. The handle turned and the door swung inward, the hinges squeaking noisily.

Gwynnie's breathing grew laboured, her chest heaving as she looked around for some weapon to use. All that she had was the key clutched between her fingers.

A man stepped into the room, his body turning as his eyes found hers. It was Renard, dressed head to toe in black, a cloak wrapped around his shoulders.

"Good evening, Mistress Gwynnie."

CHAPTER 20

Gwynnie held her hand behind her back, hiding the long iron key.

Renard stepped toward her, with his hand outstretched. "Do not make a sound," he warned. "If you do…"

Gwynnie had no choice. He was taller than her, stronger, and judging by their last tussle, she would only be able to escape by luck alone. She drew in a deep breath, ready to scream for help, when he planted one of his forearms across her shoulders, pressing her into the wall as his other hand latched over her mouth, clamping it shut.

She pushed against him, trying to break free, but it was no use. He was too strong.

Renard kept his hand over her mouth as he used his other arm to drag her away from the wall. Gwynnie used the opportunity to raise the key high. It was a horrible way to defend oneself, but sometimes, as Emlyn had told her, it was necessary.

She aimed for Renard's eye with the key outstretched like a blade.

A hand reached up and caught her wrist. It was a tussle of strength as Renard bent her arm backward, increasing the distance from his eye. Their arms shook, each of them fighting with as much might as they could muster. As he bent her arm, pain shot up Gwynnie's bicep and into her shoulder.

Raising both hands to the key, she drove it down toward him again. Renard was forced to release her hand to fight with her, and as he did so she stamped down hard on his foot. He grunted in pain and lashed out at her hand. She dropped the key, scurrying back and falling over the foot of her bed.

She landed heavily on her back on the floor, the pain so strong that she winded herself. Then a hand found her hair and jerked her head back.

"No —" The word just escaped as a strip of material was wrapped around her mouth. Her words muffled, she pushed herself up into a kneeling position to tear the gag off, but Renard was too fast. He caught her elbows and dragged them up behind her back.

Flailing like a caught pigeon as he dragged her down the corridor, she tried to kick out at passing doors, hoping it would draw someone from their beds, but Renard dragged her back before her boots could connect.

Reaching the stairs, Gwynnie no longer fought as much. One wrong move, and she could find herself pushed down the steps. She did not want to be found with a broken neck at the bottom of the staircase.

"*Bon*," Renard said. "At least you have realised there is no point in fighting with me."

Gwynnie could hardly answer. She was dragged out of the servants' building and into a narrow lane. Here, she started fighting him again, kicking out at nearby walls and trying to use them as leverage to get away from him. He was too strong, and in the end he wrapped an arm around her waist, holding her high with her arms pinned to her sides as if she was nothing but a log for the fire.

Gwynnie flicked her head back and forth, searching desperately for any sign of her mother. Emlyn was nowhere to be seen. In fact, the entire palace was quiet. These small lanes were all occupied by staff who by now were tucked up in bed, for they would all have early mornings.

As they approached the empty tiltyard, Renard put Gwynnie down and dragged her forward instead, so her boots created furrows in the damp ground.

The tiltyard looked almost ghostly in the moonlight. The courtiers and jousters were all gone now.

Gwynnie's eyes grew round as she realised that the tiltyard wasn't empty after all. In the middle of the yard stood a figure. He leaned against the railing, his hands gripping it tight.

"Your Grace?" Renard called.

The figure looked up, his light auburn hair revealed in the moonlight.

It was Fitzroy.

He stepped toward her, his lanky figure towering over her. Gwynnie shrank before him. Out here, alone with him and Renard in the middle of a field, she was deeply aware of what he was capable of. If she'd had the use of her hands, she would have reached up to her throat to protect it.

Fitzroy frowned and turned to Renard. "I do not see it. She is just a maid. It cannot be her."

"We both saw a woman leave your chambers that night. It is *her.*"

"Then how did she get rid of the jewels?" Fitzroy stepped back and waved a hand at Gwynnie. "You said you had this finished. That Tombstone and Pascal would have sent her to Newgate by the end of the day. Yet I see her before me still."

"Do you not see?" Renard asked. "Only a thief with a good hiding place would be able to get rid of those jewels in time."

Fitzroy stared at Gwynnie, disgust wrinkling his nose. "You're the thief?" he sneered. "I at least expected something more than a trifling maid."

Gwynnie grunted against the gag and kicked out with her leg, desperate to make contact, but Renard dragged her back.

"You want more proof?" Renard asked. "Watch." He pressed down into the small of her back.

Capitulating under the sudden pain, Gwynnie yelped and dropped to her knees, Renard still refusing to let go of her arms.

"The thief fell on her back, see? You want the guilty party? I give her to you."

Fitzroy nodded slowly. "Get rid of her."

The order made Gwynnie go still. She was suddenly aware of her isolation. She was alone, with a murderer, with nothing but the stars and the hoots of owls in the distance to keep her company.

He meant to see her dead.

Renard glared at her. "I cannot."

"Why not? You know what she is. And you know what she saw…" Fitzroy waved a hand at Gwynnie. "You have walked around for days now, claiming you can solve our problem, yet nothing has happened, has it? You have even been searched by Tombstone yourself. No. This ends now, Renard. Put her with the other one, if you must."

The other one? There was only one other person Gwynnie could think of whose body hadn't yet been found: Master Jerome Woodville. Did they intend to kill her and hide her body with his?

"She is more valuable to us alive." Renard grabbed both of Gwynnie's wrists and pulled them up so that her face was pressed down toward the ground. She didn't dare move an inch, in case her arms were torn from their sockets. "We must bide our time if we are to escape all suspicion."

"This is taking too long." Fitzroy paced, pushing his hands through his short hair. "My father stepped out of his bed this evening. Would you like to know the first person he asked for, after demanding to see that new woman of his?"

Gwynnie looked up, thinking of Jane Seymour and how she had been sent to new rooms that very evening.

"He wished to hear from Cromwell. He believes someone may have spooked his horse on purpose. He insists his riding skills are as great as ever, and that the only reason he could have fallen from his horse was if it was sabotage. You should have heard him." He laughed humourlessly. "Some madness about omens... How Battersby's death was a sign of what was to come. He fears his own death."

"I know, Your Grace." Renard cut him off. "That is why we need her alive — you need a scapegoat. You need to blame her, to make Pascal see her for what she is — just a common cutpurse." He tossed her forward.

Gwynnie fell face-first into the dirt, the jolt re-opening the cut on her chin. She snatched the gag from her mouth and knelt up, facing Fitzroy.

"I know who you are," Gwynnie said, her eyes blazing. "And I saw what you did to that poor man."

Fitzroy's nostrils flared as he marched toward her.

Gwynnie scrambled back as he halted above her, his voice booming.

"The man was a rat," Fitzroy seethed. "Nothing more than that!"

"Shh," Renard ordered. "You will be heard, Your Grace."

"Heard?" he hissed. "She heard everything that night. Renard, she *knows*."

"I know —"

"No! Not just what I did, but who I..." Fitzroy trailed off.

Gwynnie said nothing. She cared not if Fitzroy preferred the company of men to women. It was the matter of murder that upset her.

Fitzroy took another step toward her, his hands clenched at his sides.

Renard abruptly stood in front of Gwynnie. She blinked up at him, startled that he had put himself between them, before realising that he only wanted to keep her alive long enough to see her take the blame for the murder.

"She's no good to you dead," Renard insisted.

Gwynnie looked about the tiltyard, desperate to see where she could run for her best chance of escape when she saw a shadow move.

Someone was standing at the edge of the yard, watching them. Was it her mother? Her heart thudded in her chest.

Yet the person continued to stand there, watching them. It was a beat later when Gwynnie realised this person was too short to be her mother, only a little taller than Gwynnie herself. But it was a woman. The skirt of her gown and her long cloak rippled in the breeze.

A sound must have escaped Gwynnie's lips, for Renard turned around.

"Who's there?" he called to the figure.

Slowly, the woman walked forward into the moonlight. Gwynnie blinked up at the unmistakable face of Esme Battersby.

She looked down at Gwynnie, her eyes wide. "What is this?" she asked. "What are you doing to this maid?" She reached a hand toward Gwynnie.

Gwynnie moved to her knees, reaching for the proffered hand, but Renard batted her arm down.

"Sir." Esme stood tall. "You must understand how this appears from my perspective." Her eyes settled on the other man, and she must have realised for the first time just who it was. "Your Grace," she whispered and dropped a deep curtsy.

"Ah, Mistress Battersby." Fitzroy clasped his hands together, attempting to adopt a familiar tone, as if they were talking in the banqueting hall over a great feast. "It is nothing important. Merely a misunderstanding. You are out late tonight. May I escort you back to your rooms?"

Esme shook her head. "I cannot sleep these days, not since…" She blinked back tears as her gaze returned to Gwynnie. "Release the maid into my care. If you have a complaint against her, then it should be made to the steward."

"Now, truly —"

"Hand the maid to me, Your Grace."

Gwynnie felt a rush of admiration for the lady. It didn't matter to Esme that Fitzroy was the son of the king. She was not going to back down.

Gwynnie also knew that the lady deserved to know who had killed her husband. She should know that the man before her was to blame.

"I am afraid I cannot do that." Fitzroy pinched the bridge of his nose. "Renard, I have had a thought." He pointed to the breast of Renard's doublet. "Do it."

Renard reached into his doublet, finding a secret pocket that must have been missed by Tombstone, and pulled out a thin glass vial with a cork in the top. The vial was thrust before Gwynnie's face as the cork was removed.

All too late did she realise what was happening. Renard's hand caught the back of her head as he forced the vial toward her lips. She caught the end and stopped it before it could reach her mouth.

"What are you doing? What is that?" cried Esme.

Renard shoved Gwynnie's hand away, just enough to tip the vial and force the liquid into her mouth.

It tasted overly sweet. Gwynnie gagged on the mixture and tried to spit it back out, but Renard took hold of her nose, and she was forced to swallow it. Coughing and spluttering at the bitter aftertaste, she retched into the ground, hoping to make herself vomit.

Esme pushed Renard aside and knelt before Gwynnie, lifting her head up.

"What was it? What did they make you drink?"

"I…" Gwynnie couldn't describe the taste. She had never had it before in her life.

"Mistress Battersby?" Fitzroy called to her.

Esme released Gwynnie and turned around on her knees.

Renard struck out hard. His fist connected with the side of her head.

"No!" Gwynnie screamed and reached out, grabbing Esme to stop her from falling to the ground. She cradled her in her lap, tears threatening as she noticed the lady's eyes slide shut. "What have you done?" she shouted. "She did nothing to you. Nothing!"

Renard and Fitzroy ignored her.

"You have to wake up, Goodwife Battersby. You must," she whispered, yet something strange was happening. Esme's face was no longer in focus.

A tingling feeling spread down the left-hand side of Gwynnie's body. She released Esme, slowly lowering her to the ground and planting her own hands in the dirt. She could no longer raise her head. It felt strangely heavy, and she wanted nothing more than to close her eyes and go to sleep, but to sleep now would be madness.

"It will do its task," Renard muttered. His voice sounded distant. "Something I saw used on the Continent in my youth. Soon enough, she will not be able to do anything."

Gwynnie glared back over her shoulder, wishing to defy him.

She saw Fitzroy move to stand beside Esme Battersby, towering over her unconscious form.

The last thing she remembered was Fitzroy's gaze, resolute and unflinching, then the world slipped into darkness.

CHAPTER 21

There was a bright light overhead. Gwynnie grimaced, screwing up her eyes tight. Was it morning already? Surely not. She could at least spend a few minutes longer in bed, but the bed was not as warm as she had expected. In fact, it was cold and damp, and not a bed at all, but soft ground. There were sods of earth beneath her fingers.

Gwynnie blinked, opening her eyes wide. She was outside, still in the tiltyard. She could see the staggered seating to her right. Angling her head to the left, she sought out the jousting rail. She remembered at once what had happened the night before, how Renard had tackled her in the bedchamber and dragged her out here, forcing her to kneel before Fitzroy.

Neither man was here now.

Gwynnie shivered in the cold and rolled over onto her front. She felt sick. The taste in her mouth brought up bile, the bitter aftertaste acrid.

Something soft brushed her arm. Gwynnie raised herself onto her knees, looking down to see there was another woman beside her on the ground.

The embroidered skirt of Esme Battersby's russet gown was billowing in the wind, and that was what had brushed her arm. Esme's eyes were closed.

"No!" Gwynnie scurried forward on her hands and knees, hardly caring that she was now covered in mud and shivering so much that her teeth were chattering. There was blood under Esme's head, spreading across the ground. Gwynnie reached for her wrist, desperately trying to find a pulse. She tried again, reaching for Esme's neck this time. Her skin was cold, but there it was, at last! There was a flutter beneath the skin. As soft as the beating of a butterfly's wings, but undoubtedly present. "You are alive. Thank God."

Gwynnie gently shook Esme's shoulders. "You must wake up! Goodwife Battersby, please, you must wake up!" But it did no good; Esme's eyes stayed closed.

There was a sound across the tiltyard. Gwynnie looked up. In the distance, she could hear chattering voices. It may have been early, but people were beginning to rouse in the palace, and it wouldn't be long until someone walked past the entrance to the tiltyard. All at once, Gwynnie realised how the scene would look when she was found beside the unconscious Esme.

Glancing down, she saw there was not only mud on her hands, but blood too.

"They'll do me for murder." She closed her eyes, seeing herself on the gallows. She could practically feel the hangman's noose tightening around her throat, squeezing the life out of her, as the crowds jeered. Maybe some would throw tomatoes, while religious men might pray for her soul to be saved. "Which is exactly what those two knavish bastards want."

Her eyes shot open, and she stood up. With new determination, she tried to pull the unconscious woman up into a standing position, but Esme was taller than her, and larger in build, and Gwynnie fell back down to her knees again.

"Oof!" she gasped as she clutched her temple. Whatever Renard had forced her to drink the night before, it had left her unconscious for hours, and she still felt groggy.

She looked beyond the jousting rail toward the gate that led to the nearest lane. She couldn't see anyone yet, but voices were calling to one another. The cooks had risen, for someone shouted for more wheat to be brought from the tithe barn.

"Come, Esme. You are not dying out here." Gwynnie moved so that her back was to Esme and latched the woman's arms over her shoulders. When Esme was practically strewn across her back, Gwynnie gritted her teeth, forced all her weight into the ground beneath her feet and stood straight.

The toes of Esme's boots dragged along the ground behind her, but it would have to do. At least this way, she could move Esme. Struggling across the tiltyard, staggering under the weight, Gwynnie glanced back once.

The mud was disturbed and the bloody puddle where Esme's head had lain was plain to see. She gulped at the sight and moved on, shuffling slowly toward the gate. It was imperative she wasn't seen with Esme. She wasn't going to the noose for any crime that Fitzroy was responsible for.

Peering through the gate, she was careful to keep her back to the wall.

Samuel walked by, carrying a sack of wheat over his shoulder. He yawned loudly, a great hand clutched over his mouth. Behind him was a boy in training to be a cook, struggling under the weight of another sack.

"Hurry!" Samuel called to him. "We need to get the bread in the oven."

Gwynnie waited for Samuel and the boy to disappear through the doorway of the kitchens, vanishing from sight. Stepping back, Gwynnie rested both her weight and Esme's against the wall.

She could take Esme back to her chamber, but what then? Neither she nor Emlyn knew any healing practices. She needed to find someone who could help.

"Oh, no." Gwynnie sighed deeply, for she knew only one person inside the palace walls to whom she could turn for help.

She couldn't go to one of the physicians, for they were busy attending to the king and queen.

Checking around the corner to ensure the coast was clear, Gwynnie decided to avoid the courtyard entirely. She heaved Esme forward, nearly buckling under her weight, and dragged her across the tiltyard. Careful to keep to the edges of the yard, she masked their bodies as much as she possibly could in the shadows, close to the wall of the yard tower and the galleries. The time seemed to stretch out infernally. A walk that would normally have taken her two minutes at most, now took ten minutes at least. More than once did she halt, taking a breather and resting Esme against a nearby wall. Her eyes darted across the windows set in the walls of the galleries, wary of anyone watching her, but it was still early, and all the curtains were drawn.

"Nearly there, Esme," she whispered, hoping that Esme could hear her. "Nearly there."

Puffing out her cheeks, she continued. Avoiding the towers, she headed to the south wing, where the clerks and lawyers of the court had their offices. When she reached the door to the building, she heaved it forward, struggling to push it with her shoulder. The door scraped across the flagstones, and she halted, leaning against the frame to catch her breath, looking up and down the corridor in case anyone came.

The corridor was empty.

Heaving forward once more, Gwynnie staggered down the corridor. She bit her lip, her already bruised back throbbing with fresh pain.

Halting in front of the door she had sought out, she rested her forehead against the wood, both hands clinging to Esme's wrists and keeping her in place. What she was about to do was a gamble. Emlyn might even call it foolish, but Gwynnie had no choice.

She had seen one man die at Fitzroy's hands. She was not about to let that man's wife lose her life, too.

Shifting both of Esme's wrists to one of her hands, she reached for the handle and turned it, pushing the door open. She didn't expect to find anyone inside. At this time in the morning, surely the lawyer would be tucked away in his bedchamber. But she was wrong.

At the sound of her entrance, Tombstone jerked his head up off the desk. He had parchment stuck to his cheek and his copper hair was wild about his ears. His eyes widened when he saw her.

"I need your help," she gasped, halting in the doorway. "I fear... I fear she's dying."

"God have mercy!" Tombstone yelled and was on his feet.

Though he may have been fast asleep a few seconds ago, he now leapt across the room toward her, knocking his chair over in the process. Tombstone reached for Esme and lifted her easily. Relieved of Esme's weight, Gwynnie kicked the door shut behind her, leaning upon it and then slumping down onto her haunches.

Tombstone lay Esme on his desk, shoving all his papers out of the way. He checked Esme's pulse at her throat. He nodded to himself then crossed to the cabinet in the corner of the room, pulling out the same carved box Gwynnie had seen him use when he attended to the cut Renard had given her.

Gwynnie sat motionless as she watched Tombstone work. He rolled Esme gently onto her side and mopped up the blood on the back of her head.

"Who did this, Gwynnie?" Tombstone looked up from his work, his hands still moving the cotton bundles.

She said nothing and closed her eyes. What could she possibly say that would persuade him to believe her?

"Did you do it?"

Her eyes shot open. "What? No! Why would I be trying to save her life if I had done this to her?"

Tombstone was silent as he returned to his work, laying a thick linen strip across the base of Esme's head as he bound the wound.

"How is she?" Gwynnie asked quietly, her eyes filling with tears. "Will she live?"

"Her skull isn't cracked, but there's a lot of blood. She looks to have been heavily stunned." Tombstone collected what appeared to be a chamber pot from a cupboard and placed it beside Esme on the desk.

"What's that for?" Gwynnie asked.

"If she wakes, she'll need it. I've seen such head injuries before. People are often dizzy and sick. Sometimes, the sickness calms. Other times…" He trailed off, not needing to say any more.

Tears rolled down Gwynnie's cheeks. She pulled her knees up to her chest and hid her face in her hands, suddenly overcome with emotion. Somehow, by the grace of good fortune, she had not been seen carrying Esme to this building, but it might not matter if Tombstone believed she had been the one to hurt Esme.

"Gwynnie?" Tombstone came toward her, but she didn't look up. Her cries came in great, gasping sobs. He must have bent down to her level, for his hands latched onto her wrists in an attempt to prise them from her face, but she resisted, crying into her palms.

"What's that smell?" Tombstone sniffed harshly. "That scent…" He hesitated. "What have you drunk?"

"I do not know." She tried to dry her cheeks, but only succeeded in smearing mud and blood across her skin. "It tasted foul. Sickly sweet, then bitter. I felt sick."

Tombstone stood. He moved to Esme, checked her breathing, then laid a blanket over her to keep her warm, tucking a cushion from a settle bench under her head. Next, he added logs to the fire and set it alight with a tinderbox, blowing on the flames until they took hold, and warmth spread across the room. Then he opened a cupboard door and reached for a basin of water inside. He pushed up the sleeves of his doublet and dipped a cloth in the basin. He returned to Gwynnie and offered it to her.

"What's th-that for?" she stammered through her tears.

"You need to clean your face."

Gwynnie slowly stood and staggered across the room, toward the basin and the cupboard, where a looking glass was propped up inside. When she saw her reflection, her crying became greater than before.

Great smears of dirt on her cheeks and temple were mingled with Esme's blood, and her eyes were bloodshot. With frantic movements, she tried to remove it all, dipping the cloth repeatedly into the water.

"This thing you drank," Tombstone said. "Did you lose consciousness?"

Gwynnie halted with the cloth, staring into the water, then nodded.

"Sweet then bitter, you said?"

Once more, she nodded.

"I've smelled that scent before, Gwynnie. On the Continent." At his words, she turned away from the basin to face him. "It's made of bryony root and opium."

"Opium?" she whispered.

"The mixture is called dwale. It's often used in medicine to render a patient unconscious. It helps in surgery, makes it easier." He stared at her. "Why would someone give you dwale, Gwynnie?"

She bent over the basin of water, suddenly feeling nauseous.

"Quick, sit down." Tombstone moved to Gwynnie, taking her shoulder and guiding her toward the fire. She knelt down on the hearth rug and leaned toward the flames to warm herself. Tombstone put a pot of water on the fire and added some leaves that he produced from a small wooden box. She didn't ask what he was doing, but she watched every movement he made, warily. He produced a blanket and placed it around her shoulders. Tugging on the ends, she wrapped it around her body. When the water boiled on the fire, Tombstone took it off and poured it into a glass, proffering it toward Gwynnie. "Drink it."

She took the glass, wrinkling her nose as she watched the leaves dancing about in the now green liquid.

"What is it?"

"Mint leaves, among some other things. My mother always told me they were good for settling an ill stomach. Drink it. It's perfectly safe."

She lifted it to her nose and inhaled, hesitant to drink anything after last night.

"Trust me." Tombstone's voice softened.

Gwynnie peered at him over the rim of the glass. "You said before that your mother was a healer."

"She was." Tombstone nodded. Gwynnie noted the past tense. Clearly, she was no longer of this world. "She knew what she was doing, as do I. Now, drink."

Breathing deeply to find her courage, Gwynnie lifted the cup to her lips. It was hot, but nowhere near as foul-tasting as she had expected. The dominant taste was of mint, which tickled the back of her throat. The more she drank, the more the bitter taste of the dwale left her tongue.

"What else is in here?" she asked after a minute.

"Don't ask." He shook his head. "You will not like it."

She decided he was right and continued drinking, for it was helping.

"Your mother was a healer then. Who was your father?" At her question, Tombstone fell silent. He moved away from the fire and went to stand beside Esme. Gwynnie sensed the brief window she had been given into Tombstone's life had closed. Changing the subject, she said, "Please, tell me she will live."

Tombstone opened one of Esme's eyelids and peered closely at the eye. "Time will tell. I have done all that I can." He walked slowly back toward Gwynnie. "Now you can tell me exactly what happened."

"You won't believe me." Gwynnie clutched the glass with both hands, lacing her fingers tightly together.

"Try me."

She said nothing, raising the glass to her lips.

Tombstone sighed heavily. He dragged out a chair and placed it beside the fire, sitting down in front of Gwynnie. Resting his elbows on his knees, he bent toward her. "I am not Pascal," he said, with sudden strength. "He may not trust the word of a maid, but he and I are different men."

Gwynnie's fingers fidgeted on the glass, wanting to believe him.

"You can trust me."

"Trust you? You have been sharp with me enough times to make me unsure whether I should like you or not. When I offered you information, you even shouted at me for it."

He sighed and ran a hand across his face. "I never claimed to be a man of easy temperament, but you *can* trust me. Please, tell me what happened. If you do not…" He held his arms out wide. "There is nothing I can do to help."

Gwynnie's lips parted. It was a leap of faith, but here by the fire, with the mint liquid in her hands, it was the safest she had felt for some time.

CHAPTER 22

"Renard made me drink the dwale." Gwynnie didn't look at Tombstone as she said the words. She stared down, watching the green leaves floating in her glass. She wondered what her mother would say now, to hear her revealing what had happened, but there was a great gulf between her and Emlyn at this moment. She didn't even know where her mother was.

"Why would he do that?" Tombstone leaned forward in his chair again, the wood creaking beneath him.

"Not for his own gain." Gwynnie looked up, finding Tombstone's gaze level with her own. She took a shaky sip of the mint before she went on. "Renard came to my chamber. My mother had gone for a walk. He broke in. He was not particularly good at picking the lock, but he managed it."

She noticed Tombstone frowning, but she went on. "He took me from the room. I fought him, but I…" She shrugged. She had stood little chance against Renard. "He took me to the tiltyard. His master was there, waiting for us."

"Do not tell me." Tombstone closed his eyes. He sat back in his chair, sighing deeply. "Fitzroy, the Duke of Richmond —"

"I said you wouldn't believe me." Gwynnie's breath hitched. Tears pooled in her eyes once more and streaked her cheeks. She wiped them away with the heel of her hand.

"Why did they want to see you?"

Gwynnie sniffed, holding back more tears. She would have to tell him everything.

"He attacked her." The sudden sound of Esme's voice made Gwynnie drop her glass.

The hot liquid burnt her lap and she yelped at the pain. Tombstone jumped to his feet. He threw a fresh cloth at Gwynnie to mop up the tea, then he hurried to Esme's side.

"Goodwife Battersby, please, do not sit up," he urged, moving the chamber pot so it was within easy reach. "You are dizzy, yes?"

"I am," she whispered weakly.

"If you feel sick, use this."

Gwynnie just stared at Esme, overwhelmed with relief that the woman was awake.

"I ... I do not know what they wanted with her," Esme whispered, her eyes flitting up to meet Tombstone's. "I tried to get her away from them. They would not let me take her. Then they..." She inhaled deeply and reached a hand up to her bruised face.

"Who struck her?" Tombstone asked Gwynnie.

"Renard. On his master's orders," Gwynnie answered.

"It is true," Esme murmured as her eyes closed again.

"You must rest," Tombstone urged gently. "Please, rest. Call me if you need me."

She closed her eyes once more and he drew the blanket up over her body. Gwynnie watched, her lips parted. Tombstone cared for the lady with a soft touch indeed. He stepped back, returning to Gwynnie and pouring more minty water into her glass.

"Drink," he pleaded, pushing it once again into Gwynnie's hands. He placed a finger to his lips, indicating that they should talk quietly now. "To my mind, striking down Esme and leaving you beside her, intoxicated with dwale, suggests they wanted you to be found there. They wanted you to be accused of the attack."

Gwynnie's hands tightened around the glass.

"Why would they wish to frame you for an attack on Goodwife Battersby?"

Gwynnie didn't answer. She wanted to trust him, to believe that another was in a position to help her now.

"This is not easy," she whispered.

"If Fitzroy is involved, I imagine not." He scratched the coppery stubble across his jaw. "Yet there is only one way out of whatever mess you are in. That is to tell me the truth."

Gwynnie inhaled, ready to speak. "I —"

"Elric? Elric, are you in there?" a voice called from the door.

Tombstone jumped up from his chair and flung open the door, revealing a rather tired-looking Pascal on the other side. He walked into the room, carrying a cane with him and resting his weight upon it.

"You and I must talk —" He halted abruptly, his chin jerking between Esme and Gwynnie.

"Hush, we must be quiet." Tombstone took Pascal's shoulder and steered him across the room, away from Esme and toward Gwynnie.

Not for the first time did Gwynnie think there was something strange about Tombstone and Pascal's relationship. She imagined many employers would have been furious at their employee for manhandling them, but Pascal simply accepted his touch.

"By this light, what has happened?"

Gwynnie concentrated on her drink, the bitter taste now gone as she listened to Tombstone revealing how Gwynnie had come to his door with Esme, and what they had both said since.

"Will she live?" Pascal waved his cane in Esme's direction. His concern made Gwynnie's heart soften toward the man.

"I have hope, considering she has woken now," Tombstone said softly, returning to his seat beside Gwynnie, who was still kneeling by the fire. "She has not yet emptied the contents of her stomach either. It is promising."

"Good, good," Pascal said distractedly, his gaze turning on Gwynnie.

Whatever softening Gwynnie had felt toward him vanished abruptly.

"And you believe this woman's tale?" He thrust the cane toward Gwynnie.

"I do." Tombstone waved a hand toward the sleeping form of Esme. "Goodwife Battersby confirmed it."

"Poor Goodwife Battersby has been struck down. She could say anything, confused by what has happened. You know as well as I do that people with head wounds can lose their mind, no longer know their left from their right, their husbands from strangers."

"She spoke with reason," Tombstone insisted, a firmness to his tone. "I choose to believe her."

"You are a fool," Pascal spat with sudden venom. "You have her attacker here before you." He pointed the cane once more at Gwynnie. "She is covered in the woman's blood. What further proof do you need?"

"Renard did it —" Gwynnie tried to speak.

"Oh, and I should believe you, should I not?" Pascal scoffed. His eyes were hooded, his face wrinkling like parchment that had been scrunched up by strong hands. "You accuse the man of one of the greatest courtiers in England!"

Gwynnie put down her glass.

She didn't cry this time, nor did she panic. This was what she had suspected would happen, and why she shouldn't have placed her trust in Tombstone in the first place. Even if he was inclined to believe her, the man with the ultimate power was Pascal. He had already proved himself prejudiced against maids and anyone of Gwynnie's class.

"You would sooner believe the word of anyone above me, would you not, sir?" she asked, lifting her chin toward him. "Or would you sooner trust the word of any *man* over me?"

He stood straight, leaning his weight upon his cane. "You are covered in blood," he said. "Elric, arrest her."

Tombstone didn't move. He stared at Pascal, his jaw going slack.

"Tombstone!"

"You wish me to take her to Newgate? I cannot do that."

"Whyever not? She has attacked a courtier, a fine lady indeed. We have seen before what insolence she is capable of. She is hardly like her mother, a reverent woman. Now you see the true capabilities of a person of her class, Tombstone. It is before you."

Gwynnie stood. Her legs, which had been shaking, were now straight and firm.

"Take her," Pascal ordered again.

"I do not believe —"

"Take her to Newgate now, or your position here is at an end." Pascal's threat hung in the air. Tombstone glared at him, as if he did not believe his ears. When Pascal's grasp on his cane tightened, Tombstone sighed, clearly resigning himself to the inevitable.

Gwynnie moved toward the fireplace and took hold of the poker that rested against the stone hearth. She knew now that nothing she could say would persuade Pascal to believe her.

"Take her," Pascal said again.

Tombstone stood.

"I am not going to Newgate." Gwynnie acted fast. Striking out with the poker, she thrust the iron rod into the fireplace and pulled out one of the burning logs. It landed on the hearth rug between her and the two men, setting the rug alight.

"Oh! Look what she does. She tries to kill us both!"

"Hardly, Pascal."

Gwynnie let the fire burn as she darted from the room, dropping the poker and running as fast as she could. She glanced back at Esme, whose eyes still hadn't opened in the kerfuffle, as Tombstone tried to get the burning log back into the fire and Pascal waved his cane manically in the air.

Gwynnie sprinted down the corridor, picking up the skirt of her gown so she would not trip. She knew she wouldn't be able to hide easily: in this stained gown, she would be noticeable. And Tombstone would find her if she went back to her chamber. No, she had to find somewhere else to hide, somewhere that no one would think to look for her.

Rather than fleeing through the door and out into the courtyard, she took another door and darted up a spiral staircase that led to the lawyers' chambers. Glancing up and down the corridor, she searched for an empty room. She found a door standing ajar, the sunlight bathing the bedchamber in a cool glow.

Gwynnie hurried inside and closed the door behind her. At the far end of the room, underneath the mullion window, was a rather plain wooden coffer. Lifting the lid, Gwynnie reached for the black robes inside that were so identifiable as a lawyer's. She flung them over her gown, then reached for a full crown black bonnet, pleated at the front with a hawk's brown feather thrust into the hem. Gwynnie pulled the bonnet over her head and tucked the strands of her loose hair under the rim.

She looked down at her stained boots. The black robes were so long that they hid her feet. She turned to a looking glass that hung from a hook on the wooden panelled wall. Her cheeks were no longer stained, since she had washed in Tombstone's chamber, but her eyes were still red and her face was too feminine. Returning to the coffer, she shifted the clothes to the side, delving deep to find something that could hide her features. Tucked away at the bottom of the coffer, she found a white lace collar, greying with age. Wrapping the collar around her throat, she flicked it up over her chin and mouth, hiding half her face, then pulled the brim of the bonnet lower over her head.

Breathing deeply, she headed toward the door and calmly stepped out. Moving along with her head bowed, she inched toward the spiral staircase, taking the steps carefully. When she reached the lower corridor, she could see a great tumult.

Tombstone was marching up and down, asking every lawyer and gentleman he passed if he had seen a maid running by. Pascal followed, striking his cane into the floorboards in his anger and looking tempted to strike the nearest gentleman who claimed not to have seen her.

"Someone must have seen her!" Pascal boomed. Those that hadn't yet been drawn out of their rooms by the great cries now pushed their heads out of their doors, looking around in wonder. "Come forward now. Who has seen her?"

"A young woman, you say? A maid?" Although her heart was pounding, Gwynnie calmly pointed to the spiral staircase from which she had just emerged. She deepened her voice and turned her head away, her face hidden by the collar and brim of the hat. "I saw a maid running upstairs just now, sirs."

"Thank you." Pascal thrust the cane at Tombstone. "Go. Find her!"

Tombstone walked past Gwynnie, not giving her a second glance as he ran up the stairs. Pascal returned to Tombstone's office, evidently going to check on Esme.

Gwynnie released the breath she had been holding and stepped out into the courtyard. She had escaped, for now, but everything had changed.

It seemed that Renard and Fitzroy's plan had worked after all. Despite everything Gwynnie had done in the hope of pointing Tombstone toward Florian's killer, suspicion had fallen on her instead. It wouldn't be long before Pascal questioned why Gwynnie would have hurt Esme. Perhaps he would even start to question why Emlyn had been seen by Donsen Tower on the night that the jewels had gone missing.

"I'll hang for this after all," Gwynnie muttered to herself.

Knowing she couldn't go back to her chamber, she crossed the courtyards and headed to the laundry rooms. By now, her mother would have risen and no doubt be at work.

Gwynnie stepped inside the room, keeping her head bowed low.

"Sir, you should not be back here." Emlyn was sharp as Gwynnie appeared beside her. Water splashed and Gwynnie looked up to see her mother moving quickly around the room. Her face was flushed, her movements frantic, and Gwynnie could tell at once that her mother was worried. "Please, leave. I have laundry to attend to."

"Ma?" Gwynnie's voice made Emlyn stagger against the nearest barrel, causing it to tip over, the water and lye spilling across the cobbles as the chemises fell out too.

"Gwynnie? Where have you been?"

Gwynnie lifted the bonnet off her head, allowing her hair to fall down around shoulders.

"Everything has changed, Ma. Pascal has ordered Tombstone to take me to Newgate."

CHAPTER 23

Gwynnie stood by the riverbank, gazing out across the water. Her hands fidgeted beneath the thick lawyer's robes she still wore.

Her mother wore a dark brown cloak and a red cap over her head. She'd also rubbed some dirt on her chin, that at a casual glance looked rather like stubble. The heavy cross around her neck suggested she was now a gentleman of the clergy.

"Shall we just swim across, do you think?" Gwynnie said with such an ironic tone that her mother sighed audibly. "Easy, is it not?"

"I did not say it was a good idea, only that it was an idea."

"It is a knave's idea."

"I know, I know. Bite the stone, not the hand that throws it."

Gwynnie looked out over the Thames once again. It may have stopped raining, but the river was still so high that the wherrymen had not been seen out on the water. Emlyn and Gwynnie had come down to the riverbank in the vain hope that maybe one wherryman would have had the gall to work today, but their prayers had not been answered. The river was bare, and there was no way out of the palace.

"We could try the other side, Woolwich Road. The flooded lawn is retreating. We could reach the heath."

"It hasn't retreated enough." Gwynnie shook her head. "I had to swim through that icy water the other day. It arrests one's movements with its coldness. I do not believe we could reach the other side of that flood without drowning."

All day, they had been hiding in plain sight. The palace was searched not just by Tombstone, but also yeomen, in pursuit of Gwynnie and Emlyn. So far, they had not returned to their chamber, fearing that a yeoman guard might be waiting for them there.

"Even if we manage to flee, how would we survive?" Emlyn whispered as the wind whistled up from the Thames and buffeted their loose robes. "We need money. If we were to steal, we would draw attention to ourselves. We need those jewels."

"You know as well as I that we cannot risk going back to our chamber now," Gwynnie insisted. "Our best hope is to wait out the flood, and either cross the Thames or the south bank when we can."

"You think it will be that easy?" Emlyn turned toward Gwynnie, the wooden dock creaking beneath her. "You do not know what it is like to be the hunted killer. They search for you savagely. They might as well set the dogs on you. If Pascal is now convinced you hurt Mistress Battersby, and her husband before her, then you're as good as discovered already."

"Ever the optimist, Ma. You are like a ray of pure sunshine."

"Hold your tongue, girl." The sharpness of her tone made Gwynnie flinch. It had been a long time since her mother had talked to her in such a way.

Reddening almost to the colour of her crimson robes, Emlyn turned back to face the Thames. "Well, we cannot escape across there."

Gwynnie folded her arms beneath the lawyer's black cloak, staring at the water and the frozen patches that bobbed together and then parted again. She needed a new plan. Trying to frame Renard with the jewels had not worked, and telling Tombstone what had occurred in the tiltyard had failed too.

Now, she would have to do something drastic, if she and Emlyn were to ever walk away from Greenwich Palace.

"It is strange to me." Emlyn broke the silence. "I believed Pascal thought women incapable of being thieves, certainly incapable of murder. He must have changed his mind."

Gwynnie looked back at the palace in deep thought. It was true that Pascal had not thought she could be a thief. Therefore, he must have thought that she had another reason to attack Esme Battersby.

"They're still looking for the thieves then." A smile twitched across Gwynnie's face.

"Whatever you are thinking, take care," Emlyn cautioned. "None of your recent plans have gone well, miting."

"So good to know you believe in me, Ma."

"That is not what I said. You have a good mind," Emlyn said, nodding. "You get that from your father. Yet whatever your plan is now, I urge you to think it through carefully. What we do next must be foolproof."

Gwynnie continued to smile. A plan was forming in her mind. Slowly, she turned her back to the palace, staring out over the water.

"I have had a thought. Give me the evening to think through all the possibilities. If I am right, then when night comes and the moon rises, we must act."

"It will be a new moon tonight." Emlyn lifted her chin and nodded at the horizon. In the distance, the clouds were parting as the sun drifted toward the thatched roofs of London in the distance. "My ma once told me new moons were for new beginnings."

"Perhaps they are," Gwynnie agreed, though she was not disposed to believe such superstitions. "We need to go. It will not be long before someone spots two strange men staring at the water." She pulled on Emlyn's arm, and together they retreated under the gate of the palace and back into Greenwich's grounds.

"Do it," Gwynnie ordered Emlyn.

Dressed in full yeoman's garb, at a glance Emlyn was tall enough to fool anyone into thinking that she was a man, but her sour expression and the way she struggled with the pike were not so persuasive. The uniform had been taken from the laundry room, for a stubborn stain across the front had rendered it useless to its usual wearer.

"I do not like this."

"Trust me," Gwynnie pleaded. "Just do as I ask and this time next week we'll be in France, far away from Pascal, from Newgate, and from this flood."

Emlyn didn't argue. She walked toward the top of the staircase in the queen's tower and looked down the stairs. On the very top step stood a suit of armour, one said to have belonged to King Henry VII, the king's father. It was rather short compared to Emlyn's stature. She pushed the tip of the pike into the breast plate, and glanced back at Gwynnie, who nodded. With one firm thrust, Emlyn knocked the suit of armour over.

It clattered down the staircase. The metal plates shattered, breaking apart from the bolts that kept them joined together as it crashed to the floor below, the pieces scattering widely. In the quiet of the night, the sound was cacophonous.

Voices erupted from the distant ends of the corridor.

Emlyn pulled on her yeoman's cap and hurried down the stairs, deepening her voice.

"Ho! We have an intruder!" she bellowed. "Someone has knocked over the late king's armour."

Gwynnie shrank back into the shadows, pulling the coif low over her head.

Ladies and gentlemen of the court hurried past, some appearing in little more than their nightwear, with cloaks thrown over their shoulders. Others were still fully clothed, glancing rather disapprovingly at those who were not so well dressed.

Gwynnie pulled at the deep mulberry-red gown she wore. It was a maid's dress, but finer than any that she would usually wear, for such colours were reserved for the maids that attended the queen's chambers.

She waited, glancing at the queen's door.

"Come, please," Gwynnie whispered under her breath. "Let your curiosity defy you."

As if the door had heard her, it opened. Queen Anne strode out, her face pale.

Her dark hair was loose and a cloak hung from her shoulders. Her ladies-in-waiting followed her.

"Your Highness, you are still too unwell. Please, return to your chambers."

"If the king knew you walked about —"

The queen halted and turned abruptly to glare at her ladies. "I do not believe the king concerns himself much with what I do at present." The queen moved forward once more to the top of the stairs. "What is all this commotion?"

Gwynnie waited until they had passed her by, then she stepped out from the shadows and moved toward Queen Anne's chambers. Slipping in through the door, she pushed it shut, but didn't quite click the lock into place.

Inside, the room had been transformed into what appeared to be an apothecary's back room. There were herbs dangling from the ceiling, and small glass vases full of lavender and rosemary posies, the scent hanging in the air. A large fire blazed in the corner of the room, so vast that the flames practically licked at the fire screen.

More voices sounded in the corridor.

"Who pushed the armour over? Someone must have done it."

"Quick, gather it together, before the king hears of this."

Knowing she had little time before Queen Anne returned, Gwynnie hurried into the queen's private chamber. In the corner of the room, she found a large black box resting on a buffet cabinet. The edges were carved with roses and vines. In the middle was a single falcon, the symbol for Queen Anne.

Lifting the lid, Gwynnie peered inside, gulping at the jewellery that appeared before her. She had thought Fitzroy's selection of jewels luxurious, but this was otherworldly. The jewels were spread across a crimson cushion and glittered in the candlelight from the room.

There were great brooches, with teardrop-shaped pearls dripping from their golden mantle surrounds. Necklaces glistened with blood-red rubies, and there were golden pins made for the hair, the metalwork so detailed that the beaks of the carved falcons looked pointed enough to tear the skin.

Gwynnie opened the leather pouch attached to her belt and stuffed the jewels inside, clattering them together in her haste. She didn't have time to take them all, but she took most, then drew the bag shut.

Darting back to the door, she heard voices on the other side.

"He will not be happy." Queen Anne's voice was the loudest.

Gwynnie flattened herself into the space behind the door, just as it was pushed wide open.

The queen marched in with her two ladies-in-waiting behind her.

"He must be told. I must see him."

"Your Highness." One of the ladies scurried at Anne's heels, following her into the main chamber. "He has already sent word. He … he…"

"Out with it," Anne ordered.

"He has no wish to see you. He said as much in his message."

"I am his wife!" Anne shouted. She picked up a glass vase and threw it across the chamber, where it shattered against the fireplace. As the ladies darted across the room to clear up the shards of glass, Gwynnie took her opportunity to escape.

She stepped out from behind the door and slipped into the corridor. Hastening away, she passed others on the stairwell who were still trying to put the armour back together. Arguments had erupted between the men that had gathered. Some tried to fix the plates together, dismayed when their construction ended up with three legs instead of two.

As Gwynnie reached the front door of the tower, she stepped out, passing a yeoman guard by the doorway. No ordinary yeoman, Emlyn picked up the black lawyer's robes they had left hooked over a window frame nearby and pulled them over Gwynnie's gown. Swapping her white coif for the black bonnet, Gwynnie led the way across the cobbles, her mother following behind, both of their heads bowed.

They passed through courtyards and down narrow lanes. Finding a path at the back of the kitchens, they both came to a stop in the shadows, half hidden between old crates and boxes that had been used to carry apples to the kitchens from the orchard in autumn.

"Well?" Emlyn asked, nudging up the red cap of her yeoman's garb.

Gwynnie held up the leather pouch and grinned. Emlyn reached for it, her eyes widening, but Gwynnie pulled the pouch back.

"You know these are not for us to keep."

Emlyn blinked, then nodded. "What next?" she asked, her voice rather tart.

"We wait until the feast tonight. When we are certain Fitzroy and Renard are in the great hall, that's when we plant the jewels in Fitzroy's rooms."

"You realise how dangerous this is, do you not? You are no longer pointing the finger at Renard, but at Fitzroy himself! If we are discovered —"

"They'll hang me anyway if they catch me. By God's blood —"

"Curb that tongue of yours."

"Ma!" Gwynnie snapped under her breath. "We have one chance at this. Do you truly wish to back out now?"

"No, of course not."

Though as they plotted how to gain entry to Fitzroy's rooms, Gwynnie felt her mother's eyes lingering on the leather pouch.

CHAPTER 24

Turning the letter back and forth in her grasp, Gwynnie peered through a window in the lawyers' corridor, toward Donsen Tower, waiting for the signal. In the end, Emlyn had refused to let Gwynnie return to Fitzroy's chambers. Emlyn instead took her place. Dressed as a lady of the court, she had walked into the tower as if she belonged there, in order to plant the jewels they had taken from Queen Anne's chamber in Fitzroy's rooms.

Gwynnie waited for their agreed signal, shifting the lawyer's bonnet on her head as she peered through the lead-lined glass. At last, a window opened in the tower, far higher than Gwynnie had been expecting, and a hand appeared, waving a white handkerchief in the air.

"It is time," Gwynnie muttered to herself. Walking down the corridor, she glanced over her shoulder, but no one else was around. She bent swiftly down in front of Tombstone's door and slipped the letter underneath, then walked on, as if she hadn't hesitated at all.

Darting through a doorway, she cowered near other lawyers who had gathered in the courtyard. Pulling her bonnet low, she hid her face, listening in on their conversations as she caught a glimpse of Tombstone appearing from his chamber.

Evidently having found her letter, he had hurried out in order to find who had left it. He looked around the courtyard, though his eyes never settled on Gwynnie in her lawyer's robes.

Tombstone walked past, seeking out another as he held the letter in his hand. Gwynnie was careful to keep to the back of the group of lawyers. None turned to talk to her, and fortunately, because she was so short, Tombstone didn't even appear to notice she stood there.

Gwynnie dared to lift her head an inch, watching him. He stopped to re-read the letter then stuffed it back into his robes, darting back into the building. Gwynnie allowed herself the smallest of smiles and walked away, heading toward the path at the back of the kitchens where she and Emlyn had agreed to meet.

"Well?" Emlyn asked, appearing at the far end, every bit the fine lady. Her hair was tucked under a French hood, her gown glittering in the sun.

"Did he read the letter?"

"He did." Gwynnie nodded and leaned against the nearest wall. "I signed the letter from 'a friend'. I wrote that it was time to catch the true culprit, and if he wished to find out who that was, he should look to who Renard works for. I told him he'd find the evidence for the thefts in Fitzroy's rooms."

Gwynnie sat down on a crate beside Emlyn. All that mattered was that Tombstone acted on the tip-off and searched Fitzroy's rooms. By now, people would know Queen Anne had been robbed. If those same jewels were found in Fitzroy's chambers, it would be difficult for even a man with his connections to worm his way out of the situation.

"Where did you hide the jewels?" Gwynnie asked.

"In the bible box in his bedchamber. I left the bible discarded on the side too. Let us just hope this lawyer is no great fool, and he acts on the information."

"Time will tell, I suppose." Gwynnie stood from the crate. "We need to find somewhere to hide. We cannot keep coming to this lane, and sooner or later, someone will notice a new lady of the court walking around." She gestured toward her mother.

"We need new disguises," Emlyn agreed. "I have an idea for that, and a way to get us close to Fitzroy's chamber too, so we can see what happens next."

"Stop fidgeting, miting."

Gwynnie and Emlyn stood in the upstairs corridor of Donsen Tower, wearing new disguises. Emlyn had returned to dressing as a yeoman, but rather than carrying around the ungainly pike, she carried a short staff in front of her and a small blade at her hip.

"Where did you get those?" Gwynnie asked, nodding at the weapons' belt.

"Yeomen are always sleeping on patrol." Emlyn grinned, pulling the red and yellow bonnet down across her brow. "King Henry should probably hire men that are more vigilant in their roles. I thought I told you to stop fidgeting."

Gwynnie abandoned pulling at the loose jerkin on her shoulders. She was rather short to pull off the guise of a yeoman, so they had chosen to dress her in a footman's uniform that they had found in the laundry room. She wore a large hat on her head, with such a wide, heavy brim that if she pulled it down completely it would have swamped her face. For now, it did a thorough job of casting her face in shadow, so she was unrecognisable to anyone who walked past. With gloves on her hands, the dark brown leather masked her small and feminine fingers.

"I hear something," Emlyn muttered, tilting her head to the side. "To your position, Gwynnie."

Turning away, Gwynnie pretended to wipe down the nearest window as Emlyn sat in a nearby chair, looking close to sleep, just like many of the other guards they had seen around the palace at this time of the evening.

On the staircase there were hurried feet.

"This is absurd. Surely you do not mean to search the duke's rooms?" It was Pascal's voice. "If he knew, you'd find yourself in the Tower."

"That is why I am doing it now, as he and Renard are at the feast." Tombstone appeared at the top of the stairs. He didn't glance Gwynnie and Emlyn's way, as if they were simply part of the furniture in the corridor. "Pascal, I know this is mad — perhaps I have gone mad myself — but someone has sent this letter for a reason. What if they are right? If Fitzroy does have something to do with the queen's jewels going missing, are we just supposed to ignore it?"

"I ... well ... I didn't say that. Yet one has to remember our position. Fitzroy is the son of —"

"The king. I know." Tombstone marched toward Fitzroy's door at the far end of the corridor. "Please, just watch and be sure that Fitzroy does not return. If I find nothing, then we know whoever wrote that letter was simply out to cause trouble, and we need not pay it any further heed. Fitzroy need never hear that we searched his chambers."

"Well..." Pascal sighed. When Tombstone took his shoulder, he nodded reluctantly. "I hope you know what you are doing, boy."

As Tombstone stepped into Fitzroy's chambers, Pascal leaned against the wall, his breathing fast.

Gwynnie glanced at Emlyn, who affected a rather large yawn to cover up her whisper.

"Those two seem to know each other rather well," she observed.

Gwynnie gave a small nod.

Silence followed for a few minutes. Pascal grew restless and started pacing, his cane striking the wooden floorboards. Inside the chamber there was a heavy thud, which caused him to stop pacing and fix his attention on the door.

The door opened and Tombstone's face appeared.

"Well?" Pascal barked. "Have you lost the power of your tongue?"

"You need to see this." Tombstone opened the door wider.

Pascal paused, reluctant to enter, then stepped inside the chamber.

Gwynnie and Emlyn exchanged an uneasy look.

"We are still expecting a lot," Emlyn muttered under her breath. "If they find those jewels, they'll be accusing one of the most powerful men in London."

"In the country," Gwynnie corrected her mother.

A few seconds later, Pascal burst back out of the room. In the moonlight, Gwynnie saw a resemblance to Tombstone she hadn't noticed before. They both bore the same cheekbones, even the same jawline when viewed in profile.

"They're related," Gwynnie whispered to herself.

"Shh," Emlyn hissed, yawning dramatically once more. Gwynnie shifted her focus to the window again, straining to hear what was said further down the corridor.

"Never in all my days…" Pascal was dabbing his brow. "The king's son. The king's own son! I cannot tell him. Imagine what he would do to me if I told him! No, no. Another must do it."

"It has to be reported." Tombstone stepped out of the room. He carried the jewels in his hands. "You know who we must speak to, do you not? We must go to Cromwell. He is the only one who could report such a thing to the king."

"That's if the king will see him at all. Oh, I fear this." Pascal clutched his chest. "I fear it more than I can say."

Tombstone walked toward them, and Pascal hurried to follow. Gwynnie continued to wipe down the window, waiting until the sound of their footsteps had retreated down the staircase, then she turned to Emlyn.

"What do you think Cromwell will do?" she asked. Emlyn shook her head and tipped the bonnet back across her brow.

"Let us hope he believes in justice. We need that for someone to accuse the son of a king."

"We must wait," Emlyn ordered.

Gwynnie glanced restlessly at the door. They had moved to stand just outside the great hall, listening to the sounds of the feast happening within. Tombstone and Pascal had entered the hall a few minutes ago.

But cowering outside in the corridor told her nothing of what was happening in the feasting room. Had Tombstone gone to confront Fitzroy? Or was he reporting to Cromwell after all?

The door to the corridor opened, and a line of maids walked in, each carrying a tray of sweetmeats or sugar in bowls made of gold. The maid at the back of the line tripped on the doorjamb. Hurrying to place her tray on a ledge, she bent down, reaching for the laces on her boots to retie them.

"Gwynnie…" It was as if Emlyn could read her mind, but the muttered warning was not enough to stop her.

Gwynnie checked the footman's uniform she wore, pulling tightly on the jerkin and flicking up the collar so her chin was masked, then she hurried across to the tray the maid had discarded and held it high in the air, half covering her face as she followed the other maids into the room. She heard Emlyn sigh behind her, but there was nothing she could do to stop Gwynnie now.

The scent of cooked meat and heated flagons of wine hung in the air, while cinnamon and clove spices were either floating in wine goblets or spread across the meat. As Gwynnie walked between the tables, taking small pots of honey and rosewater from her tray and placing them on the tables, her eyes furtively searched the hall.

King Henry's table was practically empty. Queen Anne sat quite alone, staring at her plate. She moved around chunks of pheasant with her fork, but from what Gwynnie could see, she made no effort to eat.

Gwynnie searched for another. At the side of the room, where the other professional gentlemen sat, were Tombstone and Pascal. They both whispered frantically in the ears of Cromwell. The privy councillor stared forward as he listened to their words. When they were done, he stood and turned to face them. Despite the distance that separated them, Gwynnie could see well enough that Cromwell was challenging the men. No doubt he wished to be certain that what they had found in Fitzroy's chambers could not be mistaken for something else.

Gwynnie walked around the hall, being careful to add one of the golden bowls she carried to Cromwell's table.

"You searched his room? If the king should know —"

"Forgive me, my lord," Tombstone interrupted, "but would the king not care more that his son might have been the one to steal from his wife, the queen? I would have thought that would be the greater concern."

"Surely you are not accusing a duke of being one of the Shadow Cutpurses? It is an outrage! You have let ideas run away with you."

"My lord," Tombstone went on calmly, "it is the whispering of courtiers that has suggested the Shadow Cutpurses were ever in this palace at all. What if the thefts had nothing to do with their legend? It is possible, is it not?"

Cromwell didn't answer for a minute. He breathed deeply, his shoulders wideset. Despite the fact he was shorter than both Tombstone and Pascal, he seemed somehow more impressive and much more intimidating.

"I do not like this. Every bone in my body, every one of my bodily humors, argues against it. My black bile runs foul," Cromwell spat darkly. "It must be done, however. There is no way to avoid it. Come."

"Where is it we are going, my lord?" Pascal asked.

"To have a meeting with the king. You will tell him what you have found, for I will not take the blame for his son's rooms being searched." As Cromwell stepped away, Tombstone and Pascal exchanged an uneasy glance.

CHAPTER 25

"They want you in the kitchens," Emlyn growled as she strode up to the door leading to the king's chambers. She leaned against the wall beside the yeoman who was standing guard.

"Now?" The yeoman frowned. "It is not time to change."

Gwynnie stayed hidden around a corner in the corridor, waiting for her mother to move the guard along. It took some persuasion.

"I am just following orders. I do not want to be the one accused of disobeying. Do you?"

The guard clearly didn't want to get into trouble. Without a goodbye, he marched off, walking past Gwynnie's hiding place. Once he was gone, Gwynnie stepped up beside her mother, who opened a cupboard door.

"Get inside," Emlyn urged. "They will not question a yeoman of the guard standing here, but a footman without a duty will raise eyebrows."

Gwynnie stepped into the cupboard. It smelled of damp. Covering her nose, she pulled the door shut, her back pressed against the bolts of linen that filled the space.

It did not take long for Cromwell, Tombstone and Pascal to appear. What shocked Gwynnie was the voice that accompanied them. Evidently, Cromwell was not content to speak to the king about such a matter without his son being present.

"What is this insanity?" Fitzroy demanded. "Cromwell, we are feasting. My father has orders not to be disturbed. His physicians are with him. You do realise how ill he is? How close to death he came in that jousting accident —"

"Your tongue, Your Grace." The sudden words startled Gwynnie. She imagined few in the palace would have the gall to interrupt a duke, but apparently, Cromwell was one of them. "I should think a man such as yourself would be wary to even mention death after what happened to your father. He is a superstitious man. Just this morning, he demanded that all the crows and ravens be scared from the palace roofs."

Gwynnie pressed her ear close to the door, straining to listen. Like a chastised child, Fitzroy said nothing. Cromwell knocked on the door to King Henry's chambers, which was opened a minute later by the master of the stool, who at first prevented their entry. When Cromwell insisted on coming in, one of the physicians attending the king also appeared at the door.

"It is imperative we see the king." Cromwell refused to back down. "It concerns his son."

"Devel seoc," Fitzroy whispered, under his breath.

Gwynnie grimaced. She'd heard such words once before, many years ago. Someone had muttered them to her mother, accusing her of being possessed, and of no longer being in control of her own mind.

"It must be done," Cromwell ordered the physician. "The king will be furious if he does not learn of this quickly enough and knows that we have sat upon such important information as I have now received."

His power was clearly greater than Fitzroy's. The physician stepped back, and the men were ushered inside. The door clicked shut, and less than a second later, Emlyn opened the door of the cupboard.

Neither Gwynnie nor Emlyn said anything as they tiptoed to the door, straining to hear the conversation inside the king's chambers. The voices were muffled at first, so they could not discern one word from another. Fortunately, Fitzroy's outrage made him raise his voice, so they could hear everything he said.

"They are accusing me of being a thief! They should be put behind bars for such an accusation. Me? A thief? I want for nothing!"

"I am not accusing you of being a thief." Cromwell raised his voice. "Yet the circumstances do require an explanation."

"Why were the queen's jewels in your chamber, Your Grace?" It was Tombstone.

Gwynnie stiffened, her hands on either side of the doorframe. Tombstone must have been the lowest ranking man in that room, yet he persisted.

"Brash of him," Emlyn whispered, clearly thinking the same thing. "Foolhardy."

"Courageous?" Gwynnie offered.

"I do not have to explain myself to a common lawyer."

"I am asking you to explain yourself to a privy councillor and to a king," Tombstone went on.

"Elric." Pascal's voice held a warning. For all the anger and stiffness he had shown previously, he was clearly cowed by power.

"It is a simple question," Tombstone continued. "Why were the jewels in your chamber?"

"I require an explanation too," Cromwell added. "Explain the matter and this conversation will be at an end."

"There is something I wish to know…" a rather weak voice interrupted. Gwynnie's eyes widened as she realised it was the voice of the king, though it was virtually unrecognisable. "Cromwell, you came to me yesterday and said your men were hunting for two women… Maids."

"The daughter is accused of attacking Mistress Battersby," Cromwell explained.

"You see? When murder is afoot, you busy yourself with theft. How ridiculous," Fitzroy cut in.

"Would you like to know how she fares?" Tombstone asked.

"Did you speak to me?" Fitzroy grew louder in his outrage.

"It is simply that you pointed out, quite rightly, that murder, or the attempt of it, is a greater crime than theft. I presumed you would be interested to know if Mistress Battersby will recover?"

"Of course, I would like to know." The words sounded forced to Gwynnie's ears, but then she knew the truth of the matter. "I would have thought your priority would be hunting down her attacker, rather than a thief."

"Even a thief of the queen's jewels?"

What passed next, Gwynnie couldn't hear. The voices grew quieter, and she assumed the king must have been speaking again, his muffled mutters weary. She pressed her ear to the door.

"You should arrest them for their accusation," she heard Fitzroy say.

"Fitzroy." The king spoke clearly. "I do not know what is happening in this palace, but I fear someone is playing some awful game with us. You shall return the jewels to Anne at once."

"I did not take them!"

"And Cromwell, have your men find these two women. Find the one who struck down Mistress Battersby. They are the priority now."

Gwynnie stepped back from the door, her shoulders slumping. It seemed that no matter what they did to shift attention onto Fitzroy, it kept coming back to them.

"They cannot find them. They have proved themselves so useless, they accuse *me* of theft. Might I suggest we enlist the services of one of my men to find them? Renard is diligent and loyal. He has proven himself many times in the past. Two maids should be an easy quarry for him."

"Yes, yes, Fitzroy. Whatever you think." The king's words were weary once more. "Now leave me to my physicians."

Gwynnie stepped back into the cupboard as Emlyn shut the door on her. As the door to the king's chamber opened, a waft of medicinal herbs emanated from the room. There was mudwort hanging in the air, and most particularly, turpentine.

"Might I suggest one more thing?" It was Fitzroy, his voice now clearly audible with the chamber door open. "That knave, that excuse for a lawyer — I recommend we remove him from his role. Any man who accuses me of theft is not sensible of his position."

The king's answer was a tired one. "Cromwell, see that it is done."

"I beg your pardon?" Tombstone's protest came out high-pitched. "You are dismissing me from my position? But —"

"Not another word." These words were quieter, uttered by Pascal in a low tone, as he evidently dragged Tombstone out of the bedchamber and down the corridor. The two continued to argue with one another as they walked away.

Gwynnie rested her head against the wall of the cupboard, her mood growing graver by the second. It seemed that in her effort to shift the focus onto Fitzroy, she had only succeeded in making the one man who potentially believed her story, lose any power he once had.

"We'll only have a minute, so be quick."

Emlyn stood guard in front of Mistress Battersby's door as Gwynnie turned the heavy iron handle and stepped into the bedchamber. It was a relatively small room in the rafters of

Greenwich Palace. The wooden beams were so low overhead that even Gwynnie had to think twice about whether she would hit her head.

Across the room, laid out on the bed, was Esme. She had no physician to attend her. In fact, she was completely alone and fast asleep, her skin as pale as curdled milk.

Slowly, Gwynnie stepped forward, being careful not to kick over the chamber pot that sat at the foot of the bed, and reached for the bedpost. The bandage across the back of Esme's head appeared fresh and neatly bound. Gwynnie thought she saw Tombstone's work in that bandage.

"Esme?" Gwynnie whispered to her, wishing the lady would wake, but she did not. She continued to breathe evenly and deeply, showing no sign of being disturbed. "I am so sorry." It was feeble, Gwynnie knew that, but she longed to say the words regardless. She wished to tell the woman before her that she had failed her. Esme had tried to save her that night in the tiltyard, and yet Gwynnie had not raised a finger to help her husband. The guilt grew steadily worse, until Gwynnie's hand shook upon the bedpost. "I..." She longed to say more, to promise that she would keep fighting for justice, but how could she now? Justice seemed an impossibility.

Backing up from the bed, Gwynnie noticed that Florian's things were still strewn around the room. There was a thick sheaf of parchment with his name written upon it, and a man's knife laid beside the papers. A white collar was thrown across the back of the chair with a black bonnet beside the inkwell. It was almost as if Florian had only just stood up and walked out of the room.

Stepping forward, Gwynnie peered at the notes Florian had made. She could barely read his handwriting, for it was so slanted, but there was a drawing she recognised. Neat and repeated across the page in a rigid pattern was a Celtic knot. Gwynnie stared at the diagram, knowing exactly where she had seen it before.

The unusual brooch she had found in Fitzroy's chamber had been wrought in the same shape. Why would it be here? Why would Florian be recreating it on these notes? Unless it was merely a common symbol, and it was a coincidence, but the chances of that seemed unlikely indeed.

Beside the table was a wad of handkerchiefs that Esme had evidently used to dry her tears. The sight of those handkerchiefs urged Gwynnie to retreat from the room. She stepped out into the corridor, closing the door softly behind her.

"Well?" Emlyn asked. "Did you find some comfort in seeing her?" When Gwynnie shook her head, Emlyn said, "I thought not. We talk of justice. We talk of what comfort it brings, but in truth, it brings little comfort at all. The desire for it eats us alive, and even if you get it, it does not bring back what you have lost."

Gwynnie blinked, struck by the sincerity of her mother's words. Emlyn was just like Esme. They had both lost a husband to murder. Yet Emlyn had taken revenge for the death of hers, while Esme was left not knowing who had committed the deed.

"We cannot give up now," Gwynnie said, determinedly.

Emlyn cursed, so strongly that Gwynnie's eyes widened.

"A sharp tongue you have there, Ma. I knew I got it from somewhere."

"Do not turn such lessons on me now. Gwynnie, you and I are backed into a corner. Our best chance now is to swim through the flood come nightfall. It is only a matter of time before people start to question why there is an additional yeoman of the guard and a footman hanging around the palace."

"If we swim through that flood, we will either drown or die from the cold."

"Sooner that than at the end of a noose!"

"And would you leave Esme so unhappy? So desperate — as you have once been?"

"Miting, please." Emlyn breathed in sharply and turned away.

"We try to leave, we most likely die. We stay, we try for justice, and we might just live. Even if I do die at the end of a hangman's noose, I'll go to my death knowing I did everything I could to give Esme justice for her husband's death." Gwynnie blinked, feeling tears prick her eyes. "I stood by that night and listened to him die, Ma. I didn't help him when I could have done."

Emlyn stood straight and nodded once. "As you wish. We shall stay. Any ideas about where we go from here?"

"Just one. Though I do not imagine he will be pleased to see us."

CHAPTER 26

Gwynnie thrust the short metal rod firmly into the lock. It gave way beneath her touch and the door swung open. Staring into Tombstone's office, she felt her mother peering over her shoulder.

"A fine room he keeps," Emlyn muttered, striding past Gwynnie and into the office. "I never trust a man who is too tidy."

Gwynnie didn't comment. She followed her mother in and closed the door behind them. On a table beside the desk was a flagon of mead, the honey-scented liquid glistening in the remnants of sunlight that shone through the window. Emlyn poured out a glass and passed it to Gwynnie. Consumed by thirst, Gwynnie lifted the glass to her lips and gulped. All day they had been hiding, avoiding the kitchens as people were more likely to know their faces there, so they hadn't eaten a single thing.

"Gwynnie," Emlyn cautioned.

Gwynnie lowered the glass and shrugged. "I am elegant, am I not?" She slurped the mead pointedly. Emlyn just shook her head. She chose the chair behind the desk and sat back, sighing deeply and looking in danger of going to sleep. Gwynnie sat on the desk itself, picking at the manchet bread that had been left out on the tray beside the mead.

They didn't have to wait long for Tombstone to arrive. On the other side of the door, he thrust his key into the lock and made a sound of surprise to find it unlocked, then the door swung open.

"What the...? Who are you two?" He marched into the room, then came to an abrupt stop as Gwynnie took off the footman's hat and dropped it onto the desk, her hair falling around her ears.

"Good evening, Tombstone." Emlyn was the first to speak, pulling off her yeoman's hat and dropping it beside Gwynnie's. "I have talked mostly to your employer in the past. I have a feeling this is the first time you and I are seeing each other properly."

Tombstone's eyes shifted between Gwynnie and Emlyn. "Do you have any idea what is happening? You are both wanted for the attack on Mistress Battersby. Even Pascal is now starting to question if you are responsible for more — if you did indeed kill Master Battersby."

"We did not." Gwynnie's voice was firm as she chewed on the manchet bread. "Though I should have done more for him than I did."

"I beg your pardon?" Tombstone stepped forward and snatched the bread out of Gwynnie's hand, then the flagon that she was still drinking form. "What are you wearing?"

"You were looking for two maids, were you not?" Gwynnie reminded him. "How else were we supposed to dress?"

"This is mad, mad," Tombstone whispered to himself, running his hands through his coppery hair.

"He's debating whether to turn us in," Emlyn said to Gwynnie, nudging her in the back with her goblet. "He might get his position back if he does."

"I do not think he will." Gwynnie looked at Tombstone. "You believed me when I told you what truly happened to Esme Battersby, did you not?"

Tombstone paced around the room, evidently unable to stand in one place for long. "Who are you?" he asked.

Gwynnie smiled. It was the most perceptive question he had asked her. She knew what answer she had to give. Right now, the truth was their best chance.

"My name is Gwynnie," she said softly. "My mother and I have been known by many names. Thieves, cutpurses. They called us jades once. You were not so flattered by that one, were you, Ma?"

"No, I was not." Emlyn took a hefty gulp of mead. She was evidently finding it hard telling a stranger what she knew after keeping her occupation a secret for so long.

"Some call us the Shadow Cutpurses."

Tombstone's jaw dropped open. He stared at Gwynnie, his eyes wide.

"I told you he wouldn't believe us," said Emlyn, breaking the silence.

"You are…?" Tombstone hesitated, shaking his head a little, then his eyes drifted down over their clothes and he grunted, as if holding back a laugh. "Hiding in plain sight."

"Lots of people do not notice maids," Gwynnie explained. "Just as they do not notice footmen or yeomen. We are just always supposed to be there."

Tombstone returned the flagon of mead to the desk and Gwynnie snatched it up again. She managed just one swallow before he took it out of her grasp. "I did not say you could steal my mead."

Gwynnie let him take the flagon back from her, but while he was distracted, she managed to steal another piece of manchet bread.

"Why are you here?" He glanced between the pair of them. "You could have taken your chance in the flood by now. You must know that I have to take you to Pascal and Cromwell. I have no choice."

"You do have a choice," Emlyn said as she put down her goblet. "You can either let us go or arrest us for stealing."

"From what I know, one of the Shadow Cutpurses is wanted for more than just theft." He leaned across the desk. "One of you killed a man, years ago."

Emlyn met his gaze. "That was not Gwynnie." Her voice was cold. "You want a thief with blood on her hands, you look to me. Not my daughter."

The silence stretched, as if Tombstone couldn't quite believe Emlyn had so willingly confessed to her crime. Gwynnie was shocked too, though she knew at once why her mother had said it. She wasn't going to risk Gwynnie being arrested for murder.

"You intend to arrest me for murder?" Emlyn asked. "As well as larceny?"

"Yes," Tombstone asserted.

"This was a bad idea."

"It was the only idea we had left," Gwynnie reminded her mother. She nudged Tombstone on the arm, knowing she had to tell him everything. "I stole Fitzroy's jewels."

Tombstone shifted his focus to her. "Your mother was your distraction, talking to the yeoman so you could sneak into the tower."

"She was." Gwynnie nodded. "I was hiding in Fitzroy's garderobe when he and a visitor came in."

"Renard?"

"No." Gwynnie shook her head. "Florian Battersby."

Tombstone sat down suddenly. He gestured for her to go on, his expression unreadable.

"Florian tried to blackmail Fitzroy. He challenged him regarding his relationship with Master Woodville."

Tombstone lowered his hand onto the arm of the chair, seeming shocked but not outraged.

Gwynnie halted, remembering how she had seen Tombstone's head turned at the joust. Not for the first time did she wonder if Tombstone and Fitzroy shared something in common.

"Florian threatened to tell the king of his son's nature. He said it was no scandal in the theatre, even in the streets of London. But the son of a king?"

"The son of a king like Henry," Emlyn added.

"Fitzroy was desperate. He started crying, stamping around the room, not knowing what to do with himself."

"All this time, you were hidden in the garderobe?" Tombstone asked.

Gwynnie nodded. "I thought of climbing out of the window, but then the accusation changed. Florian accused Fitzroy of being behind Master Woodville's disappearance..."

Tombstone was as still as his name suggested he should be — not a twitch, not a blink.

"The tumult built." Gwynnie took a shuddery breath. "Then Fitzroy put his hands around Florian's throat and strangled him to death. And I ... I did nothing to stop it."

Emlyn nudged Gwynnie in the back, prompting her to go on.

"Afterward, Fitzroy was muttering 'not again', and he was quite mad. He left the chamber, and I went to check on Florian, but..." She paused, not wishing to say the words. "Fitzroy came back with Renard, and I hid in the garderobe once more. Renard said it was like before..."

"You mean he ... he had killed before?" Tombstone's voice was strangely quiet.

"The intimation was that he had strangled Master Woodville, too."

Tombstone took a deep breath. "What happened next?"

"They heard me. I left through the window, and they chased after me, terrified of what I had seen. Ever since, Renard has been watching me, threatening me. He urged Fitzroy to keep me alive the night that Mistress Battersby found me in the tiltyard. He wanted to frame me for Florian's murder, so suspicion would not fall on Fitzroy."

Tombstone stood abruptly. He marched across the room and threw a log onto the fire, lighting it with a tinderbox and stoking the flames with the poker. He sat down on the hearth, his temple in the palm of one hand. He didn't say anything for some minutes.

"You are sure of what he said?" Tombstone asked, lowering his hand. "Regarding Jerome?"

Gwynnie moved off the desk, noting that Tombstone had referred to Woodville by his Christian name. "How well did you know Master Woodville?"

He didn't answer her. Instead, he looked down at the scorched hearth rug beneath his feet. Gwynnie, however, had a good idea of what might have taken place. She crossed the room toward Tombstone and sat beside him, on the other side of the hearth.

"You knew him well?"

"For a time." Tombstone wouldn't look at her. "We were good ... friends."

"In the manner that Fitzroy was so keen to keep hidden regarding his own relationship with Woodville?" At her words, he looked at her keenly. "I would not disapprove of such a thing," she whispered. "I had noticed at the tiltyard that your head was turned by another man."

Tombstone grimaced and looked away, shaking his head as if angry at himself.

"You are certain? Absolutely certain of what you heard? What you saw?"

"I am." Gwynnie noticed that he hadn't questioned her confession about being in Fitzroy's rooms. Clearly, he was prepared to believe that they were the Shadow Cutpurses. "When you inspected his body, you saw that Florian had walked on glass. A glass was broken in Fitzroy's room. When Fitzroy attacked him, he trampled that glass into his boots. You also said the wound wasn't right, that he may have had his throat cut after he died. I think Renard moved the body then cut his throat to cover up the bruises."

Tombstone nodded and sniffed, the only sign that he was fighting back tears.

Gwynnie nudged closer to Tombstone. "I am sorry. I didn't know you and Master Woodville were so close."

"No one did. It was only for a short time, last year," Tombstone said quietly. "A few months, then we parted ways. I did not realise he and Fitzroy..." He trailed off, waving his hand in the air.

"What sort of man was he?"

"Gentle." Tombstone sat taller. "Softly spoken, easily led. I remember seeing him in Fitzroy's company once." He grimaced. "He seemed brasher than before, more outspoken than I had ever seen him. He was Irish by birth. He had the most distinctive voice."

"Irish?" Gwynnie hadn't heard this before. "He had Celtic roots?"

"That he did."

"Did he..." Gwynnie sat forward, gesturing to her chest. "Did he wear a brooch?"

"What?" Tombstone flicked his head around.

"Did he wear a brooch? One with a Celtic knot inlaid in silver?" Suddenly things made sense. She understood why the brooch did not look as if it belonged in Fitzroy's collection. She understood why it was hidden in the lid of that box. She understood too why Florian Battersby had drawn it in his notes when he was looking into Woodville's disappearance.

"He did." Tombstone nodded. "Why do you ask?"

"Because I saw it. When I took Fitzroy's jewels, it was in his collection."

Tombstone stood up suddenly. "Show me."

CHAPTER 27

"What are you doing?" Tombstone asked in panic as they entered the building that housed the maids' chambers.

"Well, you have no power to move the guard from our chamber door anymore, do you?" Gwynnie reminded him.

As a maid walked past them, Tombstone grabbed her lawyer's bonnet and pulled it further down her brow. Gwynnie waited until the maid's footsteps had retreated before she pushed the hat back up again. She glanced at Emlyn, who shook her head in bemusement.

"I see you know how to act with perfect ease," Gwynnie muttered wryly. For a change, her mother smiled at her sarcasm.

"Leave it to me." Emlyn walked down the corridor, her stance widening as she walked, and she laid her hands on the weapons belt of her yeoman's uniform.

"What is she doing?" Tombstone stepped forward, evidently intent on following her.

Worried that his alarm would reveal their identity to the guard who stood by their chamber door, Gwynnie moved in front of him and stepped on his toe, stopping him from going any further.

"Ow! What was that for?"

"My mother is adept at getting into places that are guarded. You wish to see that brooch? Then leave it to us." Gwynnie folded her arms and stood calmly beside him.

Emlyn must have told the guard there was a shift change, for the guard nodded and headed for the nearest staircase. She took his place outside their bedchamber, leaning against the wall as she waited for Gwynnie to approach, Tombstone behind her.

"I cannot believe that worked," he said under his breath. "He didn't even look at your face."

"People see what they expect to see. They don't often look beyond to see what is wrong with the picture." Emlyn reached into her doublet and produced a key, which she passed to Gwynnie.

Within seconds, Gwynnie had the door open. Their chamber was much as they had left it, except it had plainly been searched. The covers on the beds weren't quite flat, and the coffer lid was open, with half the contents strewn across the floor. Emlyn shot an accusing glare at Tombstone as Gwynnie moved toward the stone windowsill.

"Pascal," Tombstone explained.

Gwynnie lifted the stone with some difficulty, grunting as it came away, then reached inside and pulled out the linen-wrapped bundles. She dropped them onto her bed and unravelled each one, revealing the jewels. She sifted through the glittering gold and precious stones they'd held back before she found the brooch she was looking for. Slowly, Tombstone walked forward, his jaw slack as he stared at the mound of jewels on the bed.

"I didn't think… I didn't want to think that *you…*" he hissed, glaring at her.

"What? Are you like your employer in that you do not think a woman can be a thief?" Gwynnie asked, gesturing to the jewels.

"No." Tombstone's glare was not half so level as it had been before. He constantly looked away, as if the foundations he stood upon had been shaken. "I just remember seeing your face the morning Florian Battersby was discovered."

"You noticed me that much?"

"You were the only maid around the body," he reminded her. "Perhaps I did not want to think that someone who could feel such grief, who had a heart, would be a thief."

Gwynnie's hands grew slack around the Celtic brooch. She thrust it toward him. "Being a thief does not give me a heart carved of black stone."

Tombstone said nothing. He took the brooch and moved to the window, the better to see it. He buffed the metal with the sleeve of his doublet, sniffed once more and looked out of the window. For a few seconds Gwynnie thought he was holding back more tears.

Emlyn shrugged and leaned against the closed door. Her eyes lingered on Tombstone, wary that he was going to turn them in at any second.

"Is it his?" Gwynnie asked.

"It's his." Tombstone turned back to face her. His face was red, but he didn't let his tears fall. "Very well, I believe you. I believe that you saw what you say you saw. Nothing else would explain why Fitzroy had this in his possession." He clutched the brooch so tightly that his knuckles went white. "But I can't take this to Pascal or Cromwell. At this point, neither one of them would believe me. I have no power anymore."

"Unless..." Gwynnie stepped forward. "What if we could find Jerome? Another body would force the investigation to cover two murders, rather than just one. And the first happened before my mother and I arrived. It would be impossible to blame us for it."

"Then we need to find where Jerome is now."

"You are certain of this?" Tombstone asked, his pace so fast that Gwynnie had to run to keep up with him, struggling in her footman's garb. They had left Emlyn standing in the archway, beneath Donsen Tower, as they marched across the dock on the river Thames.

"Old Rudyard saw them," Gwynnie puffed, out of breath. "He saw Fitzroy and Woodville together. They stood here, hooting at the moon, on New Year's Eve."

Tombstone came to a sudden halt in the middle of the dock as Gwynnie caught up to him. She rested her hands on her knees, breathing deeply.

"Here?" Tombstone turned on the spot.

"Yes." Gwynnie stood tall and looked out over the river, surprised at how much the flooding had retreated. More and more of the wooden dock was visible, the icy banks plain, with frosted grass on either side. She peered into the distance, toward London town, wondering if the wherrymen would soon be working again.

There was now a chance that she and Emlyn could escape from the palace, if the river continued to recede.

"New Year's Eve," Tombstone muttered, more to himself than to her.

"Did you not see him that night?" Gwynnie asked, glancing back at him.

"No. I was not here. I was on business for Pascal." Tombstone moved his hands to his hips. "If what Florian accused Fitzroy of was right, then…" He turned on his heel and looked back toward Donsen Tower.

"What?" Gwynnie said impatiently. "What is it?"

"You said Florian accused him of relations with Jerome."

"I did." Gwynnie nodded.

"Then where would they go from here?" Tombstone pointed back toward Donsen Tower. "They had spent the evening together, drank, and hooted at the moon out of their wits.

Where would they go but the closest bedchamber? Not to Fitzroy's."

"Why not?"

"Because Jerome's was nearer and fewer courtiers would have been around to see." Tombstone took off back toward the tower. Heaving, Gwynnie ran after him again, struggling to keep up. Emlyn followed them as they hurried past. Rather than taking the main staircase, Tombstone led them to a much narrower one, built of wood and hidden behind two doors.

At the top of the staircase, Tombstone stepped out into a narrow corridor built into the rafters, with low-hanging beams. He reached a door and laid a hand on the wood.

"Master Woodville's?" Gwynnie asked.

Tombstone nodded. He looked quite sick as he turned the door handle and stepped inside.

Emlyn stood guard outside the door, returning to her role as a yeoman.

Tombstone hovered on the threshold as Gwynnie stepped into the room, the better to see the place. It was a relatively small chamber, not dissimilar in size to Esme Battersby's, though the walls were draped with fine tapestries and a coffer at the foot of the bed was heavily carved and inlaid, which Gwynnie thought odd for a man who was merely a low courtier.

Gwynnie looked through the coffer, not particularly sure what she was searching for, other than any clue as to where Jerome might be now. She soon saw that Sarah had been right about this chamber. All of Woodville's clothes had been left where they were. The coffer was still full of hoses and jerkins.

"Maybe this is where it happened," Tombstone whispered, as Gwynnie turned to face him. His cheeks had paled to the colour of the frost beyond the window. "Maybe this is where

226

he…" He broke off and rubbed his face. "What was it Battersby said to Fitzroy about this night?"

"He asked if Woodville had threatened to tell the king about their relationship."

"Ah." Tombstone crossed the room. He glanced over his shoulder at Emlyn, apparently not wanting her to hear his next words. He lowered his voice so only Gwynnie could hear him. "Jerome once threatened to tell Pascal about my … tastes too." He sighed heavily. "Where do you think he got the money for these fine things?"

Gwynnie was stunned. She looked around the room again at the coffer and the fine clothes within.

"You think that he tried to blackmail Fitzroy too? Then Fitzroy panicked and he…" She trailed off and closed her eyes, once more seeing the way Fitzroy had latched his hands around Florian's throat. "If it happened here, Fitzroy would have gone to Renard, as he did after he killed Master Battersby."

"Fitzroy is practically still a child. He goes to Renard for everything." Tombstone moved to the window.

"That's right… In Fitzroy's chambers Renard said that he would remedy it. He said that he had sorted it before and would do so again." She followed Tombstone to the window. "So, where would he have taken the body if he carried it out of here? He could have dropped it in the water?"

"No. It's too public." Tombstone nodded down at the dock where they had just been standing. "On New Year's Eve, they have fireworks and grand displays on the docks at midnight. Renard would have had to take the body elsewhere."

"There is only one way in and out of this building." Gwynnie pressed her nose to the glass, gazing at the yeoman who stood by the door of Donsen Tower. It was the same yeoman whom

Emlyn had talked to, the night that Gwynnie had broken into Fitzroy's chambers. "That yeoman must have seen something."

Tombstone strode out of the room.

"Do you ever walk slowly?" Gwynnie huffed and chased after him again, with Emlyn falling into step behind them. When they reached the staircase, Emlyn took hold of Gwynnie's shoulder, holding her back.

"When all of this is said and done, we need a way out of the palace —"

Tombstone turned at the bottom of the stairs, evidently having heard. His eyes flashed with anger as they settled on Emlyn, and they all fell still.

"I have no qualms about arresting killers, Mistress Wightham. I may be working with thieves in order to find one killer, but it does not wipe away your sin."

Gwynnie blinked, feeling as if she had been kicked in the gut. "You intend to arrest us both when this is done, do you not?"

Tombstone said nothing. He did not need to. He walked away, leaving them to hurry behind once more. Emlyn's hand tightened on Gwynnie's shoulder, and she nodded knowingly. Tombstone may be helping them for now, but it was not a support that would last. He would only use them for as long as it was convenient.

They stepped out into the main courtyard, and Emlyn was careful to walk swiftly away, hiding her face from the yeoman who would undoubtedly recognise her if he looked too closely. Gwynnie stayed close to Tombstone, half hiding her face behind his shoulder.

"What's your name?" Tombstone asked the yeoman, bowing his head in greeting.

"Cuthbert, sir."

"Were you guarding Donsen Tower on New Year's Eve?"

"I was, sir." The man nodded, his large hat slipping down his brow. He nudged it back up again.

"Did you see Monsieur Renard come by here that night? Or the Duke of Richmond?"

"The duke, sir? Aye, he and Master Woodville went to look at the fireworks. Didn't see them after that."

"And Monsieur Renard? Did you see him?" Tombstone asked tartly.

Cuthbert shifted between his feet then nodded. "Aye, I did. He came out in a most strange state, just as the final fireworks sounded. I asked him if he was well, and he said he was well enough, but he looked most sick to me. Ruddy and sweating. He was carrying something too, over his shoulder, see?" He mimicked the position, pretending to have something slung across his back. "Wrapped in a heavy cloak it was."

"Where did he go?" Tombstone demanded.

"Toward the stables, sir." Cuthbert pointed under an archway.

CHAPTER 28

Gwynnie stood in the middle of the stables, listening to the horses whinnying. Night had firmly fallen, and with no light to guide them, she waited for her eyes to adjust to the darkness. To her right was a line of stalls, with some of the horses' noses peering over the tops of the doors. To her left were stacks of hay.

Gwynnie moved slowly across the stone floor, listening as Tombstone and Emlyn followed behind her.

Tombstone was struggling to light something. He repeatedly struck the flint wool from a tinderbox; the sound scratched in the air, but no light followed.

"Give it here," Emlyn ordered.

"I know how to light a lantern."

"Your hands are shaking. Little wonder. If I was searching for my lover's body too, my hands would shake."

"I did not call him that —"

"Shh." Gwynnie waved her hand at the two of them, worried that someone walking past the stables might overhear their conversation.

Emlyn succeeded in lighting the wool and pressed the orange flame to a candle set in an iron lantern. She dropped the flint wool to the stone floor, where it burnt itself out, then closed the glass door of the lantern and passed it back to Tombstone. He took it, staring at her in wonder.

"Did you think that because I am wanted for murder, I am not capable of any kindness?" She raised an eyebrow and walked past him, moving toward Gwynnie.

"Ma, this is not the time for that conversation," Gwynnie warned, but Emlyn shrugged, clearly deciding she would speak as she wished to.

"Why would Renard bring the body here?"

"It is simple enough." Gwynnie walked on. At the back of the stables, she swept aside a heavy curtain and waited for Tombstone to catch up. The light from the lantern fell on a second chamber, full of small carriages and carts. "He must have hoped to hide the body in a carriage and take it away come morning."

"That wouldn't have been possible." Tombstone stepped forward, holding the lantern higher. "From New Year's Day, any new arrivals came by the wherrymen. The flood had risen too high across the south lawns, blocking Woolwich Road."

Gwynnie glanced at her mother. They too had arrived by the wherrymen just a few days later.

"So, he's still here?" Gwynnie's eyes darted around the stable.

"It doesn't smell." Tombstone stepped forward, his gaze searching. "The stench grows worse by the day."

"You have much experience, do you?" Emlyn asked.

"It is my responsibility to investigate any strange deaths in or around the palace." Tombstone looked back at her, his expression grave. "I should think that from your past, you too know how a body can smell."

Emlyn said nothing and moved to the carriages, opening doors and searching inside.

"How would you stop a body from smelling?" Gwynnie asked.

"Covering it in something, like the cloak the yeoman described, would not be enough. You'd have to be rid of the body itself. Perhaps dump it in the river."

231

"You already said that would have been impossible with the fireworks."

"Then you'd have to bury it."

Gwynnie looked down at the heavy stone floor. At the far end of the chamber were bales of hay, stacked on top of one another. She grabbed the top bale, rolling it off the others. Tombstone held the lantern up high as she shifted the other bales.

A stone slab had been moved. It rested against the back wall of the chamber, revealing mounded earth beneath.

Gwynnie said nothing as Tombstone laid the lantern down on the nearest ledge. He disappeared out of the chamber, into another back room, where something metallic clunked. He returned a few seconds later carrying a spade in one hand and a fork that was usually used for the hay in the other. Gwynnie took the fork, though it was tall and unwieldy, and she struggled to thrust it into the ground.

Without a word, they began to dig. The earth was solid because of the cold air, though it was obvious it had recently been turned over. Emlyn joined them, and when Gwynnie grew tired, she took over, making the hard ground soft with the fork, which Tombstone then shifted to the side in a fresh pile beside the hay.

It took a long time. The candle in the lantern was burning down and Gwynnie had just replaced it with a fresh candle when Emlyn stopped, the fork in the air.

"Halt," she ordered.

Tombstone raised the spade as Emlyn reached down and shifted some of the earth with her hand.

Gwynnie stepped around Tombstone to peer in.

Emlyn had revealed a stretch of black cloth within the earth.

They both looked at Tombstone.

"Let me be the one," he whispered. "Please."

Emlyn and Gwynnie both retreated back from the earth, watching as Tombstone laid down the spade.

He took a shuddery breath as he knelt down. He reached into the hole and took hold of the black cloth. With one tug, he pulled the corner of it back.

The pale face that appeared, grey as sour milk, was a shock.

"God's blood!" Gwynnie cried. For a change, Emlyn didn't reprimand her.

A groan escaped Tombstone and he sat back. He stared into the open grave, down at the face of the man he had not only once called a friend, but something dearer.

Gwynnie bit her lip. It didn't matter that she hadn't known this man. Finding him here felt wrong indeed. He should have been buried in consecrated ground, by family and those who loved him. His cheeks were hollow, his eyes shut, and he had started to decay. Gwynnie did her best not to look at the single maggot she saw working its way across the base of the man's jaw.

A heavy sniff broke the silence and Tombstone's shoulders shuddered.

Gwynnie stepped forward. She sat down beside Tombstone and startled herself by laying a hand on his shoulder.

He kept his face turned down, refusing to look at her. The strangled cry he was clearly trying to smother came out more as a grunt. "I never thought it would come to this, not when I heard he had disappeared."

Gwynnie looked down at the grave, wondering if his fate had been inevitable. It seemed that Jerome Woodville had made a habit of blackmailing men to keep their secret. One day, he had gone too far and tried to blackmail one of the most powerful men in the country, a man who was as used to power as she was used to being ignored in the streets by those that walked by. It was almost little wonder that Fitzroy would sooner be a murderer than pay Jerome.

"Fitzroy has killed more than once now," Gwynnie whispered.

"We need to be certain," Tombstone said, wiping his cheeks with the sleeve of his doublet. "We can link Renard to the body, for he was seen. But not Fitzroy."

Gwynnie released Tombstone and lowered herself into the grave. She pulled at the cloth.

"Don't, Gwynnie," Emlyn urged. "Let the dead rest in peace."

"I am sorry," Gwynnie whispered, then pulled the cloth back from his neck.

Despite the fact that weeks had passed since his death, and the body was beginning to decay, the bruising around the pale neck was still visible.

"It is the same," she murmured quietly. "Fitzroy strangled him. It is how Florian looked, before Renard slit his throat."

She sat back on her haunches, allowing both Emlyn and Tombstone to see what she had found.

The stench was awful. Gwynnie raised her arm and breathed into the sleeve of the lawyer's robes, preferring the scent of starch and lye to the dank fetor of death.

"I can see the truth." Tombstone said, all signs of his tears now gone. "I can see it plainly before me." He waved a hand at the body. "But do we persuade the king? He will not want to believe his son capable of this. Not without proof. We need someone to say they have seen Fitzroy."

"You have me," Gwynnie reminded him. "I saw Fitzroy murder Battersby."

"And you are a maid." His deep voice silenced her. "The king simply will not believe the word of a maid."

Gwynnie retreated from the grave. She sat beside Tombstone again, as Emlyn sat down on her other side.

"Kings and their sons have power as long as they have powerful men around them," Emlyn said, rather coolly. "If you can't get the son, can you get his man?"

Gwynnie looked at Emlyn, then she turned to Tombstone.

"Renard," they said together.

"Stop Renard," Gwynnie went on, "and perhaps Fitzroy's power will be arrested. He will no longer have a man that will cover up for him."

"But how do we get him?" Tombstone shook his head. "You planted those jewels on him, did you not? And that hardly worked. He has a habit of ferreting his way out of bad business." He glanced down at Woodville's face. "Please, cover him again."

Once more, Gwynnie reached down into the grave. As respectfully as she could, she covered poor Woodville's face.

She was about to question what they should do with him when an idea occurred to her. One other person knew where Jerome Woodville was, and perhaps they could use that as a way to get him.

"What are you thinking, miting?" Emlyn asked, her eyes on Gwynnie's face.

She looked up with the smallest of smiles. "I have thought of a way," she said softly. "A way to capture Renard, but first … we will need to speak to Pascal." Her gaze shifted to Tombstone. "We need him to trust you again."

"He doesn't trust me." Tombstone shook his head and stood abruptly. "In case you hadn't noticed, your last plots lost me my position."

"And you are telling me you cannot make him listen to you now?"

"No. I cannot. I no longer work for him."

"How strange, because I could have sworn you two were connected by something more than position." She stood up beside Tombstone, watching as his jaw grew slack. "Same jawline, same eyes." She pointed at his face. "You are related, are you not?"

"God's pestilence on you! How did you know that?" He stepped back in sudden panic. "It is a secret."

"You are alike," she said. "You say he will not listen to you anymore, because you no longer work for him, but will he not listen to you when you are his own blood?"

Tombstone's eyes narrowed. "I think I underestimated that little maid I saw, crouching beside Battersby's body."

"Every man underestimates a maid. So, will you do it? Will you speak to Pascal?"

"I do not like this, miting." Emlyn sat fidgeting in the corner of the stable, pulling at the yeoman's gloves. They had scarcely moved since Tombstone had left. The hours had gone on, and morning light could not be far off now. "When Pascal comes, you and I can call ourselves hanged already."

"Shh," Gwynnie pleaded with her mother. "At least this way, justice is done."

"Hang justice!" Emlyn muttered harshly.

"Hang it?" Gwynnie repeated, looking at Emlyn. "What happened to you? What happened to the woman who came back to our attic rooms with blood on her palms, saying justice was served at last?"

Emlyn said nothing. She just rubbed her hands together, as if they still had blood upon them and she was trying desperately to wipe it off.

There were sounds across the stable and a lantern light appeared. Two figures appeared, with Tombstone leading the way and Pascal following behind, leaning on his cane. His eyes shot to Gwynnie and Emlyn in the corner.

"Good evening to you, sir," Emlyn said in her usual tone, lifting her hat so that her face was fully visible.

Pascal pursed his lips but said nothing.

"See for yourself." Tombstone gestured to the grave.

When Pascal didn't move, and seeing that Tombstone was reluctant to touch the corpse another time, Gwynnie stood up. She climbed back into the grave and pulled the cloth from Woodville's face, covering her mouth and nose to try and block out some of the stench.

Pascal inhaled deeply. The silence stretched out before he nodded at Gwynnie, and she replaced the cloth.

"You need to trust me," Tombstone pleaded with Pascal. "Everything I have told you is the truth."

"Even if it is true," Pascal croaked, "how do we prove it? How do we capture Renard as you wish to?"

Tombstone glanced at Gwynnie, nodding for her to speak.

"You wish me to listen to a maid?" Pascal gawped in sudden anger. "The word of a maid is what you're going on here?"

"Or the word of a thief," Gwynnie said, climbing out of the grave and moving toward him. "From where you are, sir, I'd say you do not have many other options."

CHAPTER 29

"This will work, trust me," Gwynnie told Tombstone. She was dressed in a footman's uniform again, carrying a tray with a flagon of mead and two goblets upon it. The sunlight streaming through the window of Tombstone's office glinted off the silver tray.

"Trust a thief, eh?" Tombstone said, adjusting the laces of his doublet as he turned to face the looking glass above the fireplace.

"Sounds like a wise idea, does it not?" Gwynnie asked, catching his eye in the mirror. He paused momentarily with his laces, before continuing. "Speaking of wise ideas," she went on, "if this works, what do you plan to do next?"

"About what?"

"About my mother and I."

He turned and lifted the flagon of mead, pouring it into the two goblets. His eyes never once met hers.

"Will you arrest us?"

"I investigate crimes," he said simply. "What do you wish me to do? Allow a killer to walk free?"

Gwynnie stiffened. He had not mentioned the thefts, nor her. He was plainly referring to her mother alone.

Footsteps sounded in the corridor.

"He comes," Tombstone said.

Gwynnie adjusted her hat and moved to the side of the room, still carrying the tray, as Tombstone crossed to his desk. A light knock sounded at the door.

"Come!" Tombstone called. The door opened and a familiar figure walked in.

It was Renard, his face more haggard and tired than when Gwynnie had seen it last. She presumed he was suffering some sleepless nights now he could no longer find Gwynnie. He didn't even glance her way as he stepped into the room.

"You sent for me," Renard said, his accent thick. "I do not have time to discuss matters with a man who no longer has his position. I need to do what you could not and find those two women."

"It is them I wished to speak to you about. Please." Tombstone gestured to the chair in front of his desk. "I only wish to help at this time."

Renard seemed to weigh up his options. Eventually, he closed the door behind him and went to sit down.

Gwynnie stepped forward and placed the two goblets on the desk, alongside the flagon of mead.

"Thank you." Tombstone gave a curt wave, the signal for her to leave. Gwynnie stepped out of the room, closed the door, then pressed her ear to the wood, listening intently to the rest of their conversation.

"What is it you wish to say?" asked Renard.

"I have found them."

"What?"

"I have found Mistress Wightham and her daughter, but there is a problem." Tombstone paused. "Pascal does not believe me. Alone, I cannot bring them in."

"Not strong enough to defeat a couple of maids, eh?" Renard sneered.

"They have evaded your capture for long enough, have they not?" Tombstone reminded him. "I wish you to help me bring them in."

"Why?"

"If I can be of use, then there's a chance I will get my position back."

"Self-gain. Now I understand you." Renard's voice steadied, as if he was more ready to believe the claim than before. "Where are they?"

"That I can tell you later. Meet me tonight in the main courtyard, and we'll go together to find them. Midnight."

"Why not go now?"

"Because they like to hide," Tombstone said offhandedly. "They move about, but I know where they sleep at night. There is, however, one impediment."

"What is that?"

"The daughter, Gwynnie Wightham. She claims to have found Jerome Woodville's body."

"What? His body? But she can't have... He left. Everyone knows he walked out one night."

"Well, it seems Mistress Gwynnie's claims might dispute that." Tombstone hurried on. "She intends to use her knowledge of where the body is to bargain for her freedom. So, I give you this warning. You and I will bring her and her mother in, but we must accept the fact that they might not stay behind bars, if the exchange of information is made."

"I see. You are putting me on my guard."

"I am. Do we have an understanding, Renard? We help one another, and we both please our masters."

There was a long pause.

A lawyer walked down the corridor and Gwynnie shifted, standing with the tray in her grasp as if she was waiting to be called into the room, rather than eavesdropping on the conversation inside. The lawyer didn't even look her way but hurried on.

"Midnight? Very well," Renard said coolly on the other side of the door. A chair creaked, as if he stood, and Gwynnie darted down the corridor in the shadow of the lawyer, hiding as quickly as she could.

"What if Renard does not come?" Emlyn asked, peering over the stall in the stable. She was dressed in her maid's gown once again, though Gwynnie was still dressed as a footman. Struggling to peer over the side of the stall, she kicked an empty pail over, placed it on its open end, then stood on top, so she was at her mother's height.

Ahead of them, through the shadows of the dark stable, they could just about see the haystacks. They had reburied Jerome Woodville in the early hours of the morning, then returned the haystacks to their place on top of the grave.

"He will come," Gwynnie whispered. "He will not take the chance of the body being discovered, fearing it will link Fitzroy to the death. After all, it is known that Fitzroy was seen in Woodville's company on the night he went missing. There will be questions to answer."

Footsteps echoed through the stable and they both ducked down, hiding behind the stall once more.

"It is us!" Tombstone called, and they both popped their heads above the stall again.

Tombstone walked alongside Pascal, who seemed to be struggling with his cane, his cheeks puffing out as he breathed heavily.

"Take your position," Tombstone urged Pascal and pointed to the stall where Emlyn and Gwynnie were hiding.

He didn't move but glared at the pair of them.

"I am no monster, sir," Emlyn said calmly. "I am still the woman you comforted so kindly."

"We do not have time for this." Tombstone kicked open the stall door and as good as pushed Pascal inside.

Gwynnie glanced at Pascal. There was some alarm in his expression, but no anger. Whatever the relationship between the pair of them, he had to be used to Tombstone by now.

In the end, Pascal took up his place in the far corner of the stall, as far from Emlyn and Gwynnie as he could get. Gwynnie closed the stall door as Tombstone moved to the other side of the stable and passed under an arched beam, where he had retrieved the spade and fork the night before. Once inside, he must have blown out the candle in the lantern, as all turned dark.

Gwynnie latched her hands over the stall ledge, her fingers gripping so tightly, she was in danger of getting splinters. Beside her, Emlyn was tense, seemingly ready to leap out and run at any minute.

They stood there for what felt like an hour, staring into the darkness and waiting for something to happen.

"He will not come," Pascal muttered behind Gwynnie. "This is all some terrible misunderstanding, a mistake, yes. Renard will not come, for he does not know the body is here."

"Shh," Gwynnie ordered him.

"How dare you —"

"Shh!" Emlyn seconded. This time, he obeyed, though Gwynnie rather thought he could have been stunned into silence.

In the distance, a horse neighed. Then another whinnied, as if objecting to something. There was a scuffed footstep on the stone floor. Someone was coming this way.

Gwynnie sank down a little, as did Emlyn, both peering over the edge of the stall. A single shaft of moonlight through one of the stable windows fell on the hay.

A stocky figure appeared before them with a shovel resting on his shoulder. As he moved into the moonlight, his wiry hair became noticeable and Gwynnie elbowed her mother in confirmation. It was Renard.

He stared at the hay for a full minute, as if debating with himself what to do next, then he acted suddenly. He grabbed the haystacks and tossed them to the side as quickly as he could. Once the earth was revealed beneath, he started digging. Gwynnie winced with each thrust he made, fearing that he might strike Woodville's body.

They let Renard dig a short way into the hole, before Tombstone made the first move.

"Put the shovel down, Renard."

Renard halted, the shovel frozen in mid-air. Tombstone appeared under the timber arch, a spade in his hand. It was a makeshift weapon, if needed.

Gwynnie stepped down off the pail and took a lantern up from the floor, lighting it using a tinderbox. She followed Emlyn out of the stall, with Pascal behind them.

Renard's eyes widened when he saw Pascal, and he realised just how trapped he was.

"I…" He tried to talk. "I…" Then he gave up, dropping the shovel to the stone floor with a heavy clunk.

"How did you know where to find this body, Renard?" Tombstone asked. "You must have been here when it was put in the ground. Why would you be trying to move it?"

Renard's head flicked toward Gwynnie. She saw the light of recognition in his eyes as his gaze settled on her face, followed by a flash of pure fury. She had led him to this moment, and that seemed to cut deeply, as much as being caught.

"Did you kill Woodville?" Pascal abruptly stepped forward. "Did you do it? Did you strangle him? Did you strangle Florian Battersby too?"

"No. It was not me." Renard moved his hands to his hips.

"Yet you know who did do it." Tombstone's voice grew louder, his anger building. "You know what they do to murderers, Renard? You must have been to a hanging or two. It is not a fair sight, is it?"

A muscle twitched in Renard's cheek, and he raised a hand, scratching his jaw. There was a look of understanding on his face.

"You can avoid the noose," Tombstone said, stepping forward. "You can avoid it if you tell us the truth."

Renard's head lifted slowly, his eyes widening.

"Put down in writing who did the deed, and you will not feel the noose."

Renard looked at Pascal, as if waiting on his confirmation.

"It is the deal we offer," Pascal seconded. "Will you do it? Will you name the killer?"

Renard turned to Gwynnie. He said nothing for a minute, seeming to weigh up his options. He must have known that with another in the room able to point the finger at Fitzroy, he stood a chance of being believed if he did reveal the truth.

Gwynnie smiled when she saw him part his lips. A maid's word may not have been believed in court, but a man of the gentry would stand a better chance.

"It was Henry Fitzroy, the Duke of Richmond."

CHAPTER 30

"Do not say a word." Pascal waved his cane between Gwynnie and Emlyn. "You understand? Not a word."

Emlyn nodded as Gwynnie raised an eyebrow, hardly appreciating being told to hold her tongue.

"Please, do not," Tombstone said, evidently reading Gwynnie's expression. "This will be a hard enough meeting without a thief speaking against the king's son."

Reluctantly, Gwynnie nodded. She knew what he said was true. Her position counted against her, and her best bet now was to leave the speaking to another.

They stood in the withdrawing chamber, tucked behind the great hall. It was a much more private room, with the walls cloaked in tapestries, and rather than a throne or any large chair, there was a much smaller seat placed on a platform. Canopies hung from the ceiling behind it.

"It's a room for private audiences with the king," Tombstone whispered in her ear.

"The king?" Gwynnie breathed out the words. "He is coming?"

"If he can walk," Tombstone added, looking uneasy at the idea.

Gwynnie and Emlyn stood behind Tombstone and Pascal at the far end of the room, opposite the chair. Beside them, down on his knees, was Renard, as Gwynnie had never seen him before. He constantly looked around, his body hunched. He was a different man to the one who had threatened her with a knife that day on the dock.

The door to the chamber was opened by two yeomen and Cromwell walked in. He grunted as he moved, either in pain or muttering to himself, Gwynnie couldn't be sure. He walked first to Renard, nodded unsatisfactorily, then moved to Pascal's side.

"You are certain this time?" he asked under his breath.

"We are." Pascal spoke for both him and Tombstone.

Cromwell's eyes darted over Gwynnie and Emlyn before he turned away. His eyes, like glass beads, were unreadable.

Another door opened between two tapestries and a tall thin man walked in. Judging by the scent of turpentine on his clothes and the bag that hung from his shoulder, practically bursting with glass vials, Gwynnie judged him to be one of the king's physicians. He stepped up to the platform and waited beside the chair.

The next person to walk in was Queen Anne. Strangely, she was not accompanied by any of her ladies-in-waiting. She walked alone, moving to stand on the other side of the chair. Her face was as pale as when Gwynnie had seen her last, and her body still carried the extra weight of having been with child. Anne didn't look at any of them but kept her gaze on the empty chair.

Another entered the room.

King Henry couldn't heave himself through the door. Instead, he was pushed through by another physician, in a chair on wheels that looked to be far too small for him. He was placed in front of the platform and was not moved to the chair behind him.

He croaked and yawned, hardly seeming dressed to have any audience. There was a loose shirt around his body, and a long embroidered robe that hid his shoulders and waist. His leg was bound thickly in bandages, right down to the toes, and the other foot had been thrust into a court shoe that hardly seemed to match the rest of his outfit. On his head was a crimson and gold cap. He blinked wearily, his eyes shooting to Cromwell.

"Well?" he snapped. There were no niceties, and scarcely any formality at all, as Cromwell stepped forward and bowed. "Speak, Cromwell. I need to return to my rest. You said you had news. You said you had proof as to who was behind Florian Battersby's death. Well? Speak, man, in the name of God's blood, speak!"

"As you wish, Your Majesty," Cromwell said quietly. "Renard —" he nodded down at the man kneeling beside him — "was seen this very night digging a hole in the stables. A hole ... where Jerome Woodville had been buried."

Queen Anne looked up. She moved forward, standing beside Henry, who didn't turn his head to acknowledge her. If anything, he moved his body slightly away from hers.

"Woodville never left the palace on New Year's Eve," Cromwell continued. "We now know he was strangled. Renard covered up the death. He was seen by one of the yeomen carrying the body out of the palace and into the stables. Tonight, Renard was trying to move the body, to prevent its discovery."

"Bile and blood," Henry cursed, a hand to his chest. "What have you brought him here for? Arrest him. Be done with him. Hang him!"

"He did not do the killing, sir," Cromwell said, his voice soft and patient. "He merely hid the true killer."

"Then who is the killer?" Queen Anne stepped forward as she spoke, her eyes on Renard. "He works for..." She trailed off as Henry held up a hand sharply.

"Do not say it. Do not dare say those words, Anne."

"I am afraid the queen's suspicion is true, Your Majesty," Cromwell said gravely, hanging his head. "Renard, speak."

Renard lifted his head, staring into space. "I covered up the Duke of Richmond's actions. I hid Master Woodville's body, and I put Master Battersby's body in the courtyard too." He glanced at Tombstone, who nodded at him, urging him on. "I cut Battersby's throat to mask the bruising on his neck. Both men were strangled."

An eerie silence fell upon the room. No one said anything.

Gwynnie glanced around, seeing that she was not the only one looking from one face to the next. The two physicians kept glancing at one another in shock, and Queen Anne stared at her husband, waiting for him to say something.

Henry heaved. His hands gripped the arms of his chair as his small, beady eyes glared at Renard.

"Where is my son?" he muttered eventually. "Cromwell, where is my son?"

"He is in his chamber." Cromwell kept his calm tone. "He does not know of this meeting."

King Henry nodded.

Gwynnie glanced at Tombstone. He looked back at her, his shoulders lifting in the most subtle of shrugs.

"And the maids?" Henry looked at Gwynnie and Emlyn. "Who are they to this?" Cromwell gestured for Tombstone to explain.

"They are the thieves, Your Majesty."

Gwynnie took hold of Emlyn's arm, rather fearing she was going to run from the room. To do so now would no doubt result in an arrest.

"Mistress Gwynnie Wightham witnessed the second of the murders," Tombstone explained. "The night Goodwife Battersby was attacked, it was because Fitzroy and Renard were trying to frame Mistress Gwynnie for it. They wished to point the blame elsewhere."

Cromwell nudged Renard in the shoulder, who nodded in agreement.

Another silence fell upon the room. Gwynnie held her breath. Her eyes moved to Queen Anne, seeing her breathing was laboured. She was the first to tire of the silence.

"My husband," she whispered, leaning toward him. "We must do something about this. It is murder … oh, murder most horrid." She clutched her necklace, her hand shaking.

Henry lifted his head, his eyes narrowing in Cromwell's direction.

"Have this man arrested for murder." He thrust a finger at Renard. "Send him to the hangman tomorrow."

Gwynnie's mouth fell open. Tombstone stepped forward, though Pascal took his arm and jerked him back.

"Your Majesty?" Cromwell's voice shook for the first time. "Renard did not kill. Let him be punished, but to hang him tomorrow… The killer was —"

"Not another word." Henry moved to his feet, grunting in pain. The two physicians ran forward to help him, but he shrugged them both off with a sharp swipe of his arm. "Speak another word to me, Cromwell, and you will find yourself at the gallows too. Get this man out of my sight."

He tried to waddle away, struggling with the pain he was in.

"Your Majesty!" Queen Anne reached for his arm. "You cannot ignore this. Your son… Look at what your son has done. He must pay for his crimes. It is the law. It is God's law on this earth. Husband —"

The king struck Queen Anne across the cheek with the back of his hand. She fell to the floor, cradling her bruised cheek.

Henry's eyes darted around the room, as if daring anyone to speak. The physicians approached him warily once again, not daring to touch him.

"No one must know," the king spat the words. "Cromwell! You hear me? No one must learn of this. Bring my son to me. Order him to my chamber. See that man —" he thrust a finger toward Renard — "is hanged tomorrow. See it done!" He limped from the room.

The two physicians ran after him.

Cromwell moved toward Renard and took his shoulder, urging him to stand.

Gwynnie found herself moving forward. She slipped between Pascal and Tombstone's shoulders, and reached Queen Anne, bending down beside her.

"Your Highness." She offered her hand to the queen to help her stand.

Anne looked up. Her dark eyes glistened with unshed tears as she lowered her hand from her cheek. She took Gwynnie's hand and stood, struggling with her vast gown and farthingale. She was a changed woman from the one Gwynnie had seen the night she had broken into the tower. Where she had once been impressive, commanding, she now trembled like a frightened pup, her hand lifting repeatedly to her cheek.

The queen's ladies must have been waiting outside the door, for they hurried into the chamber a few seconds later and swept Anne away, taking her from Gwynnie's grasp.

She stared after the queen, watching as she stepped beyond the door and suddenly cried aloud. The door was thrust shut behind her.

"Pascal!" Cromwell's voice was suddenly full of fire. "Have Renard taken to Newgate, and those two as well." He pointed a thick finger toward Emlyn and Gwynnie in turn.

Emlyn stepped back as Gwynnie looked at her. Neither Tombstone nor Pascal made an argument against the matter.

"Guards?" Pascal called and the door opened.

Two guards walked in. Gwynnie moved back, fearing now that she would run too. Yet the yeomen were not the only ones to walk into the room. Esme Battersby walked between them.

She was pale, but she was on her feet. Any relief Gwynnie felt to see the woman standing was overwhelmed by the fear she felt.

"Take Renard to Newgate," Pascal said distractedly to one of the guards. "For the murders of Jerome Woodville and Florian Battersby. Take those two as well, for larceny."

Gwynnie felt her arm taken by a yeoman, but she couldn't look at him. She was too busy staring at Esme Battersby. Her eyes were on Renard as he was dragged to his feet by one of the guards.

Renard fought all the way, but he was much smaller than the yeoman, and could not fight him off.

Esme stepped forward, the heels of her shoes striking the floor so loudly that they competed with Renard's cries.

"You cannot do this! We had a deal! If I told the truth, I would not hang. You told me so. You cannot hang me!"

Esme continued forward and pulled something out of the billowing sleeve of her gown. The candlelight glinted off the blade.

"Ma?" Gwynnie called to her mother. Emlyn was the only one who had ended up between Esme and where Renard stood fighting with the guard. "Ma!" Gwynnie shouted, unable to move as the yeoman took hold of both of her arms.

Emlyn looked between Esme and Renard. She had clearly seen what Gwynnie had seen.

"Ma, stop her!" Gwynnie bellowed.

But Emlyn stepped to the side, giving Esme the clear path she had been looking for.

She marched toward Renard, who did not notice her advance, for he was too busy fighting. Without hesitation, Esme lifted her arm, revealing the dagger in her grasp. She thrust it down into Renard's back.

"Argh!" Renard's cry of pain erupted as everyone turned to face them.

Tombstone, Pascal and Cromwell broke off from their panicked conversation.

Gwynnie hung limply in the yeoman's grasp, unable to make sense of what she had seen.

Renard's body slumped forward as the yeoman released him. He dropped to his knees, the dagger planted in his back, blood seeping through the thick doublet. Then he slumped forward, hitting the floor face-first. There he lay dying, his shoulders growing still.

"For my husband," Esme said, stepping back. There wasn't even a tremble in her hand. "Justice has now been served."

Gwynnie looked at her mother, shocked as Emlyn stared back at her. This wasn't justice. Esme had overheard a lie. She had overheard that Renard was the killer, when he was not. Emlyn could have stopped the wrong man dying, but she had chosen not to.

"What did you do?" Gwynnie shouted, unsure if she was calling to Esme or Emlyn.

"Arrest them all!" Cromwell snarled.

CHAPTER 31

"Some prison," Gwynnie muttered as the yeoman pushed her into a cold chamber.

The flood was still too high and there were no wherrymen on the water. Since the guards were unable to send them to Newgate, Gwynnie and Emlyn were thrust into the palace bread store, a chamber deep below ground, underneath the kitchens, with a curved stone ceiling and no windows. A single candle was left with them, the flame shuddering in its tall holder as the yeoman shut the door behind them.

Gwynnie stood in the middle of the room, wondering where they had taken Esme. Mistress Battersby had also been dragged beneath the kitchens to be locked in another room, though Gwynnie had not seen where she had been placed.

"This is it, miting," Emlyn mumbled as she slid down the wall and onto her haunches, where she sat on a hessian sack. "You have that justice you so craved, and where has it got us? They hang for larceny as well as murder — you know that, do you not?"

"Justice? You call this justice?" Gwynnie rounded on her mother, outraged. "This is not right, Ma. A man has died for murders he did not commit, and the king plainly has no intention of seeing the real killer punished for what he did."

"Fitzroy is the king's son. What did you expect? Did you think he would be paraded through the streets of London in disgrace before they chopped his head off on Tower Green? The world does not deal a fair hand of cards. That's why we have lived the lives we have lived. In order to survive, you must cheat the cards."

"Cheat the cards? Ma, you stood back today and watched a man die for a crime he did not commit."

"He could have killed you." Emlyn's eyes narrowed. "Renard attacked you and was prepared to frame you. He was guilty of attempted murder, even if he didn't manage it."

Gwynnie stood back, her body trembling. She leant against the wall and slipped down, landing on another hessian sack opposite her mother. She stared at Emlyn.

In a way, what Emlyn had claimed made sense, but there was still something that made Gwynnie's heart shudder. Her mother was perhaps capable of more brutality than she had realised.

"You said once…" Gwynnie swallowed, before continuing. "You said that the night you took justice for my father, it was self-defence. That in the end, you had no choice but to kill in order to save your own life. That you went to confront him, and the confrontation turned sour. Is that true?"

The woman she had glimpsed today, the woman she had seen step out of the way to allow Esme to plunge that blade into Renard, was a different woman.

"It is true," Emlyn said simply.

Gwynnie was not sure if she believed her or not.

"One minute, that is all I ask," a voice ordered on the other side of the door. Gwynnie scrambled to stand, the hessian sack getting caught on her gown. She threw it off and moved to the middle of the room.

The door opened and a yeoman's face appeared.

"You." He thrust a finger at her. "Come. Someone wishes to speak to you."

Gwynnie hastened from the room, glancing back at her mother. She saw the twitch around her eyes. Emlyn was terrified of what would come next.

As she stepped through the door, Gwynnie's gaze adjusted to the bright morning light that shone through the nearest window. Tombstone stood before her, the neck of his doublet loose and his cloak thrown haphazardly over his shoulders, with his copper hair wild.

The yeoman moved a few paces away, giving them a chance to speak alone.

"Is it true?" Gwynnie asked in desperation. "The king will not send his son to the Tower?"

Tombstone nodded.

Gwynnie groaned. A part of her had believed that catching Renard would be enough to force Fitzroy to pay for his crimes.

"Renard is dead," Tombstone said simply.

Gwynnie staggered away and reached for the wall.

"I can get you out of this."

Gwynnie lowered her hand, glowering at Tombstone, not daring to believe it. "What did you say?"

"I can get you out," he repeated, his words fast. "We only have a minute —" he glanced at the yeoman — "so listen carefully. You have been an informant in this palace for me. I can persuade Pascal and Cromwell that you are of use. You are only guilty of theft. I can bargain for your life."

"What is the bargain?" Gwynnie held her breath, fearing what was coming next.

"That you continue to act as my informant."

She brushed his hand off her shoulder. He held up his hands, as if he was dealing with a wild animal, and took a step back.

"Work for me," he continued, speaking quickly. "I always need someone listening in the palaces. You'd be shocked at what goes on. Agree to work for me, be my informant, and they'll let you live."

Gwynnie held a hand to her throat once more. It was freedom, was it not? Not the sort of freedom she craved, not a life in France living off the sale of the jewels they had stolen, but at least she would not be dead at the end of a noose. Surely, she had little choice.

"What about my mother?" she asked, gesturing back to the cell.

Tombstone grimaced and shook his head.

"You cannot leave her in there."

"It is not within my power. Your mother is wanted for murder. It has been known for years that one of the Shadow Cutpurses killed, and she confessed that it was her to protect you. The tales are written in ballads, and the body was found. I have seen the papers that talk of it. It cannot have been you, Gwynnie. You are too young. It must have been your mother."

Gwynnie turned on the spot, her hands in her hair. She couldn't do this. She couldn't accept Tombstone's bargain, agree to work for him, only to watch her mother hang for murder.

"It was justice," Gwynnie muttered, but there was little feeling in the words now. "It was what she always said."

"I cannot do anything," Tombstone said. "I shall come to you tomorrow morning." He looked up, for the yeoman was walking back. "Give me your answer then. It will give me time to make the arrangements."

The door was unlocked.

Tombstone released her and Gwynnie stepped past the yeoman. Her eyes flitted over his weapon belt, and she saw a small dagger hanging by his hip.

She acted fast, pretending to trip on the threshold of the door.

"Oh, excuse me." She grabbed onto the yeoman's arm, steadying herself.

"Get in," the man ordered and shoved her off him.

Gwynnie kept her hands by her sides as she staggered into the room. She caught a brief glimpse of Tombstone's face, then the door was shut.

"What was that about?" Emlyn asked, sounding defeated.

Gwynnie turned to face her mother and held up the small dagger she had taken from the yeoman's belt. "A way out of here."

The tall tallow candle had nearly burnt out, with the flame close to the stub and all the wax having dripped onto the stone floor. Gwynnie used a hessian sack as a cloak, and she and Emlyn leaned against one another, trying to stay warm.

"I do not wish to do it." Emlyn broke the silence between them.

It had to be dark outside now, judging by the fact that no shaft of light shone beneath the door. They had discussed their plan for hours, but as soon as darkness had fallen, they had both gone silent, until now.

"What choice do we have?" Gwynnie asked under her breath.

They had overheard about an hour or so before that Esme was to be moved to Newgate. The yeomen had argued loudly about the best way to get her out of the palace and to the wherrymen on the dock. It had given Gwynnie and Emlyn the confirmation they were looking for, that the wherrymen were working again.

"If you stay, they'll take you to Newgate and hang you."

"It means leaving you." Emlyn swallowed uncomfortably. "I cannot imagine that."

Gwynnie smiled sadly. She did not want to think about it either. Since they had lost her father, they had never spent a day apart.

"What is the alternative?" Gwynnie asked. "If I come with you —"

"I know."

They had already discussed their limited options. It would be easier for one woman to sneak out of the palace than two. Easier as well to get a boat across the Thames. There was also the possibility that if Gwynnie stayed here, and Tombstone or Pascal ever caught wind of Emlyn's whereabouts again, Gwynnie could interfere with the information. She could secure her mother's freedom, in a way that she couldn't if she ran with her now.

"I cannot deny one thing." Emlyn took Gwynnie's hands, gripping so tightly that it hurt Gwynnie's knuckles.

"Well, that's a soft touch," Gwynnie said with sarcasm. "Ow!"

"I cannot deny it pleases me to know you will not be hunted. Not anymore." Emlyn smiled for the first time. She wrapped her arms around Gwynnie's shoulders, pulling her into a tight embrace. "You have your freedom now, Gwynnie."

Gwynnie was not so convinced. She was walking into a trap, a trap where her masters would be Tombstone and Pascal, two men she was not certain she could completely trust, even if their intentions were sometimes good.

Gwynnie nodded, knowing this was the bargain. She wouldn't have to hide, fearing that her thieving would one day catch up with her. "It must be time," she whispered, turning her eyes to the door.

They stood, neither one of them releasing the other as they moved to the door.

"You should go to France still," Gwynnie urged Emlyn. "Take a jewel from someone, enough to get you passage, and start again. Please, Ma. Do this for me. Turn your back on our lives here, and no longer be a cutpurse. It is for the best."

Emlyn brushed some of Gwynnie's hair back behind her ear. "Ah, miting. It's in my bones, as it is in yours. It is not so easy to turn your back on as you may think it is."

Gwynnie chewed her lip, fearing what would become of her mother now. Perhaps Emlyn never intended to stop thieving at all.

"I do not want you to die in gaol someday," Gwynnie said, her breath hitching with sudden tears.

"I know. That is why you are right, and this is for the best." Emlyn embraced her another time. "But it is I who dreads *you* dying in a gaol, Gwynnie. This way, that will never happen. You'll be too important to powerful men."

Gwynnie sobbed against her mother's shoulder, not wanting to release her. She didn't know how long she stood there, clinging to Emlyn, but in the end the hoot of a distant owl confirmed her suspicion that it was the dead of night.

"I must go," Emlyn whispered. "Come. Do what you must."

Gwynnie turned to the door. She sniffed, not bothering to dry her tears as she retrieved the dagger from a pocket in her gown and pressed her ear to the door. She could hear soft snores beyond, suggesting the yeoman had fallen asleep. Quietly, she pressed the blade into the lock and started to move it around.

It was an old lock, for these storerooms hardly needed to be locked securely. She rather suspected that if they had just thrown their combined weight against the door, they could have broken it open, but that would have woken the guard.

Tilting the blade high in the lock, she felt the latch and turned it. The lock slid back, and the door opened.

It swung on its hinges, creaking until Gwynnie grasped the door and held it still.

The yeoman was still sitting against the opposite wall, his heels crossed in front of him, fast asleep.

Emlyn turned to Gwynnie and kissed her on the cheek. "My heart is with you, miting. Stay safe, for me."

Gwynnie longed to say the same to her mother, but Emlyn had already released her and pressed a finger to her lips. She took the blade from Gwynnie's grasp and held it down by her side as she ran lightly down the corridor, heading toward the nearest set of stairs.

Gwynnie stared after her mother, feeling the tears threaten once again. Slowly, she stepped back into the bread store and closed the door behind her. As it shut, it created a wind that blew out the small flame of the candle, leaving her in darkness.

Resting her head against the door, Gwynnie stared into the shadows, longing for someone to talk to, though she knew there wouldn't be anyone, not anymore. She and her mother were separated, and there was a chance that she might never see Emlyn again.

CHAPTER 32

A door creaked open.

Gwynnie blinked. In her dream, she had seen the door of the attic rooms where she and her mother used to live in the backstreets of London, and how that door would creak as it opened. She saw Emlyn stumbling through it, with blood on her palms once again. She saw the determination in her face, then Gwynnie realised it was just a dream.

She opened her eyes wide, pushing herself up on the floor from where she had used a sack of wheat grain as a pillow. In the doorway stood Tombstone. She could not see his expression, for the morning light fell on his back.

"Where is she?"

Gwynnie didn't answer. She pulled herself to her feet, stretched and yawned.

"Gwynnie? Where is your mother?" he asked again.

"Is she not here?" Gwynnie looked around the room, her hands on her hips. "Perhaps she went searching for a privy. It has not been easy to find a chamber pot in this room, you know." She wrinkled her nose, thinking about how difficult a night it had been.

Tombstone stepped back out of the door, jerking his head, a silent instruction to follow him. She did as he asked, walking out and noting that the yeoman was no longer standing guard. She hesitated on the threshold, half expecting someone to appear and demand she return to her makeshift prison, but no one did.

"This way." Tombstone moved toward the staircase and Gwynnie hurried to keep up behind him. "Where is she?" he asked again.

"Maybe she didn't go in search of a privy. Maybe she just longed for a more comfortable bed."

"You think this is the time to make jests?" He turned at the top of the staircase, so suddenly that Gwynnie wobbled on the top step, in danger of falling back down again.

Gwynnie adopted a more serious expression. She had cried for a long time during the night. It somehow made it easier not to show any emotion now as she stared back at Tombstone.

"You have an arrest for murder, do you not? Esme Battersby. Do you need another? Has it not all been enough to regain your position?"

"I have my position again." Tombstone huffed and walked away, demanding she followed him with a flick of his wrist. When they reached the kitchens, he halted by an open hatch and nodded at Samuel, who produced a tray and laid it down on the ledge. His eyes widened when he saw Gwynnie.

"Gwynnie? What has happened to you?" he asked in panic.

"It was a misunderstanding," Tombstone answered before she could, nudging the tray toward her and urging her to eat. Gwynnie tore into the bread hungrily. "Gwynnie and her mother were held in the storeroom by mistake."

"See? I knew it. I knew the news of you being locked up had to be by some error." Samuel called over his shoulder. "Rudyard? That's another bet you've lost to me." He turned and reached through the hatch, good-naturedly taking hold of Gwynnie's shoulder. "You well, lass?"

"I'll be well," she assured him, forcing a smile, though she didn't feel any sense of true happiness at all. Her mind was whirring with questions, wondering where Emlyn was now, and if she had gotten away on a wherry after all.

"Eat up," Tombstone encouraged at her side. "I need to take you to Pascal."

Samuel winked at Gwynnie and returned to his work, leaving her to gulp down a cup of small beer and bite into an apple.

"Pascal will be furious when he hears your mother has gone," Tombstone whispered. He blinked, as if realising something. "If your mother got out of that storeroom, why did you not get yourself out?"

"I was not the one who was to be hanged," Gwynnie reminded him. She had no intention of telling him that it was part of her plan. He and Pascal were now two of the few people who knew who the Shadow Cutpurses really were. She planned to keep a close eye on who they told.

Tombstone rubbed his eyes and yawned, clearly having had as sleepless a night as she'd had.

"You agree to my deal then?" he asked, checking over his shoulder that no one was paying attention to them through the kitchen hatch.

"I do." Gwynnie firmly nodded, eating a piece of ham. "I will be your informant in the palace, and you will keep my name off the lips of those who whisper about the Shadow Cutpurses."

"We have our bargain. Come, bring your food. Pascal will be growing impatient by now."

Gwynnie hurried to follow behind him. As they stepped out from the kitchens and into the courtyard, the air was not so cold today and the frosted puddles had melted, leaving behind damp cobblestones. People walked by, shaking their heads and muttering between them. They passed two ladies who were gasping with great shock.

"Esme Battersby. I heard it. They say she took revenge on her husband's killer. What a tale!"

Gwynnie's gaze darkened as she followed behind Tombstone. It would be the tale that was told, even if it was far from the truth.

Tombstone didn't lead her toward the lawyers' chambers as she had expected, but out to Donsen Tower and under the archway, onto the dock. Gwynnie looked at the river, imagining her mother stepping out onto a boat in the middle of the night, and making her escape.

Gwynnie bit into her apple again as they came to a halt on the riverbank.

Pascal was standing off to the side with another group of lawyers, a group that included Cromwell, all whispering together. Beside a vast barge on the water, a man was taking his leave of the palace. When Gwynnie saw his face, she dropped the apple onto the riverbank, where it rolled away and splashed into the river.

It was Fitzroy.

He took his leave of his friends on the dock, patting them on the backs and enjoying deep, rather flamboyant bows, as he moved onto the barge.

"Goodbye, my friends. I am sure we shall see each other again soon. You will not miss me for long in palace life, I am sure." He took off his thickly plumed hat and used it to wave to his friends as the barge pushed out onto the water, the silken blue peacock feathers shimmering in the morning light.

He halted in his waving, the false smile faltering as his eyes found Gwynnie's across the water.

"That is not a kind look," Tombstone muttered under his breath to Gwynnie.

"I think I am his new favourite person," Gwynnie said, earning a reprimanding look from Tombstone for her sarcasm. "You have the same dismissive expression as my mother."

Gwynnie could not smile at her jest though, as she watched Fitzroy turn away and wave once again to his friends.

"This is outrageous." She looked around for her apple, but it was long gone. "A guilty man is escaping. Tombstone, you must do —"

"Do what?" he cut her off, shaking his head. "There is nothing I can do. The king has ordered he goes to the country, to spend time with his wife whom he sees so little of."

"Why are you not more upset? Considering that he..." She just waved a hand in the air, uncertain how to refer to the relationship he'd once had with Woodville, and how that had ended with Fitzroy killing the man he had once cared for.

"My anger serves no purpose other than keeping me company at night. He cannot be sent to the Tower. Do you need me to remind you of Fitzroy's position?"

"Pray, do not. I am tired of people repeating the words 'he's the king's son,' as if that makes murder forgivable."

"Shh!" Tombstone waved a hand at her, looking around the riverbank. "Do you wish to be overheard? If anyone hears you say such a thing, it will cause great trouble. You will probably be accused of treason." He sighed deeply. "My mother used to cling to an old saying: laws are like spiders' webs, they catch flies, but let hornets go free. I'm sadder than I can say that she turned out to be right." He looked at Pascal, who was now talking to Cromwell. "I shall tell Pascal of your mother's escape."

"I expect him to be no happier than you are."

Tombstone glared at her again.

"What did you expect?" she whispered. "Did you expect her to prepare herself for death? She is not the monster you seem to think she is."

"I never said she was a monster, but I am a lawyer. I expect people to pay for their crimes."

Gwynnie waved pointedly in the direction of the retreating barge which carried Fitzroy away.

"*Almost* everyone," Tombstone corrected himself. "The order came through this morning that Fitzroy was to spend the rest of the winter in his country house. I do not know if he'll ever be invited back to the palace again."

"How comforting," Gwynnie muttered wryly, folding her arms across her chest.

"Stay here."

Gwynnie bit her tongue, already disliking being ordered around by Tombstone as if she were a pup at his heels. She watched as Tombstone reported to Pascal and Cromwell about her mother's escape. She saw the fury, the barked orders as yeomen were sent off in search along the palace's perimeter. Eventually, Pascal nodded, as if resigned to the matter. He shot an uneasy glance in Gwynnie's direction, but must have relented to something, for he waved Tombstone away with a cursory flick of his fingers.

Tombstone returned toward her, shifting his cloak as he walked, as if it was dropping from his shoulders.

"They are searching for your mother. Fortunately, Pascal has agreed that we will still use you as an informant."

"What a fortunate day this is." The wind whistled up from the river as the barge moved away, but Gwynnie didn't shiver in the cold. It wasn't half so icy as it had been before. "Who are you and Pascal to one another then?" Tombstone shifted his weight between his feet, nervously.

"I think you and I know enough of each other's secrets, do we not?" Tombstone reminded her. "I'll keep yours, and you keep mine. Do we have an agreement?"

Gwynnie stared back at him, sensing the subtle fear in his face. He shifted his cloak again and she caught sight of something silver and gleaming on his doublet. It was the Celtic brooch. He must have worn it in memory of Woodville. An ache developed in her chest, remembering the way he had cried at Woodville's graveside.

"All your secrets are safe with me," she said softly. "I guess you and I hold much power over one another now," she said with a trace of humour. "Either one of us could reveal something we do not want others to know. It means we cannot quite be friends, does it not?"

"Friends?" He laughed, as if perplexed by the idea. "I am now your employer, Gwynnie. We cannot be friends."

"Perhaps not, but neither do I think you have a black heart." She stared at the river and the retreating figure of Fitzroy. She now knew what having a black heart truly looked like.

"Speaking of black hearts, there's something I've been wanting to ask you." Tombstone nudged her arm, trying to get her attention back from the water. "Why did you not take your chance in the flood?"

"What?"

"After you had seen what Fitzroy had done, you must have known either you would end up dead or framed for the murder. Why did you and your mother not run?"

"The flood made it impossible. We would have struggled to survive, and…" Gwynnie paused. She knew the truth, deep down. "Even if we had, by some miracle, managed to make it to the other side, what then? Poor Esme Battersby wouldn't have had her justice, not that she particularly has it now."

"Hmm." Tombstone grunted. "A thief with a sense of right and wrong? That doesn't make sense to me."

"Maybe the world is not as you perceive it to be." Gwynnie looked at Fitzroy once again. He sat at the stern of the barge, his feet lifted on the gunwales as he smiled out over the river, clearly congratulating himself on his escape. "It's certainly not what I perceived it to be."

"Have you not heard? Oh, it's too horrible!" a lady gushed to another as she ran under the archway of the tower, out onto the riverbank. "It is true. I would not lie about such a thing. I heard it from the queen's lady-in-waiting just now."

"What is all this?" A gentleman broke off from the group that had waved Fitzroy off. He moved up the bank, joining the ladies where they stood between the group of lawyers, and where Gwynnie stood with Tombstone.

"It is shocking, truly shocking indeed," cried one of the ladies. "The king this morning has said that he believes the queen ensnared him into marriage by *sortilege*."

"*Sortilege*?" Gwynnie repeated. "What does that mean?"

Tombstone didn't answer her right away. He was too busy staring at the lady who had spoken.

"Tombstone? What does the word mean?"

"It is a French term. It can mean power, divination, but it also has another meaning entirely. It implies witchcraft, bewitchment or manipulative deceit." He pulled his bonnet low over his temple as he turned back to face Gwynnie. "King Henry said such a thing of Queen Catherine once, before their marriage was annulled."

Gwynnie stared as people gathered in groups on the bank. The gossip spread like fire, the words passed between the people so fast, the sparks could practically be seen in their conversation.

It seemed the woman who had been struck by the king was about to be pushed out of her position.

"Do you think he will do it again?" Gwynnie asked. "Do you think he will divorce another wife?"

"We shall see." Tombstone stepped away.

Gwynnie purposefully slowed her pace as she followed him. She glanced back at the ladies, listening intently to every word they uttered.

"It is as before," an elder woman said to the younger beside her. "You mark my words. The past is to repeat itself again. We must be wary. We must be vigilant. All these deaths, all this ice and the flooding, it is all an omen." She held a hand up to her throat, where a cross hung around her neck. "It is happening all over again."

HISTORICAL NOTES

This book is designed to entertain. Though elements of the book are inspired by true events, such as the turmoil that led to the breakdown of Henry VIII's and Anne Boleyn's marriage, including his jousting accident in January 1536, please note that this book is a work of fiction. I have taken facts and used them to inspire a story meant for entertainment. I truly hope you have enjoyed the creative aspects of this story.

Henry VIII did indeed have an acknowledged illegitimate son, Henry Fitzroy. The true historical figure I have used as inspiration for the Henry Fitzroy in this story. From my reading, there is no suggestion about Fitzroy's sexuality, nor was he known to be the violent figure I create in this tale.

Chief to this story is its setting, Greenwich Palace, or Palace of Placentia, which was built in 1443. Believed to have been extensively rebuilt by Henry VII in the latter years of his reign, it was a palace often visited by Henry VIII and his wives. It featured heavily in Henry VIII's reign, being both his birthplace and the birthplace of his daughter, Mary I. During the Civil War, the palace fell into disrepair and was eventually demolished on the orders of Charles II, to make way for a new building. The site has undergone many changes since and a lot of what we know of the building has been discovered in historical records and through archaeology. Using this research, and inspiration from other royal palaces, such as Hampton Court, I have created a unique version of Greenwich Palace for this story.

I hope you have enjoyed the historical references in this tale.

A NOTE TO THE READER

Dear Reader,

Thank you for taking the time to read *Murder at Greenwich Palace*. I truly hope that you have enjoyed reading it as much as I have enjoyed writing it. Gwynnie will be back in a new adventure soon.

Reviews by readers these days are integral to a book's success, so if you enjoyed *Murder at Greenwich Palace* I would be very grateful if you could spare a minute to post a review on **Amazon** and **Goodreads**. I love hearing from readers, and you can talk with me through **my website** or **on Twitter** and follow my author page **on Facebook**.

I hope we'll meet again in the next adventure.

Adele Jordan

Sapere Books is an exciting new publisher of brilliant fiction and popular history.

To find out more about our latest releases and our monthly bargain books visit our website:
saperebooks.com